SANTA ANA

ADDISON J. CHAPPLE

WITH RACHAEL FLANERY

Published by:
Level 4 Press, Inc.
14702 Haven Way
Jamul, CA 91935
www.level4press.com

Library of Congress Control Number: 2019957817
ISBN: 978-1-64630-515-5

Printed in the United States of America

Large print edition.

Other books by
ADDISON J. CHAPPLE

The Man Who Would Be King
Rambling with Rebah
Con Crazy

DEDICATION

To Casey. Have a great summer and stay sweet.

PROLOGUE

Good help is hard to find. Here I am covered in blood and fingertips, having just delivered an epic speech and slit three throats like a total badass, and Jared, my tech guy, informs me I've been on mute the whole freaking time.

"What the hell do I pay you for, Jared?" I don't wait for an answer before shooting him in the foot.

Drug cartels, like all big business, evolved due to the COVID-19 pandemic. Why gather a small army for a protracted turf war when you can communicate the same message with a kidnapping and virtual execution?

But murder and mayhem only work on Zoom when you turn the fucking mic on, Jared! I have to do it. I have to shoot him in the other foot. With these young guys, you really need to take the time to mentor and mold them. Yeah, it'd be easier to just kill him, but his sister's super hot.

"Are we good now?" My guys can't hear me whisper under my devil mask. Jared whimpering like a bitch isn't helping. "Hello?"

Yeah, I wear a mask. It's movie quality, no big deal. Today I'm in my entire Santa Ana get-up: a red latex devil face with expertly placed horns and eyeholes, and a black suit. I try to keep things classy in a suit but I don't always make it to the dry cleaners. For this meeting, I made sure to be on point.

"Jared." It comes out as a hiss. "Go fucking cry in the corner. Are we good now? Can anybody fucking hear me?" I hate repeating myself.

Dennis, the fat one, is brave enough to answer. "Yeah, boss?"

"Is the fucking sound on?"

Dennis shrugs and squints toward the screen blocking my masked face.

"The camera is on."

Sweet Jesus, give me strength. "Yes, but can they hear me?"

The inside of Dennis's left nostril fills the screen as he struggles to maneuver it with his sausage fingers.

"It's not a touch screen." I push him out of the way so I don't have to kick his face in. Goddamnit. I've got to get some better guys.

"We can hear you, Devil Man."

"Good. Well . . . listen up, assholes, tell your boss—which, by the way, it's very rude he isn't here. We specifically picked this time because it worked for him. You tell that inconsiderate fuck that LA is mine. Always has been, always will be. I'm not interested in any deals or shar-ing shit with Meda Lucas."

"You don't scare us, Santana."

"It's Santa space Ana. I don't play the guitar."

"Think about it. Don't be too hasty. Maybe the market could use a little competition? We can take turns jacking up prices—"

"The only thing that's going to get jacked up is your ass if you fucking take one step, I swear, just one fucking step into Los Angeles."

"Why do you hide behind that silly mask? Let us see your face."

"Silly? You think this is some sort of joke?"

I'm losing them. Fuck these guys, my mask is badass. I grab my machete and hack off one of the dead guy's arms.

"Where should I send this, huh?" Under the blood and tattoos I notice this severed forearm is covered in track marks. I hold it up to the camera in disgust. "What kind of operation are you running? You got junkies for captains?"

"You did us a favor."

Shit. I cannot catch a break today. I throw the arm toward the camera and it hits Dennis. Flesh goo splashes on his face and he dry heaves. I have got to end this meeting.

"You want to go to war? We'll fucking go to war."

"Meda Lucas does not take kindly to threats. You would be wise to think about a partnership."

A little blue box pops up on the screen telling me the host has ended the meeting. Goddamnit, Dennis. Did they just get the last word? Son of a bitch.

ONE

Rain Man

Don't be confused. Hi. Hello. This is somebody new. Tristan. I'm glad you're here. I don't have a lot of friends.

If I were a disabled person, sorry, person who is disabled, I would have friends. People would invite me to brunch so they could tell their other friends they had eggs Benedict with a retarded guy, sorry, guy who is retarded. My broken brain would charm over crepes and fascinate the quiche out of everyone. Their other friends would smile and nod and feel shitty about themselves listening to their superior friends retell my cost analysis breaking down the buzz-to-dollars ratio of a bottomless pitcher of mimosas versus ordering by the glass. Bottom line, you're better off with a Bloody Mary.

But I'm not on the spectrum (what I wouldn't give for a smidge of Asperger's), and I understand no one wants to hear a statistical analysis of their beverage order. So, I say nothing. Ever. People think I'm rude, boring, a serial killer. I'm just trying to spare them the hassle of ghosting me after I open my mouth.

I've tried to turn off my brain and talk about the weather or perhaps a nice pair of slacks I recently saw on sale. It doesn't work. I always end up circling back to life expectancy rates and global warming. Do you know how much the sea level rises from each pair of khakis mass-produced in a sweatshop? I do. I've worked hard over the years learning how not to be myself. The problem is, I never learned how to be anyone else.

I was invited to happy hour once. After determining that, at best, the experience would be of neutral benefit to my health, mood, and social status, I politely declined. After running through each possible scenario, I had a one in three chance of drinking too much, which would result in a pounding headache, being ostracized from my cubicle squad, and at least seventy-two hours of clinical depression. If I veered away from beer and tossed back some shots, there was a 17 percent chance of public vomiting.

Hold on, why am I thinking about chickens? Oh, right, brunch! Yes. Brunch. Eggs. Chickens. Thank God no one asks me to a meal that leans so heavily toward eggs. I can't support factory farms. A full 98.2 percent of chickens raised for eggs are in factory farms. Don't make me tell you the failure rate of organic restaurants. No one is paying for that farm-to-table shit. Each omelet contributes to an industry that dumps waste into over 145,000 miles of fresh water. Male fish living downstream from these mass-produced horror shows have developed ovaries. Ovaries. I can't be a part of that. Not that there's anything wrong with hermaphroditism. I support all fish. It's the garbage water that bothers me.

I suppose I should get ready for work. Sometimes my morning routine doesn't feel like it's real. Instead, I'm watching the opening montage to a poorly attended but critically acclaimed movie. A sad bachelor methodically moves through his sad apartment. Everything is clean and in its place. Nothing is soft or lived-in. He's a little man alone in a big square box sparsely and unceremoniously populated with other, smaller boxes. Every morning, the same bleak and tired eyes stare into the mirror as he shaves for 306 seconds. Every morning he buttons up his nonthreatening patterned button-down and puts one leg into his business

casual pants at a time. He pours Raisin Bran
into his one bowl and shovels it into his mouth
with his one spoon. He doesn't eat because he
wants to but because he has to. He slams eight
ounces of tap water from a cloudy glass and
heads out the door. It's too depressing to be
mundane and too mundane to be entertaining.

I've been told I look like a Mexican Jimmy
Fallon. I guess that's a good thing since the
woman who said that let me have sex with her.
It was her idea and she was a bit pushy about it.
She moved in and after nine months I ended
up with her cat when she left me for someone
who looked like an Italian Ewan McGregor.
For the last year or so, I've been alone. The cat
died, natural causes, of course. I really miss her.
Or maybe it was a he? So hard to tell with cats.

These are the things I think about on my walk
to work. I try to walk everywhere. It's beyond
insane to me that anyone risks their life by getting into a vehicle. There are 16,438 car crashes

a day in the United States. I know women are preoccupied with serial killers. They should really be listening to podcasts about Toyota Camrys and distracted drivers.

So, I'm a walker. We are slightly less annoying than bikers (spandex not leather). Los Angeles with all its sunshine isn't exactly a pedestrian's paradise. These days I'm living the dream (Christ, I can't believe I just said that. What's next, I start each sentence with, "At the end of the day . . ."?) in Los Feliz. It's not too bad. There's a famous murder house. Unfortunately, I don't have murder-house money. I rent a one-bedroom apartment above a bowling alley, Les Miserabowls Bowling Alley and Dinner Theater. They also do the occasional musical. *H.M.S. Pinafore* was recently staged on lane eight. They did a lovely job and I got a free ticket, which was great. Living above a bowling alley and sometime community theater doesn't have many perks. It's unbelievably loud. I had more peace and quiet the brief stint I lived across the street from LAX. City noise ordinances don't apply to bowling balls.

I make a lot of money. If I could, I would spend more of it on rent. Believe it or not, this was the best I could find within my walking radius. Money, that was something my dead cat's former mother was excited about. We accumulated some nice things. She took them with her when she left. Joke's on her. We lost money on the furniture protection plan. Insurance is a ridiculous bet. I should know, my job is to make sure the house always wins.

I'm an actuary. Get two or more of us in a room and you've got a group of actuaries. I'm a fellow actuary, which, if you know anything about actuarial science, you'll know I'm kind of a big deal. I moved from associate to fellow status in under three years. Totally unheard of in statistical circles.

Monday through Friday I walk six blocks

from the small square box I live in to a huge rect-
angular box to sit in one of 100 cubes. I work
for mega-insurance company Longus Life. It's
been my first and only job. I should be a manager or CEO by now, but I have a very low tolerance for other people. Or, at least, the part of
me that controls my sweat glands and power of
speech has a very low tolerance for people. Do
you know the human face has approximately
20,000 pores? That's 20,000 microscopic open-
ings for germs, dirt, and disease. We should be
walking around with a welcome mat under our
chins. I don't have time to ask about your weekend as I'm calculating your waist-to-hip ratio
and deducting those inches from your life span.
It's exhausting. Spreadsheets are my safe space.

My boss and my boss's boss love me. There's
something about being the best and sticking
around the bottom that really endears you
to the higher-ups. I easily do the work of ten
people and will never be hauled into HR for

groping an intern. I don't ask for raises. I've gotten plenty. Sometimes they toss me an extra vacation day, which is kind of shitty. They know I have nowhere to go. All in all, it's a fine place to spend the next 71,725 hours of my life.

I'm about to cross paths with Jerry. He lives under a shopping cart at the third and final intersection on my way to work. He's standing at the ready to push the walk button. That's his job and he does it very well. He greets each pedestrian with a smile and says, "I'll get that for you." Each morning I hand him a banana and granola bar. It must be warm out today. He's normally in a heavy green wool coat, but right now he's in only a button-down with the sleeves rolled up. We're wearing the same shirt. It looks better on him. I must have passed it along with a banana some morning. If I find something that fits, I buy in bulk. We both chuckle, acknowledging our twinsies status.

"Have a great day, Tristan, my man!"

I won't. But it most likely won't be awful. Just the same. Always the same.

The office building is long and flat. The landscape is concrete. There's a squirrel eating a sandwich blocking the main entrance. I expect it to scurry as I walk closer, but it keeps eating contentedly. Huh. I wait a minute. It looks me up and down as it makes its way through soggy bread. I take a step to the side and it mirrors me, keeping the path to the door guarded. I step to the other side. Same.

"Excuse me?"

It keeps chewing. Is that a Quiznos? A delivery guy walks out the door. My furry friend tosses its lunch at my feet and runs away. The guy in brown shorts shoots me a dirty look.

"Dude, the garbage is right there." He points toward an overflowing receptacle.

Classic squirrel misunderstanding. "Oh, that's not mine."

He shakes his head and goes on with his day.

It's clear customers never step foot in here. The walls are bare and white. The carpet is thin and gray. The chairs are all Swedish and ergonomically correct. You have to be a fighter pilot to figure them out. A few jackasses have standing desks. I understand it extends your life expectancy, but why? You work here.

I weave my way to my desk. I could make the trip blindfolded. Nod at Cheryl. Avoid eye contact with Bill. Knickknacks and paddywhacks adorn my coworkers' half walls. My space is a bland oasis. The best thing about my work space is the view. I look directly into Lacey's cube.

Lacey Hahn is a brilliant accountant. She's worked across from me for five years. By the way she dresses you would assume she's single, into cats, and good at math. You would be right. She also loves collegiate wrestling, peppermint tea, and carnival rides. The deadlier the better. A Tilt-A-Whirl with a few loose bolts is her drug of choice. She's younger than me by quite a bit, but you wouldn't know it by looking at us. She's the type of person who at first glance could be fifteen or fifty. I think she's about to turn thirty. I should ask. I wonder if she's the type who cares or notices when they move into a new decade.

Lacey looks like a photograph before cameras were a thing. She has a soft round face with flushed cheeks, a tiny smile, and big eyes. Her eyelashes are little spikes under thick glasses and there's one interesting freckle beneath her left nostril. She's not thin. This bothers her. It shouldn't. The internet has convinced her she won't be pretty until she loses fifty pounds, or a hundred, depending on what you're into. I like her exactly the way she is. Though as previously stated, I'm not particularly into people.

"Oh, hello, fine sir." She's back from the copier.

"And a fine sir to you, madam." I don't know why we're speaking with British accents.

She's wearing a baggy brown sweater over an ill-fitting skirt. Her brown sweater from yesterday is hanging over the back of her chair. Her shoes are sensible. She looks like a teenager who is dressing ironically.

I saw her hair once. At the Christmas, sorry, holiday party. It was mandatory fun when companies still imposed such things. I had no choice. I nursed a beer at my cubicle while crap got crazy with a rented karaoke machine in the conference room. Lacey joined me, and we ate a plate of fudge under her desk. She's weird about eating in public. She also brought an armful of beers, and I'm pretty sure the fudge was loaded with pot. I don't remember whose desk she grabbed it from. If it was from anyone in customer service, it was definitely loaded with weed. I don't blame them. How else could you possibly talk to people all day? Needless to say, we let our hair down. Literally. I had never seen her less occupied by the way she looked.

Part of her bun unraveled, and brown hair hung past her shoulders. It was thick and shiny. We stayed on the floor for hours. Or maybe ten minutes. I had a lot of that fudge. She told me she lost her virginity to a Beatles impersonator. The Faux Four were a hot ticket on the carnival circuit the summer of her sophomore year at college. She couldn't remember if it was John or Paul. She ended by saying, "That's the one time I felt important."

I didn't reciprocate with a story.

We don't often share our personal lives.

Lacey has homework in her hands. Like me, she should be running this place but would rather not. She can do eight hours of work in about two and spends the rest of her day taking online classes. Last year she became a dog psychologist. Or almost became a dog psychologist. She didn't take her last exam. She rarely finishes. I believe she's also very close to becoming an antiquities trafficking specialist; CAD, HTML, and Java designer; sommelier (that was a hard one to study at work); and herbalist.

By the looks of her reading materials, she's going a more traditional route this time. A glossy magazine cover in her stack of copies catches my attention. It's a no-thrills trade magazine of sorts: *Law Today*. There's a blonde in a power suit on the cover. She's too pretty to be dressed in all gray. There's something familiar about her face. Is that a model or an actual per—

Excuse me, hold on a sec.

Shoot, where is my computer cover thingy? I do not want to break in a new monitor. I just adjusted this one to optimal brightness. Phew, here it is. And just in time.

It rains in the office, multiple times a week. We're prepared. We have our Longus Life–branded computer covers and primary-colored umbrellas with giant L's screen-printed on top. I know exactly when the sprinklers are going to go off. I cover my computer with time to spare, so my nearest cube mates get a heads-up. It wasn't hard to figure out. I won't bore you with the details. Observations, square roots, a smidge of high-level math. I don't use an umbrella. First, seven years of bad luck, and second, it's my fault this happens. I deserve to get wet.

When the sprinkler system started malfunctioning, I chatted up the building engineer and discovered it'd be much more cost-effective to mitigate the damage than attempt to eradicate the problem. This flat coffin we're all rotting in was built sixty years ago. If no permits are pulled, the toxic building materials slowly killing us are safe from modern legislation. Sure, maybe the lobbyists are right and if left undisturbed we're all safe from sucking in cancer all day. I tend not to believe "experts" who get paid in lump sums.

Move one ceiling panel and the company could be on the hook for an abatement bill that's ten times the building's property value.

Not to mention commercial sprinkler systems designed after 2008 are notorious for constant repairs and hard-to-get (i.e., expensive) replacement parts. Every third night industrial fans are rolled out to dry the carpet. Every few days the umbrellas go up. On average, three computers are replaced each month. We can go on like this for sixty-two years and still come out ahead.

After a couple seconds—okay, it's more than a couple—after ten seconds of being drenched by dusty, lukewarm ceiling water, Lacey realizes that in her hurry to open her umbrella she knocked over half the items on her desk. She never takes my cue to prepare, and her desk ends up soaked and tossed multiple times a week.

She bends over to gather up her now-soaked magazines.

"Damn it." She apologizes instantly for swearing. Lacey rarely swears. These must be important copies.

I reach down and grab the wet *Law Today* at her feet. Where have I seen this blonde before? I'm studying it while I wait for her to take it from my outstretched hand. She's embarrassed once she notices I'm waiting.

"Thanks." She takes the magazine and shakes off the water.

"What is that?"

She's surprised by my question. I don't often ask them. Did I mention that Lacey is my only and most trusted friend? Which isn't saying much. It's a position she claimed by default.

"Nothing. Just a dumb magazine. *Law Today*. My professor recommended an article."

I didn't know you could get a JD online. "You're going to be a lawyer now?"

She laughs nervously. I don't know why she's so nervous around me. I bought her tampons once. But that's a story for another time. Right now, I have to figure out what's up with this new career path, and who is that woman? I sound crazy, but I swear I know her.

Direct questions make Lacey blush. She answers in a hurry to change the subject. "No. No, I could never be a lawyer."

"Why not? You're smart enough."

"No one listens to me. Look." She holds up the magazine. "This is the type of woman people listen to."

Why does that model look so flipping familiar? Oh, no. Oh, God. Oh, my God! "I know her!"

Lacey is not expecting my mini freak-out. She answers cautiously. "Breanna Davies?"

"Yes! Brea Davies! We went to high school together. She was in all my classes." This flash from the past is a total punch to the nuts. "What is this? Is she just a cover model?"

Lacey shakes her head and points to the title in serious-looking font arranged above Brea's smartly arched eyebrow. "She just argued her eighth case in front of the Supreme Court."

"Did she win?"

Lacey shrugs. "I haven't read it." She studies the cover. "She was in *your* classes?"

I don't appreciate the way she emphasized *your*. "Yeah."

"So, she's really good at math?"

"Sure. And science. History. English. She's obviously really good at most things if she's arguing cases in front of the Supreme Court."

"Duh. I know she's smart. But Tristan-smart? That's a lot. Those boobs, with your brain? The rest of us don't stand a chance."

I'm done with this conversation. I turn my back to Lacey and shake off my computer cover.

"Was she nice?"

If I say something rude to Lacey now, whose fault is that? Clearly, I'm signaling with my body language that I am no longer interested in continuing this conversation. Ninety-three percent of all communication is nonverbal. She should be getting this loud and clear.

"I have to go to the restroom." I toss the wet plastic under my desk and leave her standing there without looking back.

TWO

Some Clarification

So, what did you think of Tristan? He's a bit much, I know. He'll grow on you. Or not. Let's hope. Tell you what, next time you're with him, ask him what the odds are of anyone giving a shit about any of us by the end of this book. Did he talk about the fish? I don't know how he does it but an unbelievably high number of his conversations involve hermaphrodite fish.

Oh, and if you read that juicy prologue and were like, *What the hell was that?* Don't worry. We'll loop back around to Santa Ana in a bit.

I hope you're not confused. That's not a great way to start a book. Let me clarify. A few of us are going to be popping in to tell this story, and I'm one of them. How do I fit into this mess? Am I a neighbor, old friend, coworker, a squirrel just trying to get a sandwich? I don't know. Maybe? It doesn't matter. You'll like me best. I know how this craziness ends.

Anyway, back to Tristan. He's always been like this. How do I know? Because I know everything. Tristan was an only child to old parents. It wasn't for lack of trying. Miguel and Elena Melendez waited a long time for their baby. Tristan's mother was an engineer who loved him very much. His father was an asshole. Miguel was a professor who spent most of his time with books and research. He was short and fat. His wife was slightly taller and slim. Everything about Elena Melendez was perfect, except for her choice in husbands.

She constantly tried to give his foul moods

context: His work was isolating and stressful. Funding was always up for debate and he never got the respect he deserved within his department. Even though his own father was demanding and strict, it was hard for both of them to be so far away from their families in Mexico. Perhaps all valid explanations but excuses nonetheless.

He never hit Tristan. He left a space in between his words that would have been a perfect pause for a smack or a shove, but Miguel kept his hands to himself. Even so, Tristan often flinched in his presence. The old man went downhill fast after Elena died. The start of his dementia had probably been overlooked because his wife took such good care of him, right up to the end.

Tristan was destroyed by his mother's death. She succumbed to aggressive breast cancer not long after he left for college. She was sixty-one, just a year shy of the median age for diagnosis.

That didn't work for Tristan. There had to be something more. He stayed up for days after her funeral trying to sort it out. He knew she was sick—it's hard to keep chemotherapy appointments a secret from your teenage son—but she spared him the reality of her condition. She was purposefully vague and almost cruelly optimistic. None of it made sense. She took good care of herself, did all the preventive stuff, was a bit of a hypochondriac, actually. What are the chances she would end up in the 3.49 percent of women over sixty who develop invasive breast cancer? And of the 330,840 women who are diagnosed with breast cancer each year, why was she one of the 43,600 who died?

Tristan didn't know much about his extended family. That impeded his research. Both of his parents left Mexico as children, leaving most everyone behind. He did some digging, and I mean digging. This was over twenty years ago, before social media and Ancestry.com. He tracked down his mother's family, living at the bottom of a mountain in Veracruz. He discovered that his grandmother and three out of his five aunts had died from breast cancer. This led him to surmise that Elena carried the BRCA gene mutation, which gave her an astounding 72 percent chance of developing breast cancer. Given that the cancer was hormone resistant and had spread, she had a 12 percent survival rate. Phew! Now it made sense. These were odds he could live with. He used math to manage his heartbreak.

Tristan can tell the future using numbers. He understood probabilities while he was still gurgling in single syllables. He's not often a man of action, but on the rare occasions he makes a decision and does something, a big something or a little something, whatever it is, he knows exactly why he's doing it. Senior year he went to school on Halloween in the *Scream* mask, not because he thought he'd be original but because he knew he wouldn't be. He spent the day in blissful camouflage. Sitting in the cafeteria, Tristan did his best trying to blend in, but his slumped shoulders and choice of seating three tables from the nearest human were a dead giveaway, and his onetime best friend knew exactly where to find him.

I should back up. This is a flashback. Let me set the stage. It was 1997. Y2K and flying cars were only three years away. The world had made it through the OJ trial and was mourning Tupac. Mass shootings were not quite as mass, bird flu didn't catch on, the USA was sitting pretty in between wars in Iraq, and 9/11 still stood for emergency services. Life was good.

Azusa High, where Tristan was sent to blossom into a fine young man, was like any other teen purgatory in the Valley. Open air quads and halls that resemble prison yards. Stuffy classrooms with that obnoxious half desk welded to a plastic chair, which always had a crack just big enough to pinch your butt cheeks. Azusa is only twenty miles from East LA, but might as well have been on Mars. White, Black, Brown, no parent was going to let their kid hop on the bus to party in Bum Town.

Tristan never found a proper place within the quad hierarchy. He wanted to belong somewhere but was too terrified of everything to ever figure out where that place might be.

There were the jocks, of course; there are always jocks. Goth posers, stoners who thought they were the first to discover the Grateful Dead, their horrible offshoot brothers of Jam Band Douchebags. White kids in dreads. No, thank you. Some girls did pigtails and belly shirts, while others still buried themselves in flannel. I mixed and matched, myself, but this isn't my flashback.

It was early in the day. Tristan's best friend, Frankie DeLeon, still had hope they would catch word of a Halloween kegger. After spotting Tristan's distinctive posture, he crept up behind his masked friend and yelled, "Guten Tag!"

"Jesus, Frankie!" Tristan was not amused. He turned, taking in his friend's homemade costume, and went from not amused to completely mortified. "What the hell! Are you some sort of Nazi?"

I should mention Frankie was wearing lederhosen.

"*Europa Europa*!"

"You're what?"

"The movie." Frankie squeezed in next to him. Sure, he could have picked from any of the four open benches around the table, but he always got off on invading Tristan's space. He knew how much human contact messed with his friend's nervous system. In a way, he was providing a much-needed service, a sort of immersion therapy.

Frankie didn't have to see his face to know

Tristan was rolling his eyes. Hard. Frankie didn't let this dampen his Halloween spirit.

"*Europa Europa*, it won the Golden Globe for Best Foreign Film in '91, no, '90."

Tristan was not impressed. "I don't care. You look like a Hitler youth."

"Exactly! Only I'm a Russian Jew orphan disguised as a Nazi dickhead." He snapped his suspenders for effect. Frankie was a movie geek. Poor guy didn't have YouTube back then to monetize his awkward yet slightly charming mega fandom. Tristan would not have been a subscriber.

On a normal day after some witty banter like this the two would play cards, usually King's Corner, until the bell. That was smart of them to have something to pass the time. Oh, my God, can you even imagine sitting with some-one now and not scrolling on your phone? Like, what did we do with our hands? Touch each other?

This lunch period stands out not just because Frankie was in short shorts and suspenders but because the haves and have-nots of teen society were forced to mingle. Most days, those with a car and friends left campus for lunch. They got a leg up developing the necessary workplace skills of being able to eat a burger and smoke as many cigarettes as possible in under fifty minutes. Today they were all in lockdown to prevent the pumpkin parties from starting too early.

It wasn't long until the quad was packed. The natives were restless. And there were natives. It was 1997; sexy Pocahontas was still a thing. Sexy Inuit. Shirtless Seminole. Yes. Back when America was still so great.

A guy in a *Scream* mask and Freddy Krueger hat and sweater, which for a film lover like Frankie was grossly offensive, dropped onto a seat next to Tristan. "What's up, No Pubes."

That was one of Tristan's many nicknames. No Pubes, Edward Scissornuts, Unabomber.

The assface proceeded to eat Tristan's fries and berate him for taking AP courses.

"Leave the virgin alone!" A booming command from Zeus himself silenced the crowd.

Harrison Sullivan and his sex-bot girlfriend, Brea Davies, dressed in togas and golden crowns, parted the hormone sea to come to Tristan's rescue.

"Sup, Harry and the Hendersons?" Tristan's tormentor wasn't afraid of Harrison.

"Hey, Josh?" Brea's voice was sweeter than Splenda.

"Yeah?" Assface sat up in attention. When a sex-bot talks, you listen.

"Get fucked."

His cheeks burned red under his stupid mask. He snatched one last fry and moved on.

Brea certainly never looked threatening. Quite the opposite. Most would agree her long, bouncy blond hair, smattering of freckles, cat-shaped blue eyes, and mouth that was slightly too big for her face were rather inviting. But she ruled that school with an iron fist.

"Don't let 'em get to you, Virgin." Harry was a human golden retriever. Fit, tan, friendly.

Virgin. Forgot about that one. Another of Tristan's pet names. A simple yet devastatingly effective choice for a title.

"Shut up, Harry." Brea sat next to Tristan and grabbed a fry. "These are nasty." She frowned as she continued to eat from his plate.

"Seriously, dude. Those dickweeds are going to be cleaning your Bentley one day." Harry also helped himself to Tristan's fries.

"Babe! You're so sweet." Brea kissed Harry for an uncomfortable amount of time.

"Babe, we gotta jet."

The two stood and straightened their robes.

"Hey, Tristan?" Brea was admiring her own cleavage. "You still coming by Sunday to compare trig notes?"

Tristan replied with a nod. Now, his cheeks were burning hot under his mask.

"You know, you can always stop by tonight. Harry's folks are out of town. Bring your friend, Freddy."

"It's Frankie." Frankie snapped his lederhosen enthusiastically, and Tristan shook his head in embarrassment. He had never appreciated his sidekick's assertiveness.

"I know." Brea didn't look back as she and Harry sauntered away.

And scene.

Brea wasn't only alarmingly attractive; she was also freakishly smart. She took all the same advanced classes as Tristan. They had been study buddies since seventh grade. She didn't have this grand-reveal ugly-duckling moment. She was born and will die flawless. She might be an alien.

Tristan, of all people, understood the odds of hitting that type of DNA lottery. He didn't waste time dreaming of the day she would catch his gaze over their stack of books and rip her top off. Maybe if he was shot and she needed to stop the bleeding. Maybe.

Unbelievably, but completely on-brand, Brea left high school for the Ivy League and prestigious fellowships abroad where she dated race car drivers and a duke. She's since argued and won eight cases in front of the Supreme Court. When a sexbot talks, people listen.

Harry was not nearly as exciting. The one almost-surprising thing about him was picking the shortened moniker "Harry." He was a Harrison through and through. His father was a Harrison and his father's father. You get it. Harry's face was almost too symmetrical. In high school, any grown woman would have gladly left her family to make a *Dateline* episode with him. Even the lesbian gym teacher. We should ask Tristan how many gym teachers are lesbians. Lesbians or guys who spent one day in the minors and then got fat. And before you get all huffy with me about tossing out stereotypes, I want you all to sit and think about your former gym teachers. It's a legitimate question.

Brea was always inviting Tristan places. A party at Harry's house. Beer bash at the moon tower. Drinking in the woods. He never accepted. He thought she treated him more like a puppy than a person. Frankie thought he was insane, even if he was right.

THREE

A Bit More Exposition

don't work late. There's no point, there will always be something to do in the morning. This is Tristan again. Don't be disappointed. Or, I mean, whatever. I shouldn't tell you how to feel. Shit. There's a woman jogging toward me. Should I cross the street? Why is she running down the sidewalk? She couldn't find a park? I panic as she gets closer and stop walking. I look down at my feet like I lost something. No! That is stupid. What if she's nice and stops to help? I hold my breath as she passes. Thank God. Luckily the next people I pass are shouting into their phones and wouldn't notice me if my hair was on fire. I pause outside my building. They've changed the sign again:

Livin' on a Spare Bowling Alley & Karaoke Bar.

Awesome. Nothing like drunk *American Idol* to put you to sleep. Must have new owners. Good. Maybe someone will fix my leaky faucet. A man should know how to do that. I'm sure with the right tools I could figure it out, but the thought of wandering through a Home Depot gives me hives.

There's a loud group drinking out of red cups by their cars in the parking lot. Why would you tailgate at a bowling alley? I snake through them as I near the side door. The group would probably make a white person nervous with their shaved heads and brown, tatted-up skin. I'm not nervous. Okay, I'm a little nervous. I fumble getting my key in the lock. I'm trying to shield it from prying eyes like I'm entering my PIN or something.

"Hey. Hey, bro, you live here?"

"No." Fuck. Why am I lying? "I mean, yeah. Yes. I live here."

"You got a nice place?"

"No." I'm definitely telling the truth now.

"It looks like a real shithole."

"It is very much a shithole." This is the most I've talked to a stranger in years. I don't like it.

"You like to bowl?"

"Not particularly."

"Huh. You want a beer?" He holds out his red cup.

"Nah. Nope. I'm good." My voice is two octaves higher than it should be. Does he know this is torture? Is he trying to murder me with small talk? Because I literally might have a stroke from the stress of sharing the same air with somebody for this long.

Finally, the key turns and I slip into the narrow hall. Green carpeted steps lead the way to my shithole. My sanctuary.

Shutting the door upstairs doesn't keep much of the sound out. As I shuffle around, my solitude is interrupted by strangers having fun. Cheers after a strike. Groans after a split, and now, apparently, Solo Cup parties in the parking lot. On league nights, someone bowls a strike every sixteen seconds. Thankfully that's only Tuesdays, Wednesdays, and every other Sunday.

I have to eat again. Lacey sent me home with soup. I wash my one bowl and one spoon. This apartment was nice once. As nice as an apartment above a bowling alley could be. It was renovated on the cheap about twenty years ago. Cheap does not age well. An outdated oven, a stained, peeling countertop, and a loud, overzealous fridge line the wall next to the front and only door. Oh, did I forget about the sink that leaks? That's jammed in there, too. A stained butcher block island breaks up the space and gives the place some class. The grand living room is down a step that is perfect for twisting your ankle. If I lived with anybody, I'd probably buy a rug to put under the black sofa and metal coffee table. I would have done it for the cat, but besides my bedroom he (or she?) always preferred uncomfortable surfaces. I once found him sleeping on a fork.

My TV is flat and ginormous. I love watching TV. It's the only time I stop thinking. I'm embarrassed to admit it, but I'm a bit of a true crime junkie. More like addicted to bad guys. Wow. I did not mean to write a hook for my dating profile there. That's embarrassing.

Continuing on our tour—this is a real "Cribs, You Should Kill Yourself" edition—a small unlit path leads you to a bathroom decorated with burgundy towels. The small bedroom is an afterthought. It's a great size for a walk-in closet. Now, I'm sure you're thinking it's all bare walls with a stained mattress on the floor. Gross. I have a box spring and sheets, thank you very much, even a lovely collection of pillows and a very soft, fuzzy bedspread. The cat picked it out. The bottom of my bed was her favorite spot. Or his.

Lacey labels her Tupperware with Hello Kitty stickers. NAVY BEAN AND LENTIL. She thinks I need more protein. Warm beans make me gag but this is all I've got. If I can choke down three-fourths of this mess, I'll consume enough calories to not get a headache later. Would it taste better cold? It's the mush factor that I can't stand. I pick out one cool, flat oval and place it on my tongue. I instantly gag. No. Beans are not any better cold.

It would be rude of me to tell her I hate beans, right? But now that beans have been introduced it's highly probable I'll be seeing them again. I should tell her. A lot of work went into those beans. Sorry. I feel like by saying the word *beans* over and over I'll somehow train my taste buds to tolerate them. Beans.

The microwave beeps, causing me to jump. Beans. Beans. Ooohh. Ouch. Hot beans. Beans.

I recorded a show on A&E to keep me busy until bedtime. Something about cartels. I like drug deals gone bad as background noise. I wish I had the balls to break the law. I think I'd be good at it. That could give me a tolerable personality. Criminal Mastermind. Now there's someone you'd invite to Tahoe. I've never been. I haven't gone anywhere since my mother died. She's in the closet. Her ashes, I mean, sealed up in the nicest thing I own. I took my time picking out the perfect urn. My father wanted to do it but went on a bender instead. That worked out nicely for me. He doesn't deserve her ashes. She would be happy knowing what's left of her is kept close by in a platinum tube in my closet. There's not a lot of platinum final resting places out there. Most containers are silver or bronze. Even wood, if you're one of those granola-type people. Platinum is the most expensive precious metal, the most durable and completely hypoallergenic. I had a good mother. She deserves something hypoallergenic. When I die, someone needs to toss me in there and give it a good shake. I should ask Lacey. Wait. Could I somehow loop the beans into that conversation? You know, soften the blow?

"Will you be the executor of my estate and sole heir? And please stop giving me beans."

I'll have to workshop that.

Drunk girls are striking out below me. Good. Gutter balls are the quietest. Maybe some drunk gentlemen will attempt a #MeToo moment and they'll spend more time drinking than bowling. I'd like to hear my program, a spotlight on the most goddamn best-looking, smoothest man in all of Mexico: Meda Lucas. If I could look like him, be like him, for just a day, I'd gladly make it my last.

The show starts off with a deep voiceover on

top of violent still shots. This is going to be good . . .

"For years, drug lords Meda Lucas and the smaller but no-less-violent Santa Ana have coexisted in relative harmony. It seemed as though Meda Lucas, the head of the infamous Lobo Gris, was satisfied with owning all of Baja, California, the key to being the sole distributor of sixty percent of all illegal substances in the American drug market."

It's 63.2 percent, actually, up 0.9 percent from last year and rising at a monthly rate of 0.06 percent. But who cares? Details.

"But after recent aggressive tactics from Santa Ana, the man often referred to as the Masked Devil, Meda Lucas is no longer interested in playing nice. Hidden in the garage of this well-kept home in North Hollywood, investigators uncovered a horrifying message to the small-time nuisance."

This is going to be so good . . .

"Three low-level enforcers from Santa Ana's gang have been boiled alive and sealed in these rusted oil drums. The gruesome ritual playfully referred to as making . . ."

Turtle soup!

". . . turtle soup. Meda Lucas is known to have a dramatic flair, but once violence goes culinary it only means one thing—"

Turf war!

"A turf war. Yes. The sprawling Los Angeles area may soon be ground zero for a rather unappetizing feast. Police are still working to identify the bodies of four men discovered last week covered in mole sauce and roasted on a spit. A delicacy commonly made with pigs or chickens."

God, I love a good mole.

"And Meda's own brother recently met the unfortunate demise of being grated and plated. Tonight, we sit down with the complicated and charismatic leader to talk about life, business, and the messy road ahead."

Holy shit! Everybody shut up. I can't believe they got a sit-down with him, and holy crap I've eaten half of my beans! I better choke the rest of this down while my taste buds are distracted. Between gags, I'm frantically trying to find the remote. I've got to drown out the dickheads and their goddamn quinceañera happening outside. What the hell are they doing out there?

Found it. Let's turn this up to eleven.

Now here is a man. The man. He's so badass he doesn't bother hiding his face or fucking with his voice. Nothing scares him. He's not afraid of getting caught or cooked. He's a genius. A silver fox occasionally photographed with an underwear model and featured in the tabloids on best-dressed lists. If it wasn't for all the murdering, he could be El Presidente. His voice sounds like rough silk. He speaks perfect

English but often does interviews like this responding only in Spanish. He's noted many times it's the superior language. The scrolling subtitles are a minor distraction from his hypnotic cadence. His dark eyes are curious and deceivingly kind. His wrinkles are expertly placed. I know I sound like a thirteen-year-old girl. I don't care. He is my Justin Timberlake.

The show shifts gears from dry narration over static gore to a sit-down interview in an undisclosed modern beachfront estate.

"What are your thoughts on the rising rates of gruesome violence plaguing Southern California?"

"It is unfortunate. Nobody wants blood and gore no matter how deliciously it is executed. But one must remember. This violence, this devastation has been thrust onto my people for generations. The Europeans invented violence the moment their ships landed on these shores. What I must do to survive, to build my business and support my people, children's games compared to the brutality perpetrated by the white man."

"Do you feel your crimes are justified?"

"I don't believe what I do is criminal. I'm a businessman. Sure, I may employ more unconventional methods than, say, Microsoft or your McDonald's, but my company supports entire villages, bringing industry and wealth to places most of the world would rather forget or only know from a postcard."

"Supplying drugs, wreaking havoc on communities, and destroying neighborhoods, that's not a crime?"

"I run a corporation that manufactures a rather in-demand product. What communities choose to do with it is up to them. If you want to talk about wreaking havoc and, as you say, destroying neighborhoods, look no further than your own justice department and DEA. I am not creating the violent and biased legislation that breaks apart families and enslaves peo- ple to generational poverty and a life of crime. Seventy-four percent of the people sitting in jail right now have yet to be convicted of a crime. One out of five of these yet-to-be-prosecuted crimes are low-level drug offenses. I'm not the bad guy here."

Am I dreaming, or did he just shell out some sweet-ass stats? Yes! My man!

"Turning men into soup, doesn't that make you a bad guy? In fact, isn't that how you would like to be perceived by your rivals?"

"We're talking about apples and orang- es. I'm never going to turn the postman into carne asada."

"Just other drug dealers?"

"Yes. This is a dangerous business filled with dangerous characters. Everyone understands the risk."

"What about the harmful and illegal sub- stances you traffic, making billions? What about the dangers your product brings into the homes of everyday people?"

His sly smile gets wider. "Not billions. Not yet. Men in lab coats with prescription pads are the ones bringing death and addiction into people's homes. Most of my business is in marijuana. Three-fifths of our operation is entirely legal and thriving. However, now, with all the government red tape, it's harder to pay my employees a living wage."

"And the rest of your business?"

"The rest of my business is a variety of boutique offerings to satisfy a high-end, discerning clientele."

"Meth?"

"Yes."

"Cocaine?"

"Of course."

"Opioids?"

"The best money can buy. Our products are triple inspected, vegan, and cruelty free. I offer my customers no judgment, only the highest-quality hard drugs at an affordable price."

"Tell us how your business is changing. Why the sudden beef with local drug star Santa Ana?"

"Santa Ana is a coward and a pussy. He is no star. He is one of the forces keeping this viable trade in the shadows. What type of leader never shows his face, never reveals himself to his own men? How can you trust someone who hides behind a hideous mask?"

"You've tolerated his methods for years. What's changed?"

"I'm bringing my people and my services out of the darkness and setting up Lobo Gris and Mexico to be competitors in twenty-first-century enterprise."

"And Santa Ana gets in the way of that?"

"Yes. I've tried to work with him. To buy him out or bring him on as a partner. Did Best Buy offer that to Radio Shack? I don't think so. Did Amazon offer to buy out Best Buy? No, sir. I have always been open to an agreement that is beneficial to us both."

"Can you tell us when the violence will end?"

"Once I rip off that mask and he tells me Los Angeles is mine."

"And if he doesn't?"

"Then Santa Ana will die. Slowly."

Holy shit. That. Was. Awesome.

There's a sharp crack. You know how when you're in an accident, you can hear the impact before you feel it? A rogue bowling ball smashes up through my floorboards.

"Mother shithole!"

I scurry over the back of the couch. It takes a minute for my brain to catch up. I look down at the hole in the floor, over my shoulder to the heavy green ball rolling toward my bathroom, and then down to the beans dripping off my shirt. Right on cue, a table of bros nails a strike.

FOUR

Hi, I'm Harry

Glenn has spinach in his teeth. I don't know many men who order spinach in their omelet. Maybe this is why. He looks like a jackass. But I've waited too long to say anything. We just have to live with it now.

I spend a good chunk of my life eating breakfast with Glenn. Driving around to SoCal clinics in a Chevy Malibu, with Glenn. He's a nice enough guy. Not who I expected to be growing old with, but, hey, I can't exactly settle down in my line of work. No emotional liabilities, as we call relationships in the biz.

Glenn has a line of three moles on his right temple. He has brown spots on his hands and neck. He smells like old balls. He's got an old man nut sack that stinks like wet cigars and Sweet'N Low. When I get the old man stench? Kill me. The first whiff of crotch rot and I'm pulling suicide by cop.

This is my favorite breakfast place. All the waitresses are at least a seven. Even the busboy could pass in a boy band. Shit, this is LA; he probably *is* in a boy band. Or the Groundlings. Ugh. The worst.

This place has a half-assed retro vibe that comes off as angry. We come here twice a week on the way to Redondo Beach. The pancakes are good. The booths are sticky, and the coffee is scalding. The scenery is nice.

Our girl mopes back to the table, tugging on her itchy vintage uniform. If a piece of clothing had bedbugs, this would be it. She has a mermaid tattoo wrapped around her forearm and an expensive dye job made to look cheap. I wonder if she'd bang me.

Glenn leans in after she refills the waters. "She reminds me of my granddaughter."

Glenn, you dirty dog! You must have a smoking hot wife to pass down those leggy genes. I don't know much about Glenn's life. He talks all day. Nonstop. But I don't listen. I think he's been married to the same woman for like a hundred years. Janice. No, Jenny. Or is Jenny his second wife? He's got like four kids. All girls. Or boys. It doesn't matter.

"My son's youngest, she's got a tattoo all down her arm, can you believe that? A pierced lip, too."

Go on.

"And you know what? She works for that Google. Smart as a whip and apparently these days you can look like you just walked out of the circus and make six figures."

It's his voice. After a word or two my brain

shuts down. All I hear is background noise. A necessary Pavlovian response to years of stopping myself from screaming, "Shut up!"

Did he always have those moles, or did they pop up with the AARP stench? I really do not want to wake up one day and be old.

I down my coffee. "Should we hit it?"

We each toss some cash on the table and head out in our Trufex pullovers, rolling our Trufex sample bags.

Trufex is the pill we're peddling this quarter; you know, the wonder pill that may cause partial blindness and Bell's palsy? Or perhaps you're more familiar with our famous side effect of anal leakage? But Trufex is a weight-loss drug that actually works. A common side effect could be murdering your own children and I'd still be selling a shit ton. I'm a drug dealer.

It was exciting at first. Company cars. Bonuses. Sales retreats in Cancún. Personalized pens. Don't underestimate the pride that comes from handing out a pen with your name on it. When I flunked out of college, there wasn't much for me to do but cash in on my punchable good looks and get into sales.

People want to punch my face. I know this. I accept it. It comes with a name like Harrison Sullivan the Third. I thought going by Harry would help. Nope. I still look like every blond asshole from a John Hughes movie. I've learned to play the part well. It's not as fun in your forties. It teeters on pathetic. I should text my therapist before I spend the afternoon day drinking.

It's hot and bright outside. Glenn can still rock a pair of aviators, I'll give him that. Siri directs us to Dr. I Don't Give a Crap's office. Another day, another dollar.

Whoever drives controls the music. Satellite radio has saved my life. Nineties alt rock is programmed up and down my presets. Glenn prefers podcasts. Fuck that. I don't understand how people listen to strangers yammering all day without jabbing a pair of screwdrivers in their ears.

That's probably an extreme reaction. Sorry. I've been in a dark place lately. Work has been stressful. This asshole is all up in my junk. My crew is a joke and I spend all day driving Miss Daisy over here. Things were supposed to be much better than this. Exponentially better.

I'm jamming out to Third Eye Blind. I don't know how long I've been in this bro trance, singing out loud.

"'Do do do. Do do do do do—' Great song. Don't you think, Glenn?"

"Huh? Oh, sure. You know, my favorite—"

"Really brings me back. God. Wasn't high school the best?"

"Well, when I was—"

"I ruled the school, man. Dated the hottest girls. Made out with my French teacher. Went to the state playoffs in three sports junior and senior year. That's very hard to do in Southern California."

He should be more impressed.

"Our division, we had guys go in the first round of the NFL draft. Thank God I grew up before everyone started crying about concussions. Like, it's football, okay? You're going to get a head injury. Don't be a pussy."

"I played tennis. All-American."

I don't give a shit, Glenn. God. Does he ever stop talking?

"I was homecoming king. Can you believe that? Prom king, too, I think. I got so fucked on mushrooms I barely remember that weekend."

We found Stevie naked behind a Walmart three days later. He was a crazy son of a bitch. Wonder if he ever made it through USC? Talk about failing up. That guy had nothing going for him but his dad's cash.

"My girl, she was the hottest of the hot

chicks. Beth . . . No . . . Shit . . . Brea. Man, I smoke too much. You know what I mean? Brea. How could I forget her?"

I didn't. Brea. Those four letters are forever tattooed on the tip of my tongue. She was everything. She's the one that got away, or, more accurately, the one I never had. Nobody is good enough for her. That's not me saying it like she's got an attitude or something. No. Honestly, no living male on this planet has done enough, is hot enough or worthy enough, to stand at her side.

She dumped me sophomore year of college. She left a voice mail. I cried for three months. I'd assumed I was the only one fucking around. I was wrong. I swallowed a bunch of pills, but it didn't work. Thank God. That's a real chick way to off yourself.

"She's a lawyer now."

"My grandson is in law school."

It's not always about you, Glenn. Christ.

I used to be somebody. Me. Harry Sullivan. I was worthy of her then. For a little while. I just had to show up and underclassmen kissed my ass. Now it's a whole thing. My current guys, they listen to me because they have to. Back then, I had an army just by showing up and breathing.

The phone I keep in my left pocket vibrates. It's not supposed to vibrate between the hours of nine and three. This better be fucking good. It's a coded text message. Three smiley faces, an eye roll, and a pepper. This is bad news. Very bad news.

"Hey, ah, Glenn? I've got to make a quick stop."

Siri keeps interrupting my jams by rerouting our trip. "Shut up." I knock my other phone, the only phone traceable to me, out of the cup holder. "Damn it!"

"You all right?" Glenn doesn't like to see me worked up. He's in a twelve-step program.

Apparently, the secret to a sober life is to be in a constant state of chill.

"I've got to stop at an old friend's house. Deliver some bad news."

"Want to talk about it?"

No, Glenn. I don't want to fucking talk about it. Jesus Christ, this guy. Siri continues to announce we are going the wrong way with every turn.

"We get it! For fuck's sake."

"Harry, why don't you H.A.L.T." Glenn is using that patient-father, better-than-you tone that makes my fucking blood boil.

I shouldn't, but I can't help but engage. "Why don't I what?"

"H-A-L-T. Check in with yourself. Are you hungry, angry, lonely, or tired?"

This fucking guy. "We literally just ate."

"Are you lonely?"

"No."

"Tired?"

"Of this conversation? Yes."

Thank God he takes the hint. I really hope Glenn makes it to retirement before I kill him.

We turn down a quiet residential street dotted with lovely stucco houses and mature trees. Bad things always happen where you least expect it. I pull up at the curb, then cut the engine and slide out of the car.

"I'll be right back."

Glenn leans over to turn the ignition.

"Leave it running. I'll just be a minute."

He pauses. Why is he pausing?

"I don't mind some fresh air. Take some time with your friend."

"It's a million degrees, Glenn. Keep the air going."

And the windows shut tight. This could get loud.

I grab my heavier briefcase from the trunk and head up the steps of a two-story across the street. Maybe you should stay out here with Glenn. We're just getting to know each other. I don't want to scare you off. While I'm gone, count to a hundred and, uh, sing some Sugar Ray or something.

Don't stress about this break in narration. Just go with it.

Harry is right. You can't go in there with him. His heavy briefcase is filled with bone saws and a blow torch. Let's check on Glenn. He's a cute old guy, isn't he? Don't worry, there won't be some plot twist that has him into weirdo porn or running a puppy mill. Not everyone comes with a big reveal. His wife is Janice, by the way. She's lovely and they've been married for almost fifty years. Glenn fumbles with the volume, trying to turn the station. He's blasting Soundgarden.

"Oh, dear . . ."

Don't get worked up, Glenn! And don't turn it down, whatever you do. Behind that nice front door and manicured rose bushes, some poor guy is being dismembered and fire-roasted. The screaming is intense. Glenn looks around the car thinking the howls are part of the chorus to "Black Hole Sun."

"He calls this garbage music?"

The screams continue even after Glenn finally lands on a new station. He's confused. Is all music this bad? He shakes his head. This is what's poisoning the younger generations.

Like magic, Harry is done with his meeting just as Glenn gives up and turns off the radio. Sweet timing, huh?

Inside the empty house, Harry begins to carefully put his tools away. He does his best to avoid dripping any blood on his Trufex fleece. He needs to remember to repack his tools first, before he takes off the plastic bag he drapes over himself to shield his business casual from bodily fluids. He looks over at the red-stained ball of plastic. Should he try to put it back on? Fuck this. He takes his burner phone from his pocket and dials. It rings just once.

"Clean this shit up. I'll be offline."

He drops his phone next to a charred and bloodied body. The burnt flesh looks like a lava field. Red ooze flows down the extremities, finding its way over the bumps and through the cracks. In one quick motion Harry smashes the phone with the heel of his shoe. He wipes the front of his pants and straightens his watch. He opens the front door confidently and takes a step before realizing his red latex mask with perfectly placed eyeholes and horns is still on.

What? I told you I was a drug dealer.

Shit. We've got to get to Redondo Beach. The 405 is going to suck if we don't head home by two. How's Glenn? You all sit tight in the car like I asked? Look, that guy in there, in that empty house? Not a good person. And all that stuff, you know the torture stuff? It's not like I enjoy it. Sure, at first, but like anything, it just becomes part of the job.

Glenn jumps when I open the door.

"Thanks. Sorry about that."

"Your friend okay?"

"He's fine."

He's fine? I'm losing my edge. Ten years ago, I would have said something like "He's all torn up" or "Not sure if he'll be able pick up the pieces." Even a simple "He's a mess" would have been better than fine.

Goddamn it. It's only ten-thirty in the morning.

FIVE

Let It All Hang Out

I t's Wednesday. What's up, hump day?! Sorry. That was unnecessary. I'm in a good mood. Wednesday is my favorite day of the week. A study found that, over a fifteen-year period, Wednesday was the only day of the week that did not show a peak in any of the ten most common causes of death.

You working for the weekend? Good luck. Saturday has the highest mortality rate. Mostly due to car accidents and guns. Oh, and drug overdoses. Saturday and Friday are popular days to OD. You have a slightly higher chance of being shot by your neighbor on a Sunday. If you're going to meet your maker by coming in contact with a poisonous plant or animal, that will most likely happen on a Saturday. Think about that the next time you head out to Joshua Tree. Monday is for heart attacks. Don't need to be a scientist to have guessed that. Most people who die from the flu can hold on until Tuesday and then there's my favorite, boring Wednesday. Thursday is a hodgepodge of casualties with numbers gearing up for the weekend.

Wednesdays in July or August give you the best chance of making it through the night. No one knows why but there is a seasonality to death. It's a wave that peaks in the winter. I know what you're thinking. Well, duh. Icy roads, interstate pileups, faulty furnaces, and carbon monoxide. Nope. States that don't have below freezing temperatures follow the same pattern. It's not suicides over the holidays (though Christmas through New Year's is peak carnage—more on that in a sec). Right now, there is no explanation. More people die of natural causes in December, January, and February. You can be on the beach in Hawaii or in a basement in Nebraska, your chance of having a stroke in February is the same, which is much higher than having a stroke in June. Basically, it begs the question, why bother going anywhere? Nowhere is better. Everywhere is worse.

More people die over the holidays because doctors and nurses are human. Getting sick on a special day means you'll have someone younger, less experienced, and cranky from overtime tending to life-threatening ailments. A new doctor isn't bad. But humans need repetition to refine their skills. Novel experiences are fun and all, but I don't need anyone to be forming neural pathways while my spleen needs fixing.

Lacey was sick today. She typically comes down with the Friday Flu or suffers from the occasional Migraine Monday. I wonder what ailment struck her down on a Wednesday? I'm not that worried. It's only October.

The walk home was uneventful. A continuation of a silent day. When Lacey is gone, the day goes by fast.

A small stack of mail is waiting for me in the green hallway. All my bills are on auto pay. I never get anything but junk and flyers. It's annoying that I need to bend down to gather garbage. There's a crisp square envelope peeking out from an Arby's advertisement: 5 for $5 is back. That truly is an amazing deal. But I don't like the looks of that square. I'm on every do-not-solicit list I can find. No charities, credit card apps, refinancing, alumni fundraising bullshit allowed. What is this?

It feels like card stock. Uh-oh. It's an invitation. Or an announcement. But I don't know anybody who would invite me to anything or have news to share. Do I have any cousins? How would they have found me? I'm scared to look at the address label. I don't want any clues to whatever dread is sealed up inside.

The hole in the living room floor has been covered up with a mishmash of plywood and is surrounded with yellow caution tape. I wonder how many years it will take to get that fixed. I throw the mail on the counter and turn on the news. Fingers crossed there's a local tragedy to distract me from my mail. Isn't it silly, the things we're afraid of? This is going to be a lot of buildup for nothing. I'm sure it's just fancy marketing for a new optometrist or something. Well, no, thank you. I don't appreciate companies getting cute with their advertisements. I should just open the damn thing.

The plastic blonde on the TV warns the audience the top story tonight contains graphic and violent images. Wonderful. I sit on the other side of the hole, keeping one eye on the kitchen counter.

"Blake Hernandez is live on the scene. Blake?"

"Thanks, Kyla. I'm Blake Hernandez standing in front of this beautiful home on this quiet residential street in Marina del Rey. Looking at the manicured rose bushes in bloom and the carpet-like lawn, you would never expect the grisly, horrific scene that unfolded inside earlier today."

Grisly? Horrific? Yes, please. Give it to me, Blake.

"The carnage left inside is another reminder of the increasing tensions between our home-grown drug kingpin, Santa Ana, and the largest, most ruthless cartel in northern Mexico."

The screen cuts to a sit-down with Meda Lucas. He's not messing around with subtitles. He's on a full-press marketing push and doesn't want to waste anyone's time reading. His accent is so lush and perfect it could be fake.

"I am trying to run a business. A profitable and partially legal business. This"—Meda holds out an eight-by-ten glossy and gory photo of a former captain who appears to have been barbecued—"this man here. The one who's been recently charbroiled? He has a wife. A sister. Teachers who taught him how to tie his shoes. A brother who calls him for advice. Who conducts business like this?"

Blake amps up the drama with a voice-over as the camera sweeps through the pristine vacant house with a large burnt oval where a loveseat should be.

"The man many believe is responsible for this bloody retribution is local gang leader Santa Ana, who, until recently, was a minor player on the narcotics scene and is known for conducting business hidden behind a mask representing the devil. Back to you, Kyla."

"Stay safe out there, Blake. A semitrailer carrying thousands of pounds of Lay's potato chips has overturned on the 405, killing three people and blocking the freeway in both directions."

Death by potato chip. That's a new one.

Maybe that becomes Wednesday's thing. Snack-related demise. I sure hope not.

A retirement party has taken command of the karaoke mic downstairs. Hump day is really screwing me this week. I've got to get somewhere quiet. I'll hide out in the tub. I like taking baths. It's the most relaxing thing I do. My mom always said I was half fish with my need for a good soak.

The square envelope stops me on my way to the bathroom. It's taunting me. I swear it's doubled in size. I cautiously pick it up like it's going to bite me.

To: Tristan Melendez

Blah Blah Blah Shithole Drive

You never left SoCal, USA

The return address is Azusa High Alumni Club. There's an alumni club? Huh. I'm sure they're asking for donations or something. This lowers my cortisol level some. They just want money. I bring the envelope with me and let it teeter on the bathroom sink. Something about this junk mail feels ominous, like I shouldn't leave it unsupervised.

I'm short and I still can't stretch out in my chipped and faded tub. The water heater has been in a mood lately and I can only get the bath temperature to barely warm. I go ahead with my self-care and try to relax, cold and smushed. I shut my eyes and inhale.

Before I have a chance to exhale, I sit up. I swear I just heard the envelope slither on the sink. It's definitely getting bigger. I can't relax. I have to open it. I'm letting a piece of card stock bully me. Grow some balls, Tristan.

Here we go. I dry my hands and carefully inch it over from the sink. This is going to be a major letdown. I wonder if the water has gotten any hotter? Should I check? This is when it gets tricky. I turn the tap on and I could be filling a quickly cooling tub with ice-cold water or the gremlin that effs up all my pipes is taking a nap and I'll get lucky with a scalding blast. I'm stalling. Open the darn thing. I barely slip my finger under the seal and it pops open like a jack-in-the-box. Thankfully I'm not assaulted by any confetti snakes. I wince, though, half expecting it.

I inch out the card from the envelope. Oh, shit. This is much worse. This is death by a thousand confetti snakes.

WELCOME BACK, CLASS OF 1998!

It's an invitation to my twenty-fifth high school reunion. Every muscle in my body is balled up in a mix of terror and regret. Twenty-five years, and I'm nothing but a lonely jerk soaking in room-temperature water. I have yet to make it to the stage in life when I can reliably soak in hot or even warm water. Worse, I don't think I deserve it.

That's obvious, right? I clearly have some significant mental health issues rooted in my deep and endearing feelings of worthlessness. I make six figures. I'm sitting on a Crate & Barrel pile of money and this is the life I'm willing to put up with?

Ah, but I should be making seven figures. That's the thing. That's why I don't deserve a nice bath. No. I need a sucky bath to remind me how much I suck. Some people actually make seven figures. Some people make that in a day. The tortured existence of my formative years was supposed to bring a much bigger payoff. Even the ones doing the torturing thought so.

Everyone assumed I'd figure out a way for us to live on Mars. But being good at math doesn't automatically make you good at space. That's some nerd bias. Or I'd be some nutty professor surrounded by books and covered in chalk dust. Again, not all nerds grow up to be Einstein.

But I grew up to be nothing. It's not that I want to work for NASA. I just want to *tell* people I work for NASA. Could I have worked for NASA? It's eighty times harder to get a job at

NASA than it is to get into Harvard. In 2017, they hired 12 people out of over 18,300 applicants. No. I assuredly could never work at NASA. It's spelled out in the numbers. Numbers are rarely kind and never side with optimism.

My time in high school can be described as a slouch. A skinny nobody on the verge of either tears or spewing word vomit, praying to be invisible. It was not a fun time. The boys were all a head taller and filled with gallons more testosterone. I've yet to catch up. The girls were . . . not interested. I had one friend. He was a total freak. I played a lot of chess with my mom. She was good, but I always let her win.

Right now, I just want to marinate in self-pity. I should toss this unsolicited invite in the trash and slit my wrists. No. I couldn't do that to Wednesday. I can't screw up Wednesday's stats. Oh, well. I faced my fears. It could have been worse. Why did I say that? Nothing better comes after saying it could have been worse. Fuck.

Flipping over the invitation, I'm confronted by text trying way too hard to be hip:

Beneath that, I'm slapped in the face with a memory I locked up a long time ago. A grainy senior class photo. One of the worst moments of my life.

IT'S TIME TO LET IT ALL HANG OUT. JOIN US, AZUSA HIGH SCHOOL CLASS OF 1998! CELEBRATE THE BIG 25 AND CATCH UP IRL. RELIVE AWESOME MEMORIES AND MAKE NEW ONES AS WE TOAST HOMECOMING WEEK WITH FOOD, OPEN BAR, AND RETRO FUN IN THE GYM. BRING YOUR DANCING SHOES AND GET READY FOR SOME EPIC INSTAGRAM POSTS.

It was an ordinary, mildly terrible day toward the end of senior year. The countdown was on to graduation and freedom. Even I was getting swept up in the feel-good senior vibes. I had been accepted to USC on a full scholarship. They were in need of more Mexican math majors. I was starting to believe that right around the corner might be the next day of the rest of my life.

There was just a week left of school. Everyone's fate had been decided. College or cosmetology school, parent's business or parent's basement, addict or counselor. Final exams were over. Classes had been failed or passed. Two hundred and eighty-three people were finally reduced to a number. A ranking. A statistic. A bar on a graph. We all knew it and it all made sense. For that brief period in time, I wasn't alone in crunching human numbers. We were all walking SAT scores. Even the burnouts were satisfied with themselves: 37 percent were never going to go anywhere after high school and 18.4 percent of them wouldn't have a job. They were round pegs fitting snugly into their round holes just like the rest of us.

I can still smell that day, a sticky, musty bouquet. My breakfast of Mountain Dew and Cheetos lingered on my tongue in a slick slime. I may or may not have been wearing Cool Water cologne. I promised my mother I would wear my best-fitting gray T-shirt and smoothed the tiniest bit of gel in my hair to look presentable. Frankie found me in the concrete quad and complimented my efforts right away.

"Look at you all pretty for the class picture! You clean up nice, Melendez. Is that shirt freshly laundered?"

"Shut up, Frankie."

That was the pattern of 96 percent of our conversations.

"What are you supposed to be?" I asked.

Frankie was always in a costume. He was obsessed with films and often took on the personas of his favorite characters. It was embarrassing. Today he was full-on Hunter S. Thompson, complete with a skinny cigarette holder clenched between his teeth. If he wasn't trying so hard—he was always trying too hard—he kind of looked good in the bucket hat and tinted retro shades.

"Buy the ticket, take the ride."

"What?"

"*Fear and Loathing in Las Vegas*! Johnny Depp's new movie?"

"Why can't you be more like Donnie Brasco? You know, try being inconspicuous."

He let his lame prop dangle from his mouth dramatically. He clutched his heart and put a hand on my shoulder.

"Oh, Tristan! I'm proud of you, son. That was a heck of a film reference."

I pushed his sweaty hand off my nice T-shirt. "Thanks."

"Come on, we don't want to miss the big

photo. Time to take our place in the senior hall of shame."

We were close to the exit, headed for the practice soccer field, when some ass in a Limp Bizkit T-shirt checked me into a row of lockers. I bounced hard off the metal into a recycling bin and landed on the floor, surrounded by crushed cans and empty Gatorade bottles. I got pushed around a lot, but this unexpected jolt knocked the wind out of me. Frankie hadn't noticed, or maybe he did and was too focused on his own self-preservation to help. A meaty hand reached down to rescue me. It was Harry Sullivan. Of course it was Harry Sullivan. Power couple Harry Sullivan and Brea Davies (remember her from the magazine cover?) were patrolling the halls arm in arm.

"Dude, you all right?" He pulled me to my feet, exerting little effort. "Fuck that guy. He jerks off to pictures of his mom."

"Yeah." I had nothing more to add to Harry's colorful description. He proceeded to brush hallway dirt off my shoulders like I was his little brother who fell from the monkey bars.

"Tristan, you okay?" Brea wrapped herself back into Harry's arms.

"Yeah." That's me. A real wordsmith.

Brea thanked Harry properly on my behalf by smashing her lips into his. "Babe. You're so great. Oh, my God. I can't believe he did that." She continued to talk about the horrors of my assault as they strolled to the field, then glanced briefly over her shoulder at me and Frankie. "See you out there!"

Brea was Senior Class Everything. Prom Queen, Head Cheerleader, Student Council President, French Club Ambassador . . . and here's one to throw you for a loop, All-State Math Olympian. Apparently, all that led to a very successful legal career involving Supreme

Court cases and magazine covers. Brea and I had been "friends" since seventh grade when we were separated into the advanced classes. I never understood how someone so attractive could also be so smart, but most people assume I work in landscaping. Looks can be deceiving.

I thought about hiding out in that back hallway surrounded by garbage. That would have been a much better way to cap off my high school experience. But always a rule follower, I trudged out toward the masses on the field and slid into a middle row, trying to hide. One of the parent volunteers relocated me to the front.

"Shorties in the front row, sweetie."

She placed me smack dab in the middle next to Brea and Harry, who are not short but I suppose would never stand for being anywhere but front and center.

Brea smiled, delighted at my arrival.

"You sure you're okay?"

I nodded to reassure her.

"How did you do on the final?" She intrusively began to style my hair for the photo.

"I don't know yet." I did know. I got 103 percent on our last advanced calculus exam.

"I only got ninety-nine percent. Missed the extra credit. I'm so pissed. Oh, well. I'll have to settle for an A."

Brea continued to feather my hair and smooth my shirt. I'm sure I was the only living thing in the history of human existence that did not appreciate her touch.

You want to know what happened next? Deep breath. Maybe I should have a better sense of humor. Maybe I should be more forgiving. Maybe I should consider that the actions of this random adolescent stemmed from jealousy (Brea never treated him or anyone else like a pet, only me) or was just an impulsive prank from an underdeveloped brain trying to fit into the complicated hierarchy of high school. But I reject that. Even all these years later. I reject any merciful explanation. No, what happened next is a crime that should be punished to the full extent of all legal and karmic laws. A morally repugnant and un-take-backable (I made that word up) offense.

They never caught who did it; nobody really tried to find out. Whoever was responsible for the next thirty seconds—and two and a half decades—of my life deserves a special circle in Dante's Inferno. A pit of terrors for all past and future de-pantsers (new word number two) to rot and languish for eternity. Let their eyeballs be stripped from their lids repeatedly by dragons with venomous claws. Giants with putrid boils and terrible breath should detach the lower halves of their bodies on the hour only to be sewn back together by shaking hands with rusted, worm-infested needles.

But I digress.

As the professional photographer held up his

large flash and a small crowd of parents snapped away with their digital cameras, some nameless tormenter behind me thought it was the perfect time to pull down my pants. Yes, standing there in the front row in my tighty-whities or Spider-Man boxer briefs would have been hilarious. Only he miscalculated his strength and my lack of any girth or a belt, and both my pants and underwear shot down to my ankles. Click.

Yup. There's my dick. Right there on the invitation. A yellow arrow points out my modest bits, encouraging us to "let it all hang out."

Students laughed. Teachers laughed. Parents laughed. What an innocent "boys will be boys" moment to cherish. I'm lucky I didn't have to register as a sex offender.

Look at me now, twenty-five years later in a shower cap and cold tub. Still the butt of the joke. What, are you stuck on the shower cap?

Come on, if Brad Pitt bathed with a head covering, it would be sexy. I don't have much, but I do have hair. I'm very protective of every last strand. A normal wash can send up to 200 of my precious follicles literally down the drain.

Jesus! Fuck! A shoe attached to a foot is dangling inches from my face.

A voice attached to the shoe attached to the foot in my face yells down the new hole in my bathroom ceiling. "Shit, man! You okay?"

Globs of ceiling and roof debris float around me in the tub. It takes a minute for my eyes to cut through the dust in the air. A giant metal E comes into focus.

"New sign?" I tilt my head to read the vertical metal letters: E-Bowla Bowling & Arcade.

The foot leaves my bathroom as the sign drops deeper toward the tub. A face looks down at me. "You taking a bath?"

"Yes."

"Weird."

That's what this stranger finds weird in this situation?

"I think you should get out. This whole thing can cave in any second."

"Sure thing." I slide back, submerging myself in the dirty water. Sure thing.

SIX

Big Man on Campus

Tristan might want to get out of the bath-tub. Couldn't that sign electrocute him or something? And how about that Harry, huh? What a fucking psycho. I know we were all hoping Mr. Anglo-Saxon would end up fat and bald, maybe an alcoholic, but a murdering, drug-dealing sociopath? I did not see that coming. Unlike Tristan, or 99 percent of us, Harry lives a charmed existence. He isn't a total prick, though. He's always been this perfect mash-up of James Spader and Andrew McCarthy from every late-eighties movie, and now, I suppose, he has a smidge of Tony Soprano. (By the way, Molly Ringwald is overrated. There, I said it. Anyhoo . . .) Harry was never a complete asshole, but there was certainly never any reason to root for him to get the girl. He already had the girl, along with everything else.

Sorry. Are you confused? It's me again, the one with no name, the Master of Whisperers. Don't worry. It's still early. You'll get it. Okay, back to Harry.

There's a curse that comes with being Big Man on Campus. It's easy to get stuck, peak too soon. A totally cliché plotline, but we watch the same stories over and over again for a reason. Harry growing up to be a bloodthirsty savage is a nice, dark twist, but he's stuck all the same.

These days he lives in a suburban bachelor pad. It's nicely appointed in wood and plush carpeting. The single-story mid-century is an impressive size with an eyebrow-raising Zestimate. Off the informal dining room, there are two secret spaces tucked behind what looks like a closet. One door is steel with a password-protected deadbolt. That room is mostly empty, with large metal boxes that can only be opened by the owner's thumbprint. The boxes are filled with guns, cash, Japanese steak knives, some machetes, and a grenade or two. Across the hall is a more typical man cave. Harry spends most of his nights drinking alone in this temple built to honor himself.

His pristine letterman's jacket, which has had an alteration or two over the years, hangs on display next to a full-length mirror. Trophies and pictures line heavy cherrywood shelves. There's a section of footballs from big wins and a large framed team poster. Scattered in ornate frames throughout are pictures of him and Brea. Homecoming. Prom. The senior camping trip. A pair of red lace underwear dangles from their junior prom shot. I assume that's another trophy from a big win.

Pathetic, right?

His nightly routine begins with a quick stop in his locked retreat to sneak a stack of bills out of its fortified hiding spot. A wad of cash in one hand and a Scotch in the other, he settles into his sad shrine. There he downs his drink in a leather recliner while sniffing his money. He closes his eyes and inhales his success. Then he might flip through a yearbook or two or just jump to the main event: jerking off while wearing his letterman's jacket. Why did you think the mirror was there? Once he's all sniffed and jizzed out, he'll drink some more in his chair until he dozes off.

Tonight, he has some business to take care of, too. After a hard day of murder, mayhem, and pharmaceutical sales, a surprise was waiting for him in the mailbox. He held on to the square white envelope as a treat to open after he was properly lubricated with Scotch.

The return address is the Azusa High Alumni

Club. He might be drunk enough to finally make that fat donation. One of these days, he's going to give them enough cash to name the gym after him.

He carefully opens the envelope with a silver knife that found its way into the wrong room. He pulls out the piece of card stock and his eyes get wide as his deflated wiener tingles. He reads the text out loud, almost in disbelief.

"It's time to let it all hang out. Join us, Azusa High School Class of 1998!"

Yes! This is the boost he desperately needs. The slap in the face to shake him out of his middle-aged rut. High school was the best time in his life, and in a few short weeks he gets to go back.

His mind is flooded with memories. Mostly of Brea. Her legs. Her boobs. Her smile. The time she gave him a dry hand job under his desk in World Lit. He sits up straighter thinking about how the masses would part the way to let him pass in the hall. He fancied himself a benevolent ruler. A man of the people. He'd stick up for anybody who wasn't a threat. He didn't go out of his way but had a low tolerance for pricks who picked on easy targets. He was voted Most Likely to Succeed and Nicest Dude. He also got to claim half the award for Best Couple.

He often stops what he's doing to think about his former better half. He likes to imagine her halfway across the world or wherever she's settled and think about what she's doing in that same exact moment. Are they ever both sipping a Diet Coke with lemon (her favorite and a drink he still orders in the off chance it can connect them across some cosmic timeline)? Are they watching the same breaking news on CNN or both listening to that goddamn Kars4Kids commercial?

The other day he had to step away from punching a guy tied to a metal chair to ice his hand. Pummeling someone's face is really hard on the knuckles. Looking down at his busted-open digits he wondered, did Brea have painted nails? Were they long and red or short and pink? How big was the diamond looped around her ring finger? He squinted at his swollen appendage, imagining how his battered hand would look with a gold band. Would he be doing what he's doing if Brea was his wife? Never. He'd have all the excitement he needed at home. They'd have two kids, a boy for him and a girl for her, and a cabin in Big Bear and a rambler not far from the beach. She would terrify the other PTA moms. They'd be a power couple until the end.

He runs his fingers over the edges of the invitation. She would have gotten the same square envelope. Is she sitting somewhere right now looking down at the grainy photo of that nerdy kid's dong and thinking about him?

Sorry, Harry. She's not. Brea's assistant

intercepted the invite and tossed it in the trash before it could flood her with endorphins and good vibes from her past. Brea is a very important person. She doesn't have time to open her own mail and she has made it very clear she isn't to be bothered with something as basic as a high school reunion. Let's end this chapter with a slight detour to check in on her, shall we?

It's late. She is currently holding her doomed assistant hostage in order to avoid "what's his face" waiting at home. Brea was bored once, so she got married. He's an anesthesiologist who doesn't work much. He comes from old money on the East Coast, and for a minute that felt like love. She spent a year planning an epic wedding, playing dress-up as a Kennedy. It's been a few years since the party and he's unfortunately still around. She got drunk at a BBQ a few weeks ago and told her neighbors, "Ted fucks like a grandpa."

Ted is her husband. He should get out now

before she totally destroys him. He won't. Brea has to do everything in their relationship, including leaving. The couple will probably move in order to save face from her recent digression. This is their third house. A McMansion painted in various shades of gray. They were not invited to the block's annual crawfish boil. Why do rich people love to make a thing out of eating poor people food?

Zoning out at her desk, the corner of a square white envelope catches her eye from the trash. She reaches down to fish it out of the metal bin. She flips it over in her hands. It's stained from her 3 p.m. latte.

She spies the return address. "The alumni club . . . Annabelle! Annabelle, what is this?"

Annabelle is worried by her boss's tone. She should be. "What?" She peeks her head into the office and sees the white envelope in Brea's hand. "I don't know. Junk mail."

At first, Brea assumes they are asking for

money. Maybe she's finally depressed enough to give them a buttload of cash. One day, she's going to have the library named after her. But something about the weight of this square envelope makes her think it's more important than junk mail. She stabs the stained white paper with sharp black nails. She allows her lips to spread into a wrinkle-inducing smile (she has trained her face to show zero emotion unless otherwise directed) as she slides out the invitation.

"Hey, Annabelle?"

The hopeful young woman scurries back toward the office door.

"Yes?"

"You're fired."

SEVEN

Pep Talk

Lacey was gone for two days. That's unusual. Not for Lacey. It's unusual for the average American worker. She's one of the 11 percent of workers between the ages of thirty-one and forty-five who take more than ten sick days a year. Is Lacey thirty? I feel like this has come up before. I should ask so I have accurate data. Wait. I can't ask a woman her age, right? That's still a thing? Weight, age, politics. If she's under thirty, then she's slightly less special, being one of the 16 percent of workers who call in sick more than ten times a year. I'll have to ask her.

I can't have inaccurate percentiles. This is going to keep me up at night.

In Sweden, after fourteen sick days the government pays you out of the state's insurance fund. Lacey would do well there. Here, not so much. Sometimes after an extended absence she'll come back to work with a limp or an ACE bandage wrapped around her wrist. Today she's in sunglasses. I heard her say "pink eye" as a few lookie-loos walked by.

Since getting that square envelope I've been more miserable than usual. I tried to chalk it up to vitamin deficiency, but I can't lie to myself. Sure, I've only consumed roughly three-fifths of my daily recommendations for years. Decades, I'm sure. If you offered me a million dollars to name five vitamins, I could maybe come up with three. There's C. That's oranges. D. I think that's for bones? Is there an A? A deficiency in one of those letters is a guarantee and my baseline. None of this matters.

I'm not suffering from any deficiency. Just depression. Deep depression and suffocating regret. Why couldn't I have been a normal adult and amass a pile of material goods out of spite? Sure, I'm lonely and moderately pathetic, but check out my Tesla. (Do not get me started on self-driving cars. The AI is not there, folks.) Hey, jerks, remember when you laughed at me the one and only time I showed up to drink with you in a parking lot? Well, I have a three-bed, two-bath Craftsman at the bottom of the Hollywood Hills. Go fuck yourself. You're rich and successful? Me, too, and I have triplets. The smallest one has a glass eye. My hot wife couldn't make it. She's a doctor. From Canada.

Yeah, I really should have spent more time collecting goods and people.

I have nothing to show for myself. Nothing interesting. Nothing fancy. Absolutely nothing that is hot. Of course, I'm not going to go.

Nobody will notice if I'm missing, but everyone will notice if I'm there.

"Hey." Lacey whispers toward my desk. "Tristan, you all right?"

"Huh? Fine."

"You haven't moved in like an hour."

"Oh."

Footsteps are headed our way. Goddamnit. Here comes Kevin.

"Sup, bro?"

"Not much." Take a hint, Kevin. Nothing is ever "Sup" with me.

"You catch the game?" He grabs a pen off my desk and starts flipping it around.

"Game? No."

"Do you even have a TV?"

Kevin is in the top 6 percent of intolerable people on planet Earth. He listens to music in his cubicle louder than anyone else in the office. Journey. So much Journey. I don't know if Journey is now considered retro or if he just has terrible taste. They don't have that many songs. You would know that if you had a Journey playlist on rotation three cubicles over. "Don't Stop Believin'" plays on average every forty-seven minutes. I hear that song more than eight times a day, five days a week, fifty-one-and-a-half weeks a year. If I murder Kevin, it will be because of that song. Any rational jury would acquit me on all charges.

"Dude."

I forgot he was standing there.

"Dude, you are, like, so stoned all the time!"

I clear my throat. "I don't do drugs. Especially at work."

"Whatever, stoner. Lacey, sweet glasses." He invades her space and whispers. "I'm hungover, too."

Lacey's cheeks flash red. She pushes out a smile. "Conjunctivitis."

Kevin takes a step back. "Conjunctawhat? You dudes are too much!" He saunters off to his next time-wasting adventure, pulling a wedgie from his butt cheeks.

Once we have our cubes safely back to ourselves, Lacey rolls her chair closer. "You do seem extra distracted today. Everything good?"

In a rare moment of actual communication, I once told Lacey that she asks me if I'm okay too much. So now it's "Everything good?"

"Are we doing lunch today?" The edge in my voice is Kevin's fault.

She responds with a nod.

"Sorry. I shouldn't have snapped at you."

She waves off my apology. "Lunch would be great. I brought a salad."

The next few hours I try to keep myself busy. It makes the morning go by fast, at least. Isn't that the goal? At 11:30, Lacey is waiting for me at a rusted picnic table next to the parking lot. It's a nice lunch spot. Ashtray adjacent. The tree above is half bare, which makes for some interesting shadows.

Lacey pushes some lettuce around with a plastic fork. "No wind yet. That's nice."

I sit. "Very nice."

Crap. 'Tis the season. The Santa Ana winds should be starting up any day. See, we talk about more than traffic in LA. Sometimes we talk about the weather.

She takes off her sunglasses. "I don't really have pink eye."

"I figured." I never know if I should ask her what she does on her days off. I go for it.

"Have a good day . . . days off?"

"I was sick."

I shouldn't have asked. "Right."

It's quiet. Lacey usually fills the space with chitchat. Something must be wrong. "See any good cat memes lately?"

She eats a cherry tomato without making eye contact. Something is definitely wrong.

"Tristan."

Now here's a pregnant pause. Should I respond?

"If something is bothering you, we can talk about it. I could help."

Wait, is she upset because she thinks I'm upset? This is the whole Men Are from Mars, Women Are from Venus thing, right? I don't understand why men aren't from Venus. If the point is to imply that men and women are from two different planets, it doesn't matter what the planets are, none of them have human attributes tied to a specific gender. Venus rhymes with penis. It makes more sense. I can understand no one wanting to be associated with Jupiter, a gas giant—

"Tristan! Where are you?"

Huh. Lacey must be running low on the bottomless barrel of patience she typically has reserved for me. I need to try and fix this. Whatever *this* is. "Sorry. I'm really spacing out today."

"Ya think? What's going on?"

"I have to keep my mind moving or I'll fall into a puddle of despair. Did I just say that out loud?"

"Yes." She puts her fork down and waits.

"I'm a loser."

"Is that news?"

"Ha ha." She doesn't join in my sarcastic laughing. I think she might have been serious. Harsh. "I got invited to my twenty-fifth high school reunion."

"Oh. Cool."

"Not cool. High school was awful."

"Duh. Look at us."

I'm a bit thrown off by her tough love approach. Does she have her period? Can I ask? No. I definitely cannot ask her that.

"Are you going to go?" She gets back to picking at her salad.

"No way. Why? Would you?"

She answers quickly. "I went to online school."

"I didn't know that's been around for so long."

"How old do you think I am?"

Is she mad?

She's not. "I'm messing with you. I'm twenty-eight, by the way. If you're not going, who cares? Why let it bother you?"

Twenty-eight? That's younger than expected. Is it too young? Do I need to sign something?

"Because I know it's there. I should have been prepared."

She's not getting it. "Prepared for what?"

"To show those dickholes that I made it. That I'm somebody."

She genuinely seems surprised. "Tristan, you don't care about that stuff."

This is when I would typically shrug, or, more typically, never be this deep in a real conversation. But if I'm going to share with anyone, it's going to be Lacey, and something about this moment, something about sitting next to an overflowing ashtray watching her cherry tomatoes roll around in vinaigrette, makes me word vomit.

"I was pushed around for four years. I don't know which was worse, being treated like dirt or treated like a pet. There was this one guy, Harrison, you can imagine, he hit the genetic jackpot with just enough inbred Nordic genes to be perfect. And he had everything. Quarterback. Starting pitcher. Perfect teeth. Straight-C student without ever cracking a book. Friends. Oh, my God, the underclassmen idolized him like some Greek god. His girlfriend, forget it. He had everything. He didn't need to be prom king, but he still was—"

She attempts to tiptoe into my raging rant. "Did you want to be prom king?"

I won't allow any intrusions. "Of course! Who doesn't want to be prom king? Has there ever on this planet been a person who's like 'Uhhhh, no thank you. I'd rather not be worshipped and adored. Please, let me be the peasant this time.

Yes, please, in this life you go ahead and be part of the exclusive upper ruling class and leave me to work the land.' Yes. I wanted to be prom king. Why not me? When did the world get together and vote on a list of strict attributes required of all future prom kings, and why do they all have to be some version of goddamn Harrison Sullivan? Or fine. Sure. Those *are* the rules. Why couldn't I be born with broader shoulders or blue eyes? The flipping stork couldn't throw me a little bit of swagger?"

Lacey's voice is soft as she proceeds with curious caution. "You know it's not actually like a real title. It doesn't mean anything."

I'm really spinning now. "It means everything in high school."

"But you're not in high school." She doesn't give up attempting to talk me down. "Literally one person gets to be prom king."

I sound like a teenager. "So? Why can't I be the one person?"

"It was never going to be you."

"Why not?!" Marcia, Marcia, Marcia! Lacey probably wouldn't get that reference. I can't believe she's only twenty-eight.

"Math." She leans in close. I'm not often (ever?) this open or unhinged. She looks like she's about to grab me. "How many male-identifying students did you graduate with?"

"Dudes? Two hundred and sixty-seven."

"Okay." She talks slowly. "You had a one in two hundred sixty-seven chance of being prom king. If this Harrison wasn't there, you would have had a one in two hundred sixty-six chance of—"

"I get it."

"That's a zero point three percent chance—"

"I can't face them. Not like this."

"Who can't you face? The other ninety-nine point seven percent of people who were never going to be prom king?"

"Yes." I take a long, sad breath. "Lacey, I've

got nothing. Nothing to show that I even existed the last twenty-five years."

"That's not true."

"Okay. What?"

She opens her mouth but has nothing to say. She shrugs, not certain if this is funny or incredibly sad. I don't make her come up with an answer. This is sad. Really sad. I should be coming up with more exciting and interesting words to entice you to keep reading, but I can't. Sad is the most appropriate descriptor of this moment. Of the last million and one moments.

This doesn't feel good. No. I definitely do not enjoy what happens when you give your thoughts words. I may never talk again. Thankfully, my eyes narrow and my muscles tighten. Mad. I'm mad now. This feels much better than being sad. It's amazing how the body knows what to do to survive. My new thoughts come out hot and tight.

"Brea Davies! Oh, she was the worst of the worst. You know her."

"I do?"

"From your magazine! She was on the cover."

"*Law Today*? Okay, so clearly she's outside of the ninety-nine point seven percent."

I nod and rant on. It flows out like lava. "She was always touching me. I swear she'd put me in a diaper and carry me around in a baby backpack if she could have."

"That's very descriptive."

"I didn't matter to her."

"Sure sounds like you did. Nobody has ever wanted to put me in a diaper."

"You're not getting it."

I sound frustrated because I am frustrated. Why do I have to sit here and spell out my midlife crisis for her? As my only friend, Lacey Hahn should intuitively understand what it was like to be me during those four nightmare hellscape feudal years that were high school, and she should certainly understand my urgent need for domination and thus redemption. It's a tale as old as time.

"Maybe not. It seems like you're not very happy?"

"I've never been happy. For once, I just want to be better."

"Better, like feel better?"

"Like be better than somebody. Anybody. Any single person."

Lacey is out of rebuttals. What is she going to do, tell me I'm really good at math? I'm polite and clean? She puts her hand on top of mine. It's weird to be touching. How long do I keep my hand under hers? Who moves first? Thankfully a bee buzzes by her nose and she releases my hand so she can swat at it.

"Tristan, you know, you can be whoever you want. If you don't like who you are, be something different. Most people are a work in progress."

Is she trying to tell me Kevin is actively trying to be such a major douche canoe? Or Gina in customer service with the flowy skirts and mood rings, she's doing that on purpose? Like it's a good thing? And Lacey, the Patron Saint of all the works in progress. She is constantly trying to be something different. How's that working out? I want to say something mean but I think better of it.

Luckily one bee turns into three bees, which puts an end to our lunch and conversation. Lacey mumbles something about an EpiPen as she hurries back inside. I throw out our garbage. I never unwrapped my soggy sandwich.

Back at my desk I'm in full-fledged fight or flight. I'm doing both at the same time. I'm fighting not to fly out of my chair and step in front of a semi.

Lacey is working extra hard this afternoon. She doesn't want to accidentally get me going again, I'm sure. I'm trying to avoid her gaze, but I catch her looking over the tops of her glasses at me. I wonder if I went too far over lunch. This must be what it's like to have a real friend. Someone you can word vomit all over and they still sneak a peek at you to make sure you haven't stapled yourself to death. I suppose it feels good.

It's Brea. Thinking about Brea is jamming up my whole nervous system. I have pushed some serious shit down. Way, way, way down. It doesn't often creep up. This could end up being a real Mount Vesuvius situation. It's weird, I hardly flinched when I saw her magazine cover, but that's when she was safe in the abstract. In two weeks, I'll be seeing her in the flesh. If I was going to go to the reunion. Which I'm not.

Who knows? Maybe this crisis was looming

with or without the reunion. I am overdue for a total meltdown. I was in love with Breanna Davies. It was statistically impossible to be a fourteen-year-old boy and not fall in love with her. We spent most of the school day together. We would study after school in the library. Sometimes, even in high school, she'd still come over to study at my house. My mother would creep around the dining room table, pumping us full of snacks. I was so embarrassed when she'd drop off Mexican Cokes. Just get American Coke, Mom. Jesus.

It's not that Brea wasn't nice to me. Quite the opposite. She didn't use me or try to keep our friendship a secret. She acted like we had both agreed that we would be great study buddies and super-duper friends and never not once at any time on any planet be anything else. Because I, of course, was nothing else. A guy like me should have been thrilled to be her pet and grateful for whatever bones she tossed me. I guess it hurt having so little say in my own irrelevancy.

She often wanted me around but did a good job keeping me invisible. I was so inconsequential she was literally comfortable getting naked in front of me. What should have been a total baller day that went down in teenage boy history was yet another epic defeat.

It was a Tuesday toward the end of junior year. Everyone had checked out for the summer. Class time was filled with either movies or "independent work time." Brea and I had AP Chemistry. I hadn't seen her all day. About half the class was doodling at our lab stations. We must have looked like cavemen, using such ancient tools as a pen and notebook. There I was, minding my own business working on cave drawings, when a flash of blond beckoned me from the hallway.

"Pssst. Hey, Tristan. Come here."

I fumbled with my book bag, not sure if I should take it with me.

"Leave it. Come on!" she whispered impatiently.

I shuffled with my head down toward the door. The teacher didn't look up from his *People* magazine.

"Want to have some fun?"

"I dunno."

"Come on." She grabbed my hand and dragged me down the hall.

We headed to the auditorium. It was a pretty impressive space for a high school. Big stage. Red padded seats. A balcony and tech booth. A few kids were smoking in the tech booth. Brea gave them a wave as we skipped by, hopping over seats. She was a gorgeous gazelle, giggling while breaking the rules hurdling over seats. I was a clumsy troll who couldn't understand why we weren't just walking down the empty aisles. By the grace of God, I made it to the backstage dressing rooms without breaking my neck.

I found her going through a rack of mermaid costumes. "Aren't these hot?"

The spring musical, *The Little Mermaid*, had recently wrapped up. Brea was way too cool to be a high school thespian but not too cool to play with the costumes.

"Help me with this." She tossed something sparkly at me and shimmied out of her jeans. I held the pink-scaled tail open, so she could step into it. Her bare thigh rubbed against my face. She hopped closer to a mirror and took off her Gap logo T-shirt. She turned around, not convinced that her baby-blue lace push-up bra was a good match and clearly uninterested in putting on one of the leotards that kept the look PG.

"What do you think?"

I'm getting lightheaded. Now. In the

grown-man present. Thinking about her boobs wrapped in blue lace and pushed up to her chin . . . anyway. You can imagine how my then-virgin nervous system was taking that all in.

"Let me try the shells." She slipped her bra off one strap at a time and half-heartedly attempted to cover herself with her right forearm. "Will you hand me those?" She was pointing to a rack over my shoulder.

I never gave her the shells.

The next thing I remember, Ms. Garcia, the fifty-two-year-old school nurse, was hovering over my face. I'm not a shallow person, but Ms. Garcia's unfortunate lady mustache and lopsided eyelid was a rude awakening. Once my eyes came into focus, I yelped and scooted backward.

"Honey." She crawled toward me. By this point I had lost the power of speech. "Did you hurt your skull? Let me check."

She cradled my head. "Relax. Have you eaten today? It looks like you passed out."

I blinked twice.

"Does this happen a lot?"

I blinked once.

"Oh, dear." She glanced toward my wet pants. "I think you may have had a seizure."

No, Ms. Garcia. Sweet Ms. Garcia. I did not have a seizure. What struck me down that terrible seventy-six-degree, slightly overcast with winds blowing toward the east, Tuesday afternoon was not a seizure. I had almost died from Boner-Induced Hysteria, better known as Blue-Ball Delirium in some circles. I had ejaculated so rapidly that I stopped breathing. Who knows how long I was lying there? I could have been out for hours.

At dismissal, I passed Brea in the hall wearing my gym shorts and holding a note for my mother.

"Tristan! Oh, my God, Tristan! Are you all

right?" She didn't give me time to answer. "I had to get out of there. You understand, right? No sense in us both getting busted?"

I blinked twice, and she swam down the hall with the crowd.

I want her to see me now and be dumb-struck with the possibilities. I want to be that guy, whoever that guy is, for just one freaking day. What is it like to be wanted? How would it feel if she followed me for a change instead of tugging me around on a leash? Where would I take her? How far would I let it go before I shut her down? Before I let her be covered with the thousand stings of rejection and embarrassment?

Okay, fine, who am I kidding? You're right, if she took the bait, I'd go all in. This wouldn't be a gotcha, shoulda woulda coulda situation. I'm not an idiot. You don't pass on an opportunity with Brea Davies no matter how shitty she used to make you feel.

No! This is absurd. Stop it! I am not going to that freaking reunion. It's that goddamn mermaid tail. It's doing it again. I'm losing it!

Breathe, asshole. (I'm talking to myself, not you.)

But really, what would it take to be with Brea Davies? Is Harrison Sullivan the Third the only blueprint? I'll never be blond with blue eyes. Or have broad shoulders, or impressive calves. Money. Money would help. Not being a fucking spaz would help. I've got to calm down before I hurt myself.

"Tristan?"

"What?!" I scream in Lacey's face. "Sorry." I'm burning that invitation when I get home.

"It's time to go. If we stay any longer, Tad is going to yell at us."

Or murder us. Tad is terrifying. He's half janitor, half white supremacist. You know the type. Well, hopefully you don't. Christ, I'm wasting time. We've got to go.

I jump up. "Yeah. Thanks. Lost track of time. I didn't mean to make you work late."

"I wasn't going to leave you. Tad would totally murder you."

We smile at Tad's expense and head out of the empty office. I walk Lacey to her car. I do this most nights. It's weird when she calls in sick. I walk all the way home feeling like I forgot to do something.

She breaks the silence when we are halfway across the parking lot. Lacey always parks as far from the building as possible. I don't understand it. "I hope I wasn't too hard on you at lunch. It's none of my business."

"No. Thank you. It was helpful."

Her eyes light up. "Really? Good! I am a licensed canine psychologist, you know."

Is this how she talks to depressed dogs? "You're a good friend."

Hearing this makes her smile tighten. That's

odd. Who doesn't want to be told they are a good friend?

"Tristan." Her voice is now serious.

Serious? What should I do? When in doubt, be a mirror. I learned that from an infomercial. I echo her tone. "Lacey."

It works. Her smile softens. "I thought a lot about what you said. Be whoever you want to be. Prom king, whatever. But not for Brea Davies or Garrison—"

"Harrison."

"Just as bad. Be whoever you want, but do it for you."

"I don't know *what* I want. But I know it's not this."

She unlocks her car door. "Make something up."

"You make it sound so easy."

"Why make it hard? You don't like the car you're driving, get a new one—"

"I don't drive—"

"Let me finish my metaphors. Try on a bunch of hats until you find the one that fits. Put on a happy face—"

She's losing me. "I don't think you're using the term *metaphor* correctly."

Lacey's car auto-locks itself. She's distracted digging through her purse for the key fob. "Tristan, have you ever tried being happy?"

"What do you mean?" I wish we were sitting. But then this conversation might go on even longer and I am definitely ready for it to wrap up. Damn it, why did I just ask a question?

"You put a negative spin on everything. Have you ever tried being happy?"

"I'm not always negative." Why am I arguing? Lacey raises an eyebrow. "I'm factual."

"Factual?" She sighs. I may have finally eroded her interest. "I'm just saying. What if you went to this reunion with the idea that it's going to go well?"

"There's no way I'm going."

"Okay. Forget the reunion. Try something, anything. Make yourself do it without being factual, whatever that means, and instead, I don't know, smile?"

"You sound like Mary Poppins."

"Whatever." She unlocks her car again.

"Sorry. Here. Let me try it." I smile in the creepiest way possible.

It works and makes her laugh. "You brought this all up. I'm just trying to help." She opens her door. "Why do you always think things are going to suck?"

"Because the odds are—" I'm surprised she lets me get that much of a rebuttal out.

"How do you know?" She's practically yelling. She holds up her hand, giving herself a signal to take a breath. She continues, slightly calmer. "You've never done it any other way. You're using faulty data."

Oh, no, she didn't! You don't accuse a stats man of bad data. I don't think I've ever seen her this worked up. I don't know why she cares so much about my stupid high school reunion. It's ridiculous that I care this much, why should she care at all? This is what I get for sharing my feelings. She shifts her tactics to a subject we're both more comfortable dealing with: math.

"All your calculations, you use the same variables. Makes sense you always get the same answer."

"Life's the equation and people are the variables. Now that's an excellent metaphor."

She doesn't appreciate my compliment and rolls her eyes hard.

I get out of the way so she can squeeze into her Hyundai Accent. I swear those cars are built for toddlers. She tries her best to climb in gracefully. She doesn't. Failing seems to aggravate her more. Once situated, she exhales loudly through her nose and talks out of the open window. "Fake it till you make it, you know? You think those beyotches from high school are so happy? Probably not. It's not that you're so freaking special, Tristan Melendez. You're no different than anybody else. Everyone is struggling. We're all flipping miserable but maybe the more we pretend to be anything, anything other than fudging miserable, that's when we end up being a little less miserable."

I must have pushed some buttons. "You can say *fuck*. It's okay. I'm not going to tell on you."

She smiles a big and real smile. "You know I don't swear. I don't care if you go to the reunion. It'd be nice if you were happy." She takes a second to pick her final thought. "You have to find your thing, Tristan. And with that, I bid you adieu." She waves as she puts it in reverse.

Walking home, I'm annoyed. Where does Lacey Hahn, a vision in beige, get off lecturing me on how to be happy? It's not like she's some model of self-actualization. I start making a list of some of her most notable flaws. It feels good, but I know it's mean. I don't want these thoughts to get too comfortable and accidentally sneak out in conversation. I switch to thinking about my own most-notable flaws. A greatest hits tape of cringeworthy fails. When in doubt, my brain defaults to a lifetime blooper reel often narrated by my father.

Striking out at my first Little League game.

"I knew you couldn't do it."

Bringing home an A-minus.

"You should be embarrassed."

Walking my bike home after wiping out.

"I told you to be careful."

When I was thirteen and noticed the waitress was a girl and had these wonderful things called boobs.

"Don't waste your time."

I was always too slow. Too weak. Be louder. Be a man. Be someone else's problem.

I've never gone to therapy, but I once fell asleep to an informercial selling self-help meditation tapes. To stop unwanted thought patterns,

I'm supposed to imagine a giant stop sign. The bigger the better. Okay. I need to stop walking for this. I shut my eyes, take a cleansing breath, and fill the darkness behind my eyelids with a stop sign the size of Christ the Redeemer. Fuck you, Dad.

Find my thing, what does she mean, like a hobby? What if I was a weird hobby guy? Could coin collecting or amphibians be my thing? Pickleball? Do men ever knit? A British study from 2017 estimates that it takes six weeks to get into a creative hobby and seven for an active one like yoga or paddleboarding.

I guess starting a hobby could give me something to do over dreadfully long weekends. Nah. To get good at something, become an expert, you need to do it three hours every day for ten years. A recent study looking at the life expectancy of 3.4 million people with an average age of sixty-six found people who lived alone had a 32 percent higher mortality rate than those who lived with others. Those who reported feeling lonely were 20 percent more likely to be dead in seven years than their social counterparts. In fact, sitting and loneliness are quickly becoming the leading killers of those over sixty-five. Combine that with my mother's cancer genes and my father's everything, I'll be lucky to make it to sixty.

No point in learning to play the piano now. I'll be dead in less than twenty years. It will take me half that to get any good. I don't care what Lacey says. I'm not being negative. I'm being practical.

EIGHT

The Problem

She's wrong. You agree with me, right? At home, I can't get what Lacey said out of my head. It doesn't help that I'm eating lasagna that she made for me out of Hello Kitty Tupperware with her name on it. I'm not mad anymore. Correction. I was never mad. I'm not annoyed anymore. The whole conversation was confusing. I was looking for a little misery loves company, not a pep talk. I wasn't expecting a self-reflection call to action. I hate feeling confused. It's worse than feeling like a freak. There's consistency with the latter.

After dinner, I scroll on my phone to distract myself. It mildly works. I chase an ice-cap stat down a brutal rabbit hole. Global warming. Another reason not to bother with learning new things. Before I know it, it's dark.

I have to take a leak, but I'm nervous to traverse my living (well, really, only) room. My apartment has become open concept in the worst way possible. The floor isn't fixed. There are some miscolored slats of plywood and caution tape preventing me from falling onto lane seven. Lucky number seven.

No one has attempted to do anything in the bathroom in regard to my new and definitely not up to code skylight. It's unbearably loud. I'm mildly worried a hawk is going to fly in and take up residence. Or a mountain lion. There have only been sixteen verified mountain lion attacks on humans in California since 1890. I could be number seventeen. And with my pants around my ankles. Wonderful.

In between gutter balls, I hear a group celebrating below me. Chad or Chud has just been accepted into a design program at Pepperdine. It must be Chad. No one is named Chud. From what I can gather from the different toasts in his honor, he's going back to school after a failed taco truck experiment. Once that tanked, he took his time to figure out his next move while milking goats in Italy. Design, specifically eco-friendly landscape architecture, is now his passion, and his dreams are all coming true.

This dude went from owning a food truck to goats to now whatever the hell he's talking about. Oh, wait . . . there's more. Before becoming a mobile taco enthusiast, he was a financial planner. I sneak a peek down below, being careful not to lean too far off the couch and literately crash the party I'm spying on. Renaissance Man is surrounded by a half dozen very attractive women. Lacey might be right. Reinventing himself has definitely worked for Chud.

Is that what she was getting at? I put on some headphones and blast a generic soft-rock playlist. Another tip from my infomercial. Distract your mind with music. Okay. Do your best, Marc Cohn and Rick Astley.

Never gonna give you up. Never gonna let you down. Never gonna run around and desert you.

I'm never going to be able to fall asleep. I'll probably never sleep again. I've got to make sense of Lacey's advice. I have to prove that everything she said was crap and wrong. Is that even what all that was? Advice? I don't remember asking for it.

My apartment is very still. The floor typically vibrates from bowling balls smashing into pins and thumping into the gutter. I slip off my headphones and peek down the hole again. It's dark and quiet. The soda machine and freezer are humming. Someone forgot to turn off the neon Corona sign above the bar. It's kind of beautiful. It's three in the morning. I've been rocking out for six hours. Time to break this down. I've got to mind-map my way out of this funk if I'm ever going to sleep again.

I need something big to write on. Lucky for me, half of my floor is currently a pile of scrap plywood. I dislodge a rectangle without getting a splinter or falling to my death. Okay, that's overly dramatic. I'm sure I wouldn't *die* if I ended up taking the shortest of cuts to the dark linoleum below. I'd most likely just break a few bones and crawl around until late morning when the bowling alley opens. Focus! Okay, now let's see if I have a Sharpie in the old junk drawer. Yes, even I have a junk drawer. There's not much in it, but there is a fat black permanent marker waiting for me. I take a few sniffs before getting to work. I love the smell of office supplies.

First things first, identify the problem. The reunion. That's the fuse that lit this current midlife crisis. I write it in all caps in a small circle in the middle of the board. There's a bigger problem, though. I enclose the small circle in a larger circle and write "I am a total waste of space and have accomplished nothing in twenty-five years." A little wordy. I should just write "LOSER" but we all know I'm not a very concise person.

I fill the space around the circles with random words and try to find an equation working backward to make a literal word problem that I can solve. Then I can go to bed.

Lacey and her lecture did most of the work for me. What were some of her hot takes?

Pretend.

Bitches from high school.

I'm not special.

Who cares?

I don't care.

Bad data.

Fake it.

Try something.

Be okay.

Forget the reunion.

Why make it harder?

Be less miserable.

Be better.

Put on a happy face.

Hats.

Hats? Why hats? The only thing my brain can come up with are the lyrics to "Walking in Memphis" on an unrelenting loop. Has that ever driven someone crazy? Is there a study or something about what happens when you listen to the same song repeatedly? Would certain songs lead to a quicker breakdown? Oh, my God. This marker is making me high. I like it. Back to work!

Hats.

Get a thing.

Drugs! Maybe doing drugs could be my thing. No needles or smoking anything that makes me pick my face off. Something nice that takes the edge off, like this sweet, fat marker.

Get a grip, Tristan! Wait, should I write that down? Why not?

Get a grip.

Okay, what do we have here? I prop the plywood against the wall and take a step back to study my circles and bold black words. Each letter looks like a tiny square hieroglyph.

Lacey is correct. I'm obviously not a happy person. I'm an unhappy asshole standing at a crossroads. If the invite to the reunion brought me to this unpleasant realization, is attending the reunion the only way to stop my fixation with the past? If I go and it's a success, will that change the trajectory of my next twenty-five years? If I don't go, will my level of despair go up or down? Crap. I'm rusty. I need another piece of wood.

Another quick sniff and I start jotting down my word problem:

Tristan has been invited to his high school reunion. He doesn't want to go because his life sucks. Tristan has to go in order to stop thinking about his past and maybe the next twenty-five years will suck less. How can Tristan successfully attend his high school reunion?

He can't. This is what we in the biz call a transcendental equation. Or "an equation for which we don't know a closed-form solution." It's unsolvable. Though many math minds argue there is no such thing as an unsolvable equation. Solutions do exist, it's just that you can't write down a formula for a solution in terms of well-known functions. I've never been a fan of that side of the computation aisle. Let's not turn everything into a New Age quest.

Lacey accused me—me!—of doing bad math. Having faulty data. If your variable is X, you don't get to change it to Y. I'm the X.

One plus one is always going to be two no matter what Oprah says. Numbers don't change. Neither do people.

Why don't I feel like I've won?

Fine. For shits and giggles let's take Lacey's advice and change the variables. There are two: the reunion and Tristan. Okay. I can't do anything to the reunion. That's a static part of the equation. Tristan, I have control over. (I think that's a line from one of the meditation tapes I didn't purchase.) I can plug myself into this equation pretending to be something else. Looking over at my plywood, that appears to be what Lacey was getting at all along.

Pretend. Fake it. Why make it hard? Be better.

I take a few more sniffs and scribble over the lame problem on my lap. It's slapping me right in the face. Why didn't Lacey just come right out and say it? I have to go as somebody else. Lie. Pretend. Act like a better version of myself. Being me is the problem. Always has been. I need to act like a totally different person. Yes! An impressive person. A successful person. A desirable and interesting person. I can do this for one night. It will be like putting on a mask. Hats. Mask. What's the difference?

On a roll now. I turn over the wood on my lap to make a list. Now this is a different problem. What do I need to be the best pretend Tristan?

Money. Good looks. Power. Subordinates. Friends. Fans.

I underline *money*. That's basically the key to the whole castle. Enough money buys me the rest. If I were to drain my bank accounts— wait, let's put a better spin on this. If I were to invest in myself, what do I spend it on?

New clothes? No offense, Jerry, but our clothes are terrible. What would George Clooney wear? God, I bet he has fun at re-unions. A suit. A dark suit and no tie. Italian shoes. I'll need a watch that costs at least thirty grand. That will be a terrifying purchase. Suze

Orman will appear out of thin air to slap me silly for being so ludicrous. Forty percent of the cost of a luxury watch goes right into the dealer's pocket. Less than 10 percent of all collectible timepieces ever make their money back, let alone turn a profit. Which begs an interesting question. What the hell am I going to do with this stuff after I shove it in Azusa High's face? I can't walk around in ten-thousand-dollar shoes. I'll be murdered at the first stoplight.

Security. Rich, powerful men have security. The President of the United States, the most powerful man in the world, has an entire army of Secret Service at his disposal. Don't be mad that I'm not referring to the leader of the free world in gender neutral pronouns. Yes, I absolutely pray that we have a female president, and soon. I'm just saying, right now, after 247 years, gals are oh for 46.

The amount of security correlates directly with perceived power and success. I'll get a shit ton. That won't be cheap. Not if it's real. Subordinates. I'll need a driver. Scratch that. Pilot. Meda flipping Lucas would arrive by helicopter. Yes! A driver and pilot and assistant. I can hire an actress or something. A model. Check out the big dog with the sexy secretary. Pulling this off will be easier than I thought. Lacey is a goddamn genius. Why make it hard? I'll have to give her my watch.

This is crazy. I can't get into a helicopter. Do you know why helicopters fly so low? It's not to look cool. It's so the pilot can land at any given moment. One bolt gets loose and you have about forty-five seconds before crashing and burning. Helicopter fatalities way outnumber planes and, fun fact, private rich guy helicopter trips account for only 3 percent of the yearly logged flying hours but are responsible for more than a quarter of all fatal crashes. Get serious, Tristan. Scratch the helicopter and the security. It's going to be hard enough to find a watch.

I'm excited. Like, really excited. This might be the first time I know exactly what I should do. I'm going to be absolutely nothing like myself and I'm spending all my money to make it possible. This is why people have a job. Time to buy some happiness. God, this feels good. I drop both the boards over the hole in my floor and head to bed.

Only I can't sleep. Something isn't right yet. It can't be this easy. If you can buy yourself happiness, why are so many people still miserable? What if I'm found out? If I do this, I have to eliminate all possibility for errors. If I'm found out to be a fraud, that's exponentially worse than being a loser.

Oh, wait. There's an even bigger problem. I can't spend all my money. I'll need it to pay someone to wipe my butt and flip me over so I don't get bedsores as I eventually languish, waiting for death alone in a nursing home.

Except . . . My blood stops moving. My heart

is still. Everything in this moment is silent. I've got it. That's it. This will work. If I go all in, I can make this happen. But it has to be the last thing I ever do.

I'll kill myself after the reunion. Lacey is right. Why make it hard?

Suicide? I know, I'm surprised, too. I'm terrified of dying. I spend my whole life actively trying not to die, but you know what this whole slightly embarrassing manic episode has taught me? I'm afraid of dying. I'm not afraid of being dead. It's the circumstance of how I get there that's all consuming. Each year one out of 6,336 people will die by slipping, tripping, or falling on a flat walking surface. Just an ordinary floor. Will that be me the next time I walk from my desk to the vending machine?

This is a real breakthrough. I should be proud of myself. I am proud of myself. And I didn't even have to buy those self-help tapes. I'm not bothered by what comes next. Whether I'm floating on a cloud with a harp or I'm just dust in a platinum tube, it's done. It's over. I'm not here. It happened. This horrible thing I've been waiting for doesn't have to be horrible and I don't have to wait for it. Why has it taken me forty-three years to put this together? Lacey really is a good friend. And you're great, too. This couldn't have been a joy to read. Thanks for sticking with me. The rest I think I'll keep to myself.

I've only slept for an hour when a ruckus outside wakes me up. Am I under attack? It sounds like a war zone out there. I shuffle to the bathroom, which is vibrating from all the noise. It's mechanical and rhythmic. Sitting down to pee (yes, I do that, so what?), I squint and look up through the hole in my ceiling, trying to find the source of the commotion. A large object hovers overhead, blocking the sun. Am I about to be beamed up to the Death Star? Weird. It's a helicopter. Do they always fly this close to buildings or am I noticing this odd flight pattern for the first time thanks to my recent renovations?

I hear a familiar sound cutting through the commotion. Laughter. Specifically, the kind of laughter that involves pointing and male supe- riority. KTLA's own "Eye in the Sky" is hov- ering over my toilet. I suppose it's better than a mountain lion, or a Death Star. A few more chuckles and they tilt and head off toward the tire fire or carjacking in progress or whatever breaking news is happening in the greater Los Angeles area.

The sun blasts through for just a sec and the helicopter's shadow is replaced by something blue. And squawking. With a million flapping wings. It's beautiful. A whole gaggle—or is it flock?—of bright blue jays is flying en masse overhead. Wow. There's a lot of them. A whole lot. This could be bad news for those news pricks in the helicopter.

I'm late. I don't have any spare time, but I stand in front of my closet contemplating my seven work shirts. My hand hesitates each time I reach for a hanger. This shirt's trip to the office seems more significant than most. I am settling on a green gingham no-iron button-down from Old Navy when something crashes outside. Holy crap! That was loud. My ears are ringing.

Outside about a block over, there's a huge black plume of smoke. It smells like chicken, and I don't see a single bluebird still in the sky. I told you helicopters are no good. If one thing (or a million small flapping things) goes wrong, you're toast.

Toast. Chicken. I must be hungry.

I get to the office just as the sprinklers stop going off. In my absence, my neighbors did not get their cue and are soaked.

"Thanks a lot, Tristan. I just got this monitor to the perfect angle."

Dana is not happy.

"Sorry for your loss." I keep my eyes down as I move past and assess the damage to my own work space. Yellow water swirls in the bottom of my USC mug.

"Tristan!"

Lacey spies me as she closes her umbrella.

"Lacey!" I don't know why we're using exclamation points.

She takes it down a notch. "You're late. Is everything—"

"Everything is great."

With all the hubbub this morning I almost forgot about my revelation, my plan. Seeing her face, I'm flooded with endorphins. I move my chair into her less-wet cubicle.

"You were right, Lacey."

"I was?"

I roll my chair so our knees are touching.

"About what?" Her whole body stiffens.

Is she nervous? I should move. "Sorry for

invading your space." I try to scoot back but a wheel on my chair is stuck.

"It's fine. What are you talking about?" She's still stiff as a board.

"Last night. Everything you said. Spot on. Thank you."

A little elasticity sneaks back into her shoulders. "Oh. Sure. I'm glad—"

"It's so simple. I just have to pretend."

"Pretend?"

I can hardly contain my excitement. I bet my face looks weird. "Pretend to be somebody else. Like you said—"

"That's not exactly—"

"Will you help me?"

Her face lights up. Is that from me? She's smiling but not answering. "Lacey?"

"Yes! Yes. Of course!"

Are we back to using exclamation points? Why not. "Great!"

"Great!"

A tech intern has finished switching out my dripping desktop and phone for new, dry electronics. I stand up and get ready to push my chair across the soggy carpet but turn back to Lacey before I do. "I need to go shopping."

"Okay."

"Will you go with me?"

"Okay!" She reins it in before continuing. "I can drive. Um. Saturday?"

"It's a date." There're three words I've never said before.

It takes some effort to push my chair back into the safety of my cube. Human interaction is exhausting. I catch my reflection in my new monitor. I actually look . . . okay? Let's see what an expensive suit can do.

NINE

Shop Till You Drop

Suicide. That got heavy. I hope he doesn't go through with it, but I suppose we need to respect his choice. Let's do what most of us do best and change the subject. Hilarious shopping spree, anyone?

It's the Saturday before the reunion. Lacey is on her way to Tristan's apartment. He's doing his best to tidy up the place before she arrives. He straightened the yellow caution tape around the hole in his living room floor and cleared some fallen branches from the bathroom. He wishes he had something good to offer his guest, but tap water will have to do. Hopefully she doesn't show up thirsty.

Should he put on music? He's nervously pacing. A text alert makes him jump. She's here! He hurries down the green carpeted stairs to welcome her to his humble abode.

"Find it okay?"

"Yeah. Siri knows where she's going."

It's dumb trying to make small talk while walking up stairs. They are both quickly out of breath. Tristan fumbles in his pockets for the keys before he realizes he left the door unlocked.

"Duh." He pushes the door but it sticks. "Huh?" He hits it harder, leaning with his shoulder, and flies into his apartment. This is going great.

Lacey is pleasantly surprised. She wasn't sure what to expect but this is fine. He's not a hoarder, he's not harboring illegal exotic pets. Tristan lives in a fine, normal, age-appropriate apartment. However, the hole in the middle of the living room is a smidge surprising.

"What the sharts?" She heads over to get a closer look.

Not understanding what she's looking at exactly, she's very close to falling onto lane seven. Tristan hurries to her side and holds his arm out, grazing her chest. Embarrassed, they both hop backward.

"A bowling ball did that. Can you believe it?" Tristan has his hands placed awkwardly on his hips. Being outside of the office, it feels like he's speaking a different language. He should have practiced.

"I suppose. I mean, you live above a bowling alley." She deftly changes subjects. "So, what's the plan? Want to hit up the Grove? Or there's a Burlington Coat Factory in Encino."

Tristan smiles and leads her away from the hole in the floor, toward his kitchen table. He spreads out some loose-leaf papers.

"I was thinking Rodeo Drive."

Lacey laughs. Tristan lets her finish and then hands her one of the papers, his shopping list.

She's confused. "A Prada suit?"

"Or Gucci. Maybe Versace?"

"Do you know what those words mean?"

"Expensive."

"Tristan—"

He hands her another piece of paper, this one containing a lot of zeros. "I have it all mapped out. Here's my budget."

If Tristan had offered Lacey tap water and if she were currently drinking it, she would be spraying Tristan and his budget right now.

"What? This is what you plan to spend on clothes?!"

He points to some of the line items. "And a watch. Maybe a haircut. Shoes. I don't know, should I get a cane?"

"A cane? Why? Are you injured?"

"To look cool. You know, something with jewels, maybe a skull."

Lacey shakes her head. "This is crazy." She takes a minute and skeptically surveys their current surroundings. "Do you even have this type of money?"

"Yes. It's all right here." He draws her attention to the bottom of the page that's getting wrinkled from her sweaty hands. "Liquid assets, 401(k), Roth IRA—"

"Wait. No. Tristan. You can't spend your retirement."

"Why not? It's time to go big."

She's suddenly serious. "Is this all your money?"

Tristan needs to be careful or he'll show his hand. Lacey can't know about his plan. He needs a distraction.

"Will you come with me? To the reunion?"

Lacey yelps her answer. "Yes! Or. Whatever." She completely forgets the little red flag that was starting to creep into this super fun day. "Should we head out then?"

Tristan is grateful he's got her back on safer ground. "Sure."

They both attempt to gracefully slide into Lacey's Hyundai Accent. It's impossible. Tristan jerks his seat back in an attempt to get comfortable.

"Are you going to be okay?" Lacey's hand pauses on the ignition as she remembers his distrust of automobiles.

"Um-hum. New me. Remember?" He yanks the seatbelt hard across his body. He doesn't trust that it's clicked and ejects and clicks it three more times.

"I think you're good."

Tristan answers with a thumbs-up.

Lacey is a fine driver. She's doing her best to be extra cautious but keep up with traffic. Still, Tristan clenches his fists into sweaty balls each time a car passes. They make it to the famous intersection of Santa Monica Boulevard and Rodeo Drive and pull into the parking ramp without incident. Lacey had already planned to splurge on parking. She wouldn't dare tempt fate by making Tristan ride shotgun as she attempted to parallel park. She takes a picture of their parking spot with her phone. She's learned the hard way she's not the best at finding her way back.

Tristan exits the compact car slowly. He's a little lightheaded from holding his breath for half the ride. For such a smart guy, he breathes all wrong.

It's crowded. They wade onto the paved path and submerse themselves in aimless tourists. After half a block, Tristan can't take being part of the herd any longer and pulls Lacey out of the throng. He needs to start spending money before he loses his nerve. This whole thing could fall apart at any second. They have stopped in front of a sparse storefront that has a symbol for a name.

"Should we check it out?"

Lacey nods and pushes out a smile. She would much rather be at Burlington Coat Factory.

The store "day maker" is busy organizing $400 T-shirts when they walk in. He's fit and tall in a non-aggressive way. He's a Beverly Hills seven, which is a Nebraska ten.

"Welcome."

They startle at the greeting, having failed to notice there was a person in this alien environment. Where are they? Is this a store or did they stumble through some wormhole into the future? Everything is white and smooth. Most racks have just a handful of items. There's a huge painting of a green dot hanging on the wall. That's it. One green dot.

This can't be right.

Their ambassador to this strange land sighs and approaches them.

Tristan is ready to bolt but he's not sure if he'll set off some intricate laser alarm system. "C-can we . . ." He's stammering. "Can we be in here?"

Their host takes a minute to answer, making them sweat. "That depends. Do you have money?"

Tristan nods. "Lots of it."

"Excellent." He smiles. "I'm Jake."

Without further fanfare, he beckons them to the back of the store and leads them through two large glossy panels.

It's true what they say, money really does open doors. In this case, to a closet filled with the most elite brands you can name, and plenty you've never even heard of.

Lacey tries to sit down gracefully on the only piece of furniture in the room, a stuffed red-velvet semicircle, but it's lower than she was expecting and there's no back. She wobbles a moment before gaining her balance, and then she crosses her legs, then uncrosses them, then crosses the other way, failing miserably in her effort to look both cool and comfortable.

Jake and Tristan also get off to a rocky start. Skinny cargo pants? No, thank you. Leather? Not for this vegetarian. A white silk kimono is vetoed out of fear of cultural appropriation and for being too Tilda Swinton-y. A yellow poncho over fishnets is an interesting look. Oversized sweater. Undersized sweater. Plastic, pleather, fur.

Tristan is starting to lose hope. "Just make me look rich!"

"How rich?"

"A ludicrous and mysterious amount!"

"That information could have saved us a lot of time. I'll be right back."

It's not more than a second and Jake returns

with a sharp black suit and a shoebox under his arm. Lacey and Tristan share a confused look.

"The man in black." Jake holds up the suit and caresses a sleeve. "It's bold. Timeless. A modern classic. The shoes? There are only four pairs of these Italian loafers in existence. Period. In the whole world. I could be murdered for selling you these shoes."

He hurries Tristan into the dressing room and then retreats, sinking effortlessly onto the red-velvet semicircle. Show-off.

After an awkward amount of silence, Lacey attempts small talk.

"So. What's with the green dot?"

"You wouldn't get it."

She's lived in LA long enough not to be intimidated by a failed actor who spends his days folding T-shirts in a spaceship. "It's dumb. This couch is dumb. Why is it a semicircle?"

"It's mid-century."

"It's butt-ugly."

They go silent when Tristan walks in.

"I don't know? What do you think? I guess this looks okay."

"Okay? Okay! Look at you." Jake forgets his tiff with Lacey and stands to fawn over Tristan. "You little devil, you have a sample-size body. What a waste."

Nobody disagrees with him.

Lacey can't help herself. "Tristan. Wow. Like, wow. That's a great . . . this is a good one. Yes, this is the one."

They both feel like giggling as they settle up at the register. That must be some suit. Lacey catches a glimpse of the receipt and squeaks. "Forty-two thousand dollars! Is that what it says? Forty-two thousand—I'm going to throw up."

"Please don't." Jake reaches over the counter with a bag.

Tristan gets an idea. "Where can I get a haircut?"

Haircut? Yes! Let's take this montage up a notch!

The salon Jake recommends looks more like a Bentley showroom than somewhere you'd pop in for a trim. The overdressed girl at the front desk is happy to fit Tristan in with a master stylist. His unmarked shopping bags act like a passport. Lacey waits in the lobby as he is treated to the haircut of all haircuts. After a twenty-minute deep-conditioning treatment ("It's a whole bond-multiplying system. You're going to love it!"), the stylist meticulously clips each strand. He barks orders at Tristan to tilt and lift his head as if they were training for an Olympic medal. Finally, Tristan sticks the landing. And voila! He is turned to the mirror to admire his transformation.

"It looks . . ."

Exactly the same. Tristan eyes himself incredulously.

The stylist takes that as a compliment. "Thank you. Thank you so much." He bows ceremoniously.

Tristan walks out to find that Lacey is sleeping sitting up in the lobby. "Ready?"

Her eyes pop open. "Are you . . ." She studies Tristan's head. Why does he look exactly the same? "Done?"

"Do you like it?"

The girl at the counter answers for her. "I love it. That is such a good length for your face shape. Oh, my gosh. What are you going to do now? You've got to go out and show off that fierce new look."

Tristan and Lacey again turn to each other, confused. Are they crazy?

"I don't know." Tristan takes back his credit card. "What would you do?"

The girl puckers her lips and thinks for a moment. "Probably take some selfies and grab a boba tea?"

They skip the selfies but take her advice about sitting down to enjoy a successful day with over-priced beverages. Turns out neither of them like boba tea. I don't blame them. What is up with those tapioca balls? Why would anyone want to drink snot globs? They reluctantly sip while sitting on a lovely patio. Despite the beverages, it's nice. The charming and exclusive setting. The orange and pink Southern California sky. They can't help but relax and enjoy themselves, snot globs and all.

"I guess we need to get something for you next. My treat."

"I think you've spent enough money for one day." Lacey takes a hard swallow. "Don't worry. I have a dress."

"You do?"

She does. Lacey has a fantastic red dress. She bought it years ago for her cousin's wedding. It's an A-line wrap dress with a deep V-neck. It still fits. She spends a lot of Wednesday nights walking around her apartment in that dress.

"Yup. It's sexy, too."

Tristan chokes on a tapioca ball.

She springs up. "I'll get some water."

"No. No." Tristan coughs. "I'm fine."

As he waves her off, his naked wrist catches his eye. Crap! He needs a watch. A really expensive watch. But how? Lacey won't survive another big-ticket item. They're both barely surviving boba tea. He shouldn't press his luck. Damn. Can he get a Rolex on Amazon?

Lacey is still standing. "I'm going to run to the bathroom."

Now's his chance. He won't have much time to find something. He can't imagine Lacey is the type of person to go number two in public. He needs to act fast. Once she's out of eyesight, adrenaline kicks in and he sprints across the street to a jewelry store. I know what you're thinking. "How convenient, a fancy jewelry store right across the street." Well, yeah. It's Rodeo Drive.

He busts through the doors in a frantic craze. The impeccably dressed sales staff throw their arms up in the air.

"No. No. I'm not here to rob you." He's out of breath and panting.

The sales team slowly start to lower their arms.

"Give me a Rolex! Now!"

They shoot their arms back up. Tristan, hoping to end this miscommunication, reaches for his wallet in an overly calm and exaggerated manner. "Please. May I pay for a Rolex?" He tosses his credit card in an arc through the lobby and it skids across a glass counter, spinning in place like a top before landing faceup in front of the sales team.

They look down at the card in amazement, then back up at Tristan. The alpha, an older gentleman in a ruby pinky ring, takes the lead.

"Which one?"

"I don't care. Your favorite."

The clerk raises an eyebrow and inspects the credit card.

"Your favorite that's under fifty thousand."

They aren't moving fast enough. Tristan takes out a wad of hundreds and attempts to throw the bills in their direction. They float down like faulty paper airplanes. "That's for you. All of you." He shrugs. "I'm sorry. I'm in a bit of a rush."

After a beat, they are finally on the same page.

"You heard the man! Get him a watch!"

After a flurry of excitement, Tristan is handed a small black bag and his recently maxed out Mastercard.

"It was a pleasure—"

"Yup. Yeah. Thanks so much." He runs back across the street to his empty table and beverage.

Lacey comes around the corner from the restroom and finds him there, panting.

"You all right?"

He takes a swig of boba and tries to act natural. "Great. Fine. Why do you ask?"

"I don't know. You look sweaty?"

"Too much sun. Shall we go?"

"Okay."

They gather Tristan's purchases and head back to the car. I wonder how many people leave this intersection of Santa Monica and Rodeo carrying their life savings in shopping bags?

TEN

Working Nine to Five

This fucking warehouse needs a sign. You know, one of those obnoxious YOUR MOTHER DOESN'T WORK HERE SO PICK UP YOUR OWN SEVERED BODY PARTS kind of sign? I almost broke my neck tripping over a leg back there. There are bodies lying all over the place. Nothing like having a big fucking mess to clean up before leaving town. The reunion is coming up this weekend. I've cleared my calendar. If these guys can handle melting limbs in acid and understand the mechanics of using a fucking mop, I should be able to actually be on vacay for a full forty-eight hours.

I know. This looks bad. Would you feel better if I told you all these dead people were white supremacists? They were. Look at that pile of arms over there. Nothing but swastikas. Am I a hero? Sure. I enjoyed gutting that son of a bitch. But you know what? Five years ago, hell, five months ago, I would have enjoyed it a lot more. Waiting for him to squeal his last breath today, it just felt like, I don't know, *work*.

That prick Meda Lucas thought he could get away with an ambush on my turf, and he had the nerve to outsource the job to these assholes. He couldn't be bothered to murder me himself. Fucking jerk. These skinhead assholes will work for anyone. They're cheap, too. Inbred dipshits who don't trust science and can't do basic math. What a mess. This is America, goddamnit. A small-business owner like myself should be able to thrive. Aren't we the backbone of the whole fucking thing? Here's another big box chain trying to snuff me out and no one cares. No one is going to come to my rescue. I have to do it all my goddamn self.

What's that sound? Do you hear that? There is moaning coming from a heap in the corner. Why am I the only living person in this room? Or, apparently, the second living person in this room. Where are my idiots? "Dennis!"

That fat fuck runs in with a gun in one hand and a hoagie in the other. "Yeah, boss?"

Did they leave for lunch? Nobody told me they were getting lunch. I'm fucking starving.

"Someone in your pile is still alive."

"Sorry, boss." He takes a bite of sandwich and fumbles with the gun in his left hand.

"Could you lose the fucking sandwich?"

He looks around helplessly for a clean place to set it down.

Jesus Christ. "Dennis?"

"Sorry, boss. It's from D'Amico's. My favorite."

D'Amico's is everyone's favorite. I don't know if I should shoot him or his meat lover's sub. Thankfully, Tyler, a new guy and total asshole, smacks the sandwich out of his hand and shoots three rounds into the stack of bodies. Dennis looks down helplessly at his lunch floating in a puddle of blood.

"Thank you, Tyler. Now that's the type of initiative I'm looking for." Dennis slowly reaches toward the ground. "I swear to God, if you touch that sandwich, I will murder your family."

"Sure thing, boss."

I'm too hard on Dennis. But why didn't they bring me back lunch? This fucking day can't be over soon enough. Time to make my announcement and hit the road.

"Everyone get in here! Dennis, get some fucking chairs."

He sighs each time he passes his sandwich on

the floor. It takes way too long and as the crew convenes, they argue about sitting in a closed or semicircle.

"Just sit the fuck down!" Everyone complies but Jared. He's still trying to hobble over. I shouldn't have shot him. Certainly not in both feet. He's having a hard time navigating through all the bodily fluids in those stiff medical boots. "Will somebody help him?"

Rob and Bob, the twins, are quick to grab him under the arms and carry him to a folding chair. I can't tell them apart to save my life, and neither one can aim for shit—don't get me started—so they try their best to be helpful. Our little mommies.

"I have an announcement."

Rob-or-Bob opens a cooler and hands me a cold one. "Beer?"

I grab it and continue. At least someone is interested in my well-being. "Thank you. I have an announcement—"

Jared asks for a beer. Seriously?! Did I not just . . .

"Fine, everyone take a goddamn beer!" I motion at Rob/Bob and he passes them out like orange slices at a fucking AYSO kid's game. Everyone mumbles thanks and settles back in. Deep breaths, Harry. Deep breaths. "As I was saying. I have an announcement. I'm making Tyler my number two. While I'm gone this weekend, Tyler is in charge." I squeeze his shoulder. "For the next forty-eight hours, you, my boy, are Santa Ana."

He reaches for my face. "Do I get to wear the mask?"

I smack at his hand. "No."

"But I'm Santa Ana."

Can you believe this guy? "No. I'm Santa Ana."

"You just said—"

I'm yelling now. "Forget what I said!" Let me try this again. "Tyler is in charge this weekend.

No one is wearing the mask. Don't fucking bother me."

Everyone quietly sips their beer after Daddy's little outburst. I hate drinking with this mask on. I must be stretching out the bottom, pulling it out like this. I should carry a straw.

Dennis notices me struggling. "Why don't you ever take it off?"

"Do you know who I am?" I ask him.

"Ummmm. Santa Ana?"

"Exactly. Nobody knows who is under here. You don't. The feds don't. Meda Lucas sure as shit doesn't or we would have all been dead years ago. This mask is keeping us alive and gives me a life. I take this off and I can walk into the White House."

"It hurts, boss." Dennis has the nerve to pout.

Oh, my fucking God.

He won't stop. "We want to know the real you. You can trust us."

"No, I can't."

"No. He can't." Thank you, Tyler!

Strangely, this makes me feel more confident about making him second in command. One of the Obs opens his dumb mouth.

"I think it's smart, boss."

"Thank you, Rob." He shoots me a wounded look. Wrong one. "Bob." I'm being a dick. It's not their fault I'm stressed. "Hey, guys, I'm sorry. I'm being a dick." What? Don't be shocked. It's 2023, men apologize now. "I'm stressed. We're all stressed. It's a fucking stressful situation but we'll get through it. Take it easy this weekend. All right? Unwind, do something fun."

"Where are you going?"

I was wondering if anyone gave a shit. "Thank you for asking, Jared. You want to know where I'm going? I'm going back to the greatest place on earth. High school. You know what I'm talking about. Girls. Football. More girls. The parties I would throw? Legendary. You get it." I raise my beer to toast to our youth.

"I dropped out after my dad was murdered."

Well, that's terrible. Way to keep it light, Jared.

"But your thing sounds cool." Rob. Yes. This is definitely Rob speaking. "You going to teach a class or something?"

"No, Rob—"

"It's Bob."

Fuck! Wait, when did they start correcting me? I don't like that.

"No, fuck face." Tyler's stepping into his position of leadership quite well. "He's going to party with all his old friends and shit. My grandma just went. Like, old people go back to their school and act like it's prom or whatever."

"That's right, Tyler. I'm going to my reunion. My goddamn twenty-fifth high school reunion. I'm going to the last place I was ever fucking happy or meant fucking anything." Yikes. Where has that truth bomb been hiding?

"Don't say that, boss." Dennis has a sandwich. Where the fuck did he get another sandwich?

"Please. Please don't bug me this weekend. Okay? I need this. We need this. I have to get my head on straight if we're going to have any chance taking on Lobos Gris." Is this pep talk for them or for me?

"You do you, boss. We got this." Tyler looks around, demanding confirmation from the others with a stern eye. He's good.

They're trying. It's up to me to listen to my own orders and unplug this weekend. Be in the moment. I don't know. If getting back with the old crew, back with my girl, doesn't shake this funk, maybe I need a therapist. I rest my feet on a conveniently located head with no body. It wobbles a bit. Now who did this? This might be a tad unnecessary. I half-ass kick it, and it rolls to the middle of the circle like a random piece of trash.

"Doesn't it feel like we're just going through the motions? I mean, was this even fun?" My arms gesture wide at the carnage all around us.

"A bloodbath like this used to get my motor running. We should be jumping up and down celebrating this win. But look at us. Sipping sad beers like a bunch of fat chicks. It's like, I don't know. Nothing gets me hard anymore. You know? Now it's just another fucking mess."

"They have pills for that."

"I'm using my dick as a metaphor, Tyler. But thank you for the suggestion."

"I had fun, boss."

Dennis, that fat bastard, he's a waste of space but as loyal as they come.

I've got to sack up. Things could be a lot worse. I could be that fucking head over there. A lot of people would love to use my head as a soccer ball.

"Enough about me. I don't pay you to listen to me bitch." I turn to the Ob on my right. "What are you up to this weekend?"

"My baby girl's quinceañera is Sunday."

"Congratulations." I don't know what that is. Is it the type of thing you congratulate?

"My wife has lost her mind. The whole thing is costing me an arm and a leg."

I reach into my pocket and hand him a wad of cash. "For your family. Sorry, it's wet."

His brother peels a couple of limbs off the floor and tosses them in his direction. "Here. Give her this! An arm and a fucking leg!"

ELEVEN

The Plot Thickens

Now would be a good time to introduce some good guys, don't you think? Law enforcement, maybe? I'm just saying, we're not even halfway through this book and there's been an awful lot of body parts tossed around. Lucky for us, those body parts used to sell drugs.

In spite of an endless list of atrocities perpetuated daily, drugs remain at the center of all crime-fighting business. Government agencies want a piece of that juicy War on Drugs action. The local FBI office has been desperate to stick it to those DEA pricks ever since the softball massacre of '07. Unfortunately, they have yet to beat them at fast pitch or bring in a big fish. After a few botched raids on a now-defunct Armenian dope outfit, they have been relegated to horribly boring mail fraud cases or treated to horribly horrible sex-trafficking nightmares. For years they have had absolutely zero busts that could lead to a Netflix series.

But the tides are turning. This local turd, Santa Ana, has gotten much more interesting now that Meda Lucas—*the* Meda Lucas—is involved. Ah. To put a collar around that guy's neck? That would be like winning Wimbledon as you cross the finish line first at the Boston Marathon while lapping the competition during Daytona. It would be big, and retiring Special Agent in Charge Tom Spitz is looking to go out big.

Currently, two junior agents are disobeying their boss by interrupting his special time, dress rehearsal for *Gypsy*. Tom Spitz is a total musical theater nerd. After a long hiatus while raising his children and putting people behind bars, he's recently gotten back in the game, landing the role of Uncle Jocko. Don't let this tiny black box theater that smells like piss fool you. The Santa Monica Community Players are a BFD. They might get, like, twenty people to opening night.

The two junior agents linger in the back row, waiting for the director to call a five.

Agent One: "He's totally miscast. Look at him. He's the only pro up there."

Agent Two: "Can we not? Don't be a kiss ass."

Agent One doesn't give a shit what Agent Two thinks. "I'm just saying. It's a waste of talent. Some two-bit character role? He has such gravitas, and that voice? He should be headlining. Jean Valjean. Now that, that is a role made for him."

Agent Two: "Please stick to business."

You're probably like, Agent One and Agent Two . . . what the hell is going on? Look, I only have so much bandwidth. Does every person in this story have to have a whole thing? Tom Spitz is the interesting one in this side note, and here he comes.

His stage makeup hangs on his face like cake batter. The hair under his giant and ridiculous hat is sweaty. He's a pretty big fella to be dancing and singing under those bright stage lights.

"This better be good. We open tomorrow." He removes his gigantic stage glasses.

"What a treat, sir." Agent One starts to sing. "'I had a dream! A dream about you, babe . . . You'll be swell . . . You'll be great . . .'"

"That's enough, Crosby."

Oh, look. His name is Crosby. Agent One is Crosby.

The agent not named Crosby gets to work. "It's Santa Ana, sir."

Crosby can't help himself. "Have you always been a baritone? Because I'm getting some serious second tenor vibes."

As much as he would love to talk about his vocal range, Spitz sticks to business. "And? Has he turned up decapitated in a ditch?"

"No, sir. We believe we know his whereabouts."

"Great." He pauses, annoyed at the interruption. "Go apprehend him."

Agent Two should be nicer to Crosby. He's always willing to take one for the team. "We don't exactly or not exactly know where he is now. But we're pretty sure we know where he's going to be this weekend."

Agent Two whips out the props. He opens a manila folder with 8"x10" glossy photographs of a masked man taking selfies at his crime scenes. He's wearing the mask but not his usual tailored black suit. In each photo he's wearing a different Fighting Aztec T-shirt from Azusa High. "Class of '98 Azusa Baseball Team

Captain." "Azusa Football Rules State Champs 1998." In the last shot, he appears to be in a residence posing in the infamous devil's mask and a letterman's jacket. Spitz holds that one close to his face to examine.

"Did forensics get a look at this? Could they make anything out from the background? Get a location on this fuckwad?"

Crosby has something helpful to share. "No. But we're fairly certain he graduated from Azusa High School in 1998."

Spitz grumbles. "No shit. So what? You're going to start slogging through attendance records?"

Crosby continues. "His twenty-fifth high school reunion is happening this weekend."

"And you think he'll go?"

Crosby laughs and flicks the picture in his boss's hands. "Um. Yeah. This guy? I think he'll be there."

The boys are gaining some traction with their boss. "Interesting. What's the play?"

Agent Two spills the details. "We have a guy on the inside. Graduated his class."

"Interesting." Spitz has to mull this over. How much does he invest in this scheme? And does he exit stage left or stage right at the end of Act Two?

"There's more." Crosby does a little tap dance. "Word on the street is Lobos Gris is in town, ready to make their move. We make our secret Santa Ana mission not so secret and Meda Lucas himself will come to collect. He won't be able to hide behind his lawyers or friends in Congress. He'll want to get his hands dirty with this one, and we'll be there to catch him in the act."

"What if they kill each other?"

Crosby shrugs. "We still win?"

Agent Two clarifies. "It won't be as clean as

a takedown, but we'll still be the first on the scene and can claim jurisdiction."

"That would piss off the DEA." Spitz likes it. More paperwork. But fewer bullets. "Let these dirtbags take each other out."

Crosby gives his boss a playful salute. "What's your audition piece? Do you do any Gilbert and Sullivan?"

"Not yet, but I've been told I'd make a great—"

He and Crosby say it in unison. "Major General Stanley!" Much to Agent Two's dismay, they begin to sing. "'I am the very model of a modern Major General. I've information vege-table, animal, and mineral—'"

"We should let the Special Agent in Charge get back to his practice." Agent Two can't take it any longer.

Uh-oh. He has offended his boss, though.

"It's a rehearsal, Dillmann."

Oh, look! Agent Two's name is Dillmann.

Well, that will be helpful when we revisit this little fork in the road.

Crosby is the fun one. Dillmann is the straight guy. Spitz is the grumpy gramps in charge.

And scene.

Let's use our time efficiently and now head south of the border to see if their sneaky plan has legs.

It worked! The FBI's intel traveled quickly through Lobos Gris's network and right to Meda Lucas's home base, a cement and glass square in the desert. This marvel of modern architecture is both sterile and luxurious. Aboveground is for pleasure, with all the expected amenities and then some. But deep under the earth is where business is conducted. This is where the shit goes down. A labyrinth of tunnels leads to various "offices." With its packed-dirt walls and hanging work lights connected by an impossibly long orange extension cord, it's missing a bit of charm, but it's easy to hose down and equipped with a handy self-destruct switch.

Meda Lucas is in one of his favorite "conference rooms" conducting a performance review. He really prides himself on his ability to give prompt and effective feedback. The meeting is almost over. It's not going well for the guy tied to the chair. He's a dirty cop from Puebla. His uniform is hanging from a hook on the wall, torn and bloody. He must have gotten too expensive. Or too chatty. Or maybe he held eye contact for too long. It doesn't take much to get a bad review these days.

Meda Lucas turns his back on the desperate man and drags a heavy bag of gravel to the center of the room.

The poor guy pulls at the ropes around his wrists and ankles, and the chair bounces as his body fights to get free. Blood drips down his sweat-soaked undershirt. "*Por favor*, Meda Lucas. *Lo siento mucho. Lo siento!*"

Meda Lucas shakes his head. "Shhhh."

He tips the informant's chin back and jams a plastic funnel made from an old milk jug into his mouth. The chair shakes violently as the man tries to push out an obstructed scream. His eyes are wide and pleading. Meda Lucas plunges his arm into the bag of tiny rocks, using the remainder of the cut-up milk jug as a thrifty scooper. He hoists it above the funnel and the first few morsels are about to slide out when he's distracted by the sounds of feet shuffling outside in the hall.

He looks up to see his lieutenants, dusty and out of breath, peering cautiously around the door, which is ajar. One of them, an American born and raised in Santa Monica, trips over his feet as he rethinks this visit and tries to back away. Too late. Meda Lucas has officially been interrupted. He reluctantly calls them in, addressing his countryman first out of solidarity.

"Alejandro. George." He is sure to make a

show out of pronouncing it George and not Jorge. He'd never have taken the man on, but he's an exceptional shot and a great cook. "What do you need? I'm in the middle of something."

"*Lo siento, jefe.*" Alejandro makes the mistake of looking at the man in the chair, whose lips and cheeks are stretched like a rattlesnake at dinnertime, only instead of a tasty lizard, he's about to eat rocks.

George swallows loudly. "Sorry, boss. We have news."

"*Grandes noticias.*" Alejandro knows this is big and wants his share of the credit.

Meda Lucas loses his patience. "What is it already?!" He wipes grimy sweat from his brow.

"It's Santa Ana."

That gets his attention. Even the guy in the chair perks up.

"Santa Ana?" He inadvertently tips the scooper, causing a trickle of stones to roll down the funnel. A choking cough escapes the informant's gaping mouth, but Meda Lucas doesn't notice. "Is he dead?"

"Not yet, boss." George talks fast. He would like to avoid being the next to get a funnel jammed down his throat. "But he will be. This Saturday he'll be in Azusa, California, at his high school reunion."

"His what?"

"His twenty-fifth high school reunion. He'll be alone. Drunk. No mask. It's the perfect time for an ambush."

Alejandro nods enthusiastically and the Puebla cop joins in, knocking even more gravel into the funnel.

Meda Lucas's thoughts are whirling. Santa Ana is proving to be a bigger problem than anticipated. He took out those skinheads like it was nothing. It's time to show him exactly who he's dealing with. And who doesn't like a party?

"Gracias. This could work."

He waves his lieutenants away and they

gratefully retreat through the janky door. Meda Lucas steadies his grip on the scoop and grins at his captive. *"Perdón por la interupción."*

The informant makes a last-ditch effort to free his arms, while his boss ignores his unintelligible cries.

Meda Lucas whispers his final thought as he tips the scoop and the stones tumble down the pipe: *"A beber y a tragar, que el mundo se va a acabar."*

TWELVE

Reunited and It Feels So Good

It's the day of the reunion. I offered to drive, but Tristan insisted on picking me up. I have no idea what his plan is. He could show up with a horse and carriage. He's been odd this week, even for him. But happy at the same time? It's hard to explain. Extra. He's been very extra.

Oh, sorry, you probably don't recognize me. It's Lacey! I know. Mama cleans up good. It's the fake eyelashes. I spend a lot of time watching YouTube makeup tutorials where they talk about serial killers. It's like cheese popcorn and caramel corn. The two just work together.

I'm close to getting an online certification in cosmetology. Tristan doesn't know about that. I like to keep this version of me to myself. I don't want other people to know I care about my eyelashes.

The wind is shaking my apartment. I hate the flipping Santa Anas. If you've never experienced this local weather phenomenon, the Santa Ana wind is like standing in a blizzard of dust inside an oven. Los Angeles has traffic, movie stars, and wind. Each highly problematic in its own way. Wind has been proven to have a negative effect on mood, you know. Joan Didion summed it up nicely. "The winds show us how close to the edge we are." Do I sound smart? I've been boning up on my tidbits. I want to be a good date. Anyhoo, she's spot on. I can feel it in the pit of my stomach.

Oh! Here's another gem I Googled: "It was one of those hot dry Santa Anas that come down through the mountain passes and curl your hair and make your nerves jump and your skin itch. On nights like that every booze party ends in a fight. Meek little wives feel the edge of the carving knife and study their husbands' necks. Anything can happen."

It's attributed to Raymond Chandler. I don't know who Raymond Chandler is, but he nailed it. This is straight-up murder-people weather.

Oofff. Shake it off, girl. (*Shake it off. Shake it off.* I love Taylor Swift!) Sorry. I'm nervous. I've never narrated before.

Tristan just texted. He'll be here any minute. I should leave now. It's going to take me an hour to walk down the hall in these shoes. My fat feet are crammed in these strappy torture devices like little smokies. You know, those delicious tiny sausages you cook in the Crockpot? If I have to explain myself, it's probably not an effective visual. I'm really blowing this. I hope this reunion has snacks. I've been on a liquid diet since Thursday. Goodbye, apartment. Perhaps the next time we meet, I'll be a changed woman.

I do that sometimes. Talk to my stuff. Brené Brown says every time we leave our comfort zone, there's the potential for change. Or I got that from my gratitude journal. I don't remember.

Puppies and farts! It is freaking windy out here! I have been outside for thirty seconds and I need a shower. I have ancient sands lodged between my front teeth. Ick. There's leaves down my dress. Great. This is all going— What the!? Did you see that? An aluminum trash can lid almost chopped off my head! What the heck! I literally could be dead right now.

That's weird. There are four identical black SUVs parked in front of me. I should text Tristan. I'll have to meet him at the corner or something. I'm never going to make it to the corner in these shoes and this demon-breath wind. Squirts! This just keeps getting better.

"Lacey."

Oh, my God. One of the SUVs is talking to me. Oh, my God. Oh, my God. Oh, my God. Why did I wear these stupid shoes? I can't run in these—

"Lacey! Where are you going? It's Tristan."

Tristan? I can hardly hear anything with all this crapping crap flying around. Did that car say *Tristan*?

"Tristan?" My hair is slapping me across the face. "Tristan?" Screw these luscious curls. I pull my hair out of the way and sure enough, there's Tristan peering through the open window.

"Are you surprised? I told you I'd pick you up." He opens the door and scoots over.

Wait, shouldn't he have gotten out? My mother is right. I might have unrealistic expectations.

"What is all this?"

We are in a total baller car. The seats are slippery and leather. You could fit half a football team in here. There are two men in the front seat. Does Tristan know these people? Is this a new ride share thing? Why are they dressed the same with *Mission: Impossible* earpieces?

I ask again. He probably couldn't hear me the first time, being all the way on the other side of the car. "Tristan. What is all this?"

"Cool, huh?"

The other SUVs file behind us. Wait. Are we taking four cars to the reunion? Am I in *The Matrix*?

"Why are those cars following us?"

"What?" Tristan looks behind him. "Those? They're just part of my detail."

"Detail?"

"Security detail."

"Makes sense." Wait. No, it doesn't. "Why do you need a security detail?"

"I've made some additions to the plan."

"The plan?" What am I missing? "Oh. Your makeover?"

"My great deception! My ruse!"

He's at, like, peak extra right now. He's vibrating, his nerves are running so hard. I've got to try to calm him down.

"How about this wind? Crazy, isn't it?"

He nods.

Don't worry. I'm not using small talk to regulate his nervous system. I'm going to use math.

"What are the odds of getting your head chopped off by a flying garbage can lid?" I ask.

"Plastic or metal?"

"I don't know. The round, shiny kind." Remember how that almost just happened to me?

"It would depend on the force of the wind and the angle at impact. The integrity of the material would matter. If it was bent or something, that would be more dangerous. It's probably safest in its original continuous form. You know. A circle."

"Okay."

He's breathing slower. This is working. Keep going, buddy.

"Let's say it's intact. No sharp edges. I think the wind would need to be close to a whole gale, going at least fifty miles per hour. If it hit you at that speed anywhere between a thirty-five- and forty-five-degree angle? Yeah. You could get beheaded."

"What are the odds?" I wonder how long this car ride is and how long I can milk this word problem and are we really showing up with rent-a-cops? Because that is fat bat crazy.

"I'd put it in the same category as getting struck by lightning. I know I don't have to tell you what those odds are."

He's still going to tell me.

"One in five hundred thousand."

I smile and he smiles back. Good. I don't think he's going to puncture a hole in the seats with his vise grip. His hands are flatter, joints relaxed. He hasn't said anything about my dress. Or my hair. Or eyelashes.

"Lacey?"

Oh, here we go. Compliment away, sir.

"Yes?"

"Thanks for doing this."

That's something, I guess. Sincerity makes me queasy. "Sure. Whatever."

I need to cut him some slack. Repeat after me, Lacey Lynn Hahn, this night isn't about you. Be a good friend. We don't have to understand someone's feelings in order to validate them. My self-reflection calendar of the day is proving to be an excellent purchase. That nugget right there was from last Thursday.

The dude up front turns around. Oh, hello. Don't you have a sturdy jaw. "We're pulling into the airport now, sir."

I'm sorry. Did he just say airport?

"Thank you." Tristan replies like this makes perfect sense.

I have no idea what's going on.

"Did he say airport? Why are we going to the airport?"

The driver puts the car in park. "The control tower has given us a twenty-minute window before the winds shift. We're going to need to hustle."

Tristan is nodding. Is James Bond in the front seat talking to us? Hustle to where? What is going on? Tristan is mumbling to himself and looks like he's about to pass out.

He grabs my hand. "I need you to not freak out, okay? I'm really fucking freaking out and I need you, right now, to be the one who isn't freaking out so when I need to look at someone to remember how to act like I'm not completely fucking freaking out, that someone I can look at will be you."

Say what? I don't have time to respond. My door is flung open (well, finally a gentleman), and G.I. Joe with the nice face puts both arms around my shoulders and runs us toward a . . . a . . . a helicopter?! He covers my head and we duck when we get close to the propeller.

Wait. What? Does it say Longus Life on the side? Are we allowed to borrow the company helicopter now? Did Tristan win some sort of prize? I'm a much better employee. Everyone knows that. I'm the one who should be winning a ride in the boss's chopper. We're handed headsets as we get buckled in.

"Tristan?" My voice is crystal clear in my headphones but I still have the urge to shout. "Is this the company helicopter?"

He nods.

"Why are we in it? How did you get it? Moreover, what in the smushed s'mores is going on?"

He squeezes my hand and offers a weak explanation as we lift off the ground. "The pilot is doing me a favor."

"And you gave me five thousand dollars." Mr. Aviators joins the party line.

"Five thousand dollars! Have you lost your freaking mind!"

"I need you to be calm. Okay? For the next seven and a half minutes, can you please be calm and act like this is all going to be fucking fine and I'm, excuse me, we're, not going to fucking die in a plume of smoke after crashing into the side of a goddamn mountain?"

I don't know what to do but nod. "Sure."

So that's that. We're helicopter people now. Sure. Sure, sure, sure. Sure. Absolutely no problem. This day continues to make perfect sense. We're not that far off the ground. I can still make out the license plates below me. I want to ask someone on the other end of my headset if we're supposed to be flying this low, but that doesn't seem like it would jibe with Tristan's definition of calm.

We've never been this close or touched for this long. Tristan smells like soap. A lot of the time he smells like he left his clothes sitting in the washer overnight. But right now he smells good. Irish Spring. That's what he smells like. That green soap.

I should tell him that. You smell nice and I love you. Wait. What? Okay, yeah, I love him. If we're about to go down, if this is it, my last chance, I do it, right?

Hold on. I'm not thinking straight. Do what? I'm not in love with Tristan. There must not be enough oxygen in here. Helicopters suck.

I am, though. It's painful and cruelly obvious. You knew, didn't you? I don't know why or when it happened. Tristan's cute but he's no Ringo. He's not exactly a smooth operator or even an above-average friend. There's something about him, though, something so specific to just him. From the minute I met him, I wanted to be around him. The more I was around him the more it hurt to be apart. Like, literally hurt. There's a zillion Reddit boards on the topic. Check out "heart sick"; I have all the classic symptoms. Maybe life would be better if we did crash. At least my death would be romantic.

"Touchdown in ninety seconds. The field is secured, sir."

Tristan says thank you into the headset and I say you're welcome. I don't know why I said anything. Whoa, Nelly . . . that ground is coming up fast. I hold my breath and wait for a thud. A crowd is gathered on the perimeter of the field and watches as we gently set down. That was slightly anticlimactic. Good thing I didn't spill the beans up there. I have lived to yearn another day.

The rent-a-cops are here. I've got to hand it to him. We are making one heck of an entrance. I feel like Jessica Rabbit about to walk out of this thing. The door opens and we're pummeled with wind and dirt. They motion for us to get down the ladder. Tristan starts descending, then sees his waiting admirers and spins around, almost headbutting me in the process. "I can't do this!"

It's a smidge late for that, bud. "Go!" I point like he's a bad dog or something. My hair is blowing like crazy! "Come on!" I'm not completely comfortable with the current amount of space that's between my head and the spinning propeller.

Neither is Mr. Aviators. "Sir, we need to get back up in the air."

"Tristan!" Oh, my God! Did he not hear that? They need to get back up in the air!

He turns back around and I push him down the last few steps. One of the cops on retainer hands me a metal briefcase and we run across the field toward a black SUV. Wait. What? Why am I holding Tristan's briefcase? Cheese and crackers! I'm having a hard time untangling the logistics of this whole operation.

We're rushed into the back of another black

SUV. Hopefully I'll get a chance to catch my breath.

The car starts moving. We drive a whopping four seconds to the front of the line of identical vehicles. A crowd has gathered. Both Tristan and I jump when two hands pound on the outside of the passenger window.

"Tristan?!" Some middle-aged dad in Crocs is pounding on the glass. He must be an old friend. "It's me—" He's tackled by a man in a suit before he can get his name out.

Oh. Cute. It's G.I. Joe from earlier. He takes his job very seriously. He pulls the guy up by the back of his shirt. Tristan is desperate to roll the window down.

"Sir?" G.I. Joe looks over expectantly, but Tristan's eyes are on the dad.

"Frankie? God. Frankie. I'm so sorry. Are you—"

"Sir, how would you like me to rectify this perimeter breach?"

"Perimeter . . . what?"

"Permission to tase, sir?"

"No!"

The driver puts his finger on his earpiece. "Roger that. They're ready for us at registration, sir."

We leave Frankie, who is hopefully not going to be tased, and drive a whole three seconds before pulling right up to the registration area. The tires stop practically on the walkway. There's a huge WELCOME BACK CLASS OF 1998 banner all twisted inside out. Half the balloons in the balloon arch have blown away. A line of papers from the registration booth take off from the table like geese in formation on their way south. More men with earpieces open our doors.

"I'll accompany Ms. Hahn to registration." One of them leads me away from the car.

"What? Hey, Tristan—" I have to yell over the wind.

"This way, ma'am."

Ma'am? I don't like that.

"I'll catch up with you later!" Tristan walks off with another suit, leaving me alone with a bunch of strangers.

This sucks. Why doesn't Tristan have to wait in line, too? There are two men in front of me and my rent-a-cop waiting to check in as the greeters desperately try to keep all their sign-in sheets and itineraries from blowing away. They look as out of place as I'm sure I do. They're dressed in matching charcoal suits and shiny black boots, and neither look old enough to be attending their twenty-fifth high school reunion. Their tenth reunion might even be pushing it. They converse quietly in Spanish as they wait. I try to eavesdrop, but I don't know Spanish. I spent a semester in Norway, which is of zero help right now. Not that I picked up much Norwegian. The men seem on high alert.

They talk in short, declarative sentences. Both keep a hand close to their belt.

A high-strung woman leans over the table. "I'm so sorry, what was your name again?"

There are two types of women over the age of thirty-five: the ones who try too hard and the ones with short haircuts. You know the look. It screams "Let me speak to the manager." This woman has that haircut. I'm sorry. I don't mean to offend anyone with short hair. It's common for us to judge harshly that which we don't understand, and I will never understand that haircut. The men are stone-faced. They each point to a name tag on the table.

She picks up the tags and reads out a name. "Jamal Washington?"

The taller of the two nods once.

"And you're Denzel Thomas?"

The other responds by reaching out to grab his sticky label. The woman hesitates and takes a step back. "Huh. You two are a lot different than I remember."

The wind takes hold of a folding chair. It flies into the parking lot, setting off a chorus of car alarms. "Here!" She shoves the name tags into the tall one's hand and runs after the chair.

"This way, miss." That's better. Get those "ma'am"s out of here. My driver grasps my arm and leads me away from the table.

"Wait, don't we need name tags?" I'm a big rule follower. Why did we even stop here?

We briskly pass the people gathered by the entrance and follow the walkway toward the football practice field, our previous landing spot. There are refreshments and seating under a white canopy tent that is trying its very best to stay tethered. My heels sink into the grass as I'm led to Tristan and a tight circle of admirers.

More and more people mill about. There's a lot of exaggerated greetings and hugs. I'm overdressed and sticking out like Humpty Dumpty trying to pass as a stop sign. Stupid red dress.

Tristan is embraced by a man and a woman I have to assume are the source of his current existential crisis. So, here are Harrison and Brea. The gruesome twosome that has Tristan's panties all in a bunch. Attractive? Yes. Very. Still, I don't get what all the fuss is about. Harrison looks like a typical handsome dude in dude pants and a letterman's jacket. That's a little sad, but I suppose if you're ever going to dig out an old letterman's jacket, it would be for a reunion.

Here's Brea. I can finally admire her in all her glory. Wait, is she wearing a cheerleading uniform?

She must have read my mind. She leans in close. "Can you believe it still fits? Don't you love it!"

There's a tan line on her left ring finger. This situation has progressed from a little sad to completely tragic. Why does Tristan give a crap about these losers? Look at them. Clearly something pathological is going on.

The three of them take this slightly awkward beat to look at me. Now would be a good time for introductions, Tristan.

"Oh." He hesitates and clears his throat. "This is my assistant. Lacey Hahn."

Ex-squeeze me? Did Tristan just say I'm his assistant? Like, a person who works for him?

"Nice to meet you." Brea clutches my hand and shakes it.

The three of them head for the tent and I stare after them with my jaw hanging open. Is Tristan expecting me to pretend I work for him all night? In these heels? This dress? I'm a secretary in this dress? What the double fudge just happened?

THIRTEEN

A Walk Down Memory Lane

I RODE IN A HELICOPTER! Can you believe that? A motherfucking helicopter. I've only been here five minutes, but things are going flawlessly. Lacey looks incredible. Why is she still standing back there in the grass? Brea—yes, that Brea—is holding my arm. Harry—yes, that Harry—is talking my ear off. I can't hear him. I'm too jacked! Is this what coke feels like? Because I get it.

We grab drinks under the tent and stand at a cocktail table. It's not offering much protection from the wind. Napkins are flying everywhere.

I'm sipping an Amstel Light. This is surreal. Harry has aged. I'm surprised. I figured his superior genes would be doing a better job fighting that off. He's still a stud. This isn't a movie. Only in movies do beefcakes shed their hot skin to reveal the ordinary, pudgy, thinning-hair loser inside. In real life, nobody ever changes. Not like that. He is softer in places. His pants tug a bit at the waist. His face is a little tired and puffy. He could use a good juice detox. The way he's successfully draining his glass, I don't think he's the type that drinks much juice. He better be careful. Another year or two on his current trajectory and he won't be able to bag college girls anymore. He'll need to shift his focus to single mothers.

Brea is rubbing her perfectly manicured nail around the rim of her glass. Is that supposed to be sexy? She's staring at me as she goes around and around. She's had Botox in all the right places. She should also be careful. A few more injections and she could start to look like the Joker or an aging news anchor. The adrenaline from my near-death entrance has given me a maximum confidence boost. I can't believe I'm actually nitpicking these two. This is why people bungee jump.

Brea's arms are expertly toned and tanned. I have no idea what her fitness routine entails but I have to believe it takes a lot more work to keep her legs in that kind of shape these days. I don't remember her being this fit. Don't get me wrong, it works. It's just different. There are more hard angles. It's clear she's trying. Twenty-five years ago, it was effortless.

What is Lacey doing? I wave her over. Harry is wrapping up a story about fly-fishing, I think, when she joins us. Wow. Look at her. Yesterday, you would not have been able to convince me that this is the same woman I've eaten 973 lunches next to a parking lot outside a brick and steel coffin with.

"May I get you a beverage, sir?"

That's an odd thing to say, since I'm holding a beer. "I got one. You look, I mean, Lacey, you look amazing."

"Is that an appropriate thing to say to an employee, sir?"

Uh-oh.

"I'll be at the bar, sir."

Is she pissed? I don't get a chance to follow her because right then Frankie runs up to the table. Good. I'm glad he's not detained somewhere. He's recovered nicely from his rude welcome, except for the grass stain on his khakis. Why does he look so, I don't know, normal? I'm about to ask him where his costume is when, out of nowhere, my taser-happy security guy whips an elbow straight back into Frankie's gut, and Frankie doubles over.

That looked like it hurt. Does this guy have a manager or somebody I should talk to? Is that me? He's got an exceptionally square jaw. Is that a good thing? Are women into that look?

"Come on!" Frankie's caught his breath and is straightening up, rubbing his lower-left ribs.

My security guy shoots me a glance that even through his dark shades clearly indicates he's willing to take it to the next level. "Is this man bothering you, sir?"

"No." I reach toward Frankie but realize I have no idea what to do with my proffered hand, so it just falls lamely back to my side. "He's a friend."

"Friend? Well, all right then." Square-jaw guy slaps Frankie hard on the back. "Have a nice time, friend."

"Hey, Frankie." I smile in apology. "Sorry about that. Again."

He waits until there are only civilians left at the table, then once the coast is clear he lunges in for a hug. "Tristan! Holy crap, man."

"Good to see you." I don't hug him back,

but I don't pull away either. This is me at peak physical intimacy.

"Hi, Freddy." Brea waves from across the table.

"It's Frankie."

"I know. So, like, look at you? You a mortgage processor or something?"

"Something. How's the Supreme Court?"

"Boring." She turns to Harry. "Babe, what did you end up doing?"

"Sales. Hey, Fred, can you believe our boy, Tristan, here?" Harry leans in and whispers. "The dude has his own security."

"I've noticed." Frankie shakes some grass out of his hair. "What exactly does one do to require such an entourage?"

Fucking Frankie. I was just thinking something nice, what a thick head of hair he's held on to, and here he goes messing this up for me. Of course, he's the one who's going to blow this. Don't ask me questions! I'm about to stammer something about bulls and bears when the tent finally loses its battle against the wind and breaks free. It doesn't go quietly. The poles knock over tables, causing screams and panic. One of them completely nails my tenth-grade lab partner. Ouch. I collect Lacey and we follow the crowd to the nearest door. Signs in the hall point to the gym: TAKE A WALK DOWN MEMORY LANE. That's a big no-thank-you.

"Let's check it out." Harry is herding us toward the gym.

I walk next to Lacey. "Are you okay?"

"Fine. It was just a little wind."

I wasn't asking about the tent. She picks up her pace.

Brea has left us for a group of women in jeggings. Even I know those aren't a thing anymore. They ohhh and ahhh as she twirls in her short skirt. It's okay that I'm attracted to this, right? She's not an actual high school cheerleader. It's completely normal and expected that I would have the beginnings of a boner right now. Harry is giving himself a boner talking Lacey's ear off. Reluctantly, I follow him into the gym.

Well, isn't this the stuff of nightmares. Blown-up pictures of the good old days. Harry is our self-appointed tour guide. I've got to get out of here.

"Shoot." I draw attention to my wrist. "I have to make a call."

"Sure thing, bro." Harry keeps blabbing to Lacey. He didn't even notice my Rolex. Should I shake it?

I hold my arm up in an attempt to catch the light on the silver band. "It won't take too long." Harry doesn't stop talking. "Ah, Miss Hahn? We've got to check in with Geneva."

"Right away, sir."

Harry holds her back. "Come on, Tristan. Geneva can wait. You need to recharge, brother."

"It's urgent. You get it, I'm sure."

"I do. Do I ever. At least give this pretty lady the day off."

Why is Harrison Sullivan touching Lacey? I'm not going anywhere. This is brutal. Harry is going out of his way to spill the tea on all my hilarious mishaps.

"This shot over here, the one of the basketball team? Tristan was our equipment manager for a week until his foot got tangled in a net of balls and he punctured a testicle."

"That's not what happened."

Not that I owe anyone an explanation, but, yes, it's true that my foot got tangled in a net of balls. Only I did not puncture a testicle, I sprained an ankle. I don't know what budding genius started that rumor or what sort of sorcery they used to describe how one large smooth round ball could end up puncturing a hole in a smaller, less-smooth round ball, but I can assure you, my balls have always been fine.

"Didn't it, like, leak for, like, three weeks?"

"My ankle? No."

He continues down the line. "This one

was taken in the north quad. Most people spent study hall making out there. I fingered Ashley Tiddlerson on that bench. More like Fiddlerson, am I right, Tristan? Oh. I forgot. Tristan was the only one who actually studied during study hall."

Up next must be an exceptionally embarrassing photo. Harry pauses to laugh. "Lacey. You got to see this. Swim team tryouts."

She turns to me, her grin of surprise a happy change from the sour looks she's been shooting me. "I didn't know you swam."

Maybe she's done calling me *sir*. That would be good.

"He didn't." Harry shakes his head with a smile. What a fun afternoon he's having reminiscing.

"Classic No Pubes."

"No what?" Lacey isn't smiling anymore.

"No Pubes. That was one of his nicknames. Remember No Pubes, No Pubes?"

I grunt. Why is Frankie being so quiet? He should be sidekicking the shit out of this. He's not even joining in at my expense. He's too busy scanning the exits and is particularly interested in two young guys lurking in the corner. Harry's still laughing. He's the only one finding any of this amusing. I step closer to examine the black-and-white memory. There's me, junior year, soaking wet in jeans and a sweatshirt. Harry is correct. I did not swim and was not intending to participate in that year's swim team tryouts. Blake Fiddlerson, Ashley's cousin, grabbed me as I was leaving the boys' locker room (which had the best bathrooms in the building) and tossed me in the diving well, shoes and all. I heard Blake overdosed. Sorry not sorry. Young Harry, glistening in a Speedo, has his arm wrapped around me, holding me still for the photo.

Lacey gets a closer look. "Huh. That must have been one cold pool."

Harry stops laughing when he realizes he might be the punch line. "Wait, what?"

The two young strangers leave the gym, and Frankie finally joins the conversation. "Hey, we should get out of here. Want to cruise the strip?" He turns, making note of their exit. What's his deal with those guys?

Harry puts his hand on my shoulder. "Cruise the strip? You guys aren't going to Coach Gerard's dedication?"

That's a hard pass.

"Tristan, we have time before the party. Let's go visit your dad."

Frankie! I like you so much more when you are silent. Lacey is not going to let this go, I'm sure.

And cue the chorus: "You have a dad?"

"Legally, yes."

Lacey is genuinely concerned. I'd rather Harry be commenting on my lack of pubic hair than me having to answer questions about my father.

Oh, good. Frankie decides to keep talking. "When's the last time you saw him? You're here, you should check in with the nurses. He's literally a few blocks away."

"Is he sick?" At least this change in topic has softened Lacey's face. She should wear makeup more often. She looks fantastic. Like herself, but a lot better. I need to make sure I keep that to myself.

Frankie answers for me. "Tristan's been taking care of him for a long time."

I correct him. "I've been paying people to take care of him for a long time."

Lacey looks me in the eyes. "I had no idea. That must be hard."

"Not really."

Harry is not interested in any of this. "Okay. Virgin, you go visit your pops and we'll hook up later." His phone buzzes in his pocket. "Fuck.

I told them to leave me alone." He complains to nobody as he walks away. "One fucking day. Can't I have one fucking day?"

Lacey gives me an encouraging look. "Are we going?"

I'm doing everything I can to avoid participating in this conversation. Frankie is now more interested in listening in on Harry's phone call.

She asks again. "Mr. Melendez?"

Fuck. "I'd rather not."

My father. Father. Dad. I've said and heard those words more in the last ten seconds than in the last ten years. It's too much. I feel like I'm suddenly at the bottom of a pool. It's cool and quiet. I'm flat on my belly, arms straight out. I can only hear muffled rumblings from the surface and see long shadows from the people around me. They're far away, experiencing the same moment but in a totally different type of matter. I'm in liquid form now. I want to stay here. I need something to weigh me down.

My hands can't grip the concrete. If only I had suction cups on my forearms.

I never intended to see my father alive again. I live less than an hour away; I don't need to pop in because I'm in the neighborhood. But like that goddamn square white envelope kicked me in the nuts and forced me to commit to this shit show, now that it's in my head—"He's literally a few blocks away"—I can't think of anything else. Just a fucking Google map with a huge red arrow pointing right to the prick's driveway. That's all I can picture.

Lacey notices I'm drowning.

"Hey." She touches my arm and looks at me for the second time since we landed. I'm relieved she's actually making eye contact. That's all I need to get back on dry land. I'm grateful but it's exhausting, continually needing to be rescued. I'm starting to realize how much time Lacey spends saving me from myself. With all the hoopla people make about boundaries and consent, maybe she should be asking me first. What's that saying . . . that quote soccer moms frame in their half-baths and wannabe deep thinkers in their twenties tattoo on their wrists? "Not all who wander are lost." Well, not everyone who is drowning wants CPR.

One of her light bulbs goes off. "It might be nice to schedule a stop. I can clear your afternoon."

What is she doing? She can drop the act. Brea isn't around and Harry is off in the corner eye-fucking his senior picture and yelling into his phone. This whole display is a bit Harrison heavy, to tell you the truth. How much money did he donate? Meanwhile Frankie's standing here like an idiot, waiting for Harrison to give him some attention. Still a little dog waiting for a bone.

What the heck does Frankie do these days? Brea mentioned something about mortgages. That can't be right. I once knew. Whatever he does, he looks like a fucking idiot and we don't have to impress him or listen to him.

"Lacey."

She stops me from stopping her. "Don't you think he'd like to see you, your father, and all your employees?" She coughs and points toward my watch.

Employees? Oh. Right. I keep forgetting about the dozens of dudes I'm paying to make me look important. She coughs again and gestures toward my wrist. Does she need to know the time?

"It's one sixteen. No. Seventeen. It's impossible to read the minute hand on this thing."

She tries again a little slower. "Don't you think he'd appreciate a visit from his successful son?"

I don't give a shit what he'd appreciate. She's looking at me like we're playing charades and I should know the answer. Wait. Holy crap, she's brilliant! How did I not think of this? I've allowed myself to be completely sucked into Brea and Harrison's orbit and can't see the forest through the trees. Yes, Lacey, a BOGO! Why waste all my flashy good fortune on these losers when I can also jam it in my father's saggy face! She gets it. We're finally on the same page.

"Frankie. We'll take my cars."

FOURTEEN

There's No Place Like Home

Lacey and I slide into the back seat. Frankie sits up front with the driver. Three teams drive behind us. Lacey was on to something. Showing up like this is pretty badass. Frankie is taking inventory of the car's security features. He's impressed. You get what you pay for. This is a sweet ride.

"When's the last time you've seen him?" Frankie doesn't turn around from the front seat.

"My father?" There's that word again. "It's been a long time."

I've tried really hard to train my brain to

stop forming mental images. It hasn't worked. Zero-point-seven percent of the world's population is thought to have a condition called aphantasia: Their brains don't make pictures. Most are born this way, or it develops after a major injury. Lucky them. If someone says *apple* they don't imagine an apple or even a red circle. They have no mind's eye. Their brain will still make instantaneous connections associating every experience they've ever had with an apple; they can describe it, but they can't see it. Their mind is literally blank.

Many with this condition are very smart people. When asked if, given the chance, they would want to be "normal" almost all say "no thanks." They know how good they have it. What a lovely detached way to go through life. How easy it must be to move on, think about something else. If this fucking flashing sign pointing to my fucking father's home wasn't plastered in every corner of my skull, I wouldn't be driving to fucking see him right now. Fuck! I don't care if I look like I invented Facebook, and I don't care how much I'm currently cussing. I don't want to breathe the same air as that asshole. My armpits are growing moist. I fucking hate sweating. I've got to get my shit together. I am four seconds away from a complete meltdown.

Frankie turns and addresses Lacey. "He's an interesting guy."

"He's an asshole." I need to not talk and focus on slowing down my heart rate. I've never wanted to smash into a semi and be decapitated more than I do right now. Thanks to Jayne Mansfield, modern regulations make it slightly harder to die instantly in a car-versus-semi accident. Still, between 1994 and 2018 more than six thousand motorists lost their heads after crashing under a semi. Shit. I bet this armored SUV might impede a quick death.

Lacey interjects. She's still here? My fingers are tingling. "I'm sure he's not that bad. He raised you." She's quick to get back in character. "Sir."

Finally, Frankie contributes something helpful. "No, he's a total prick."

I don't have anything nice to say about my father with the exception that on paper, he did all the things he was supposed to do.

This is a huge mistake. I survive one helicopter ride and think I can handle dropping by to catch up with Dad. Lacey is wrong. This is a very dumb idea. He's going to see right through all this shit and trash me like I'm some terrified kid.

We pull up at the American dream. I grew up in a neat two-bed, one-bath Craftsman on a cul-de-sac. My parents walked across the border as teenagers and multiple degrees later had slid into the professional middle class.

I'm trying to disassociate by being a reporter, an observer of my life rather than a participant. The house is a soft yellow with white trim. It looks really nice, nicer than I ever remember it looking. Are we at the right place? I'm not trying to do a bit here; I honestly do not recognize the house. It's the same, but brighter?

"Is he having a party?" Lacey's looking out the window at all the cars lining the circular dead end. The front porch of one of the neighbor's houses has the remnants of party decorations flapping in the unrelenting wind.

I point. "Must be them."

We pull into the driveway. The rest of my mini fleet of armored vehicles has to do a loop and park back near the entrance of the cul-de-sac.

Is this really my house? There are flowers blooming in clay pots framing the front door. The bushes are green and perfectly trimmed. The lawn is freshly cut and the wind hasn't disturbed any of the carefully placed perennials. Who do I pay to keep this up? I could definitely downgrade my service. My father doesn't need to shuffle around in a botanical garden. This would have made my mother happy, though. I'd like to think this house wouldn't seem so strange to me if she was still in it. I would still spend time with her even if that meant I had to see him.

"Wow." Frankie shuts the car door after we both climb out. "The place looks great."

"Your dad must be into gardening." Lacey joins us in the driveway.

"My father can't button his own pants. I pay for it."

A flock of loose balloons flies by, making Lacey laugh. We have to duck and dodge random paper plates and napkins as we approach the front door. Rough day to have an outdoor celebration. I can hear a crowd in a nearby backyard. They don't seem to mind that the wind is moving their party into the street. This must be driving my father crazy. He hates celebrations, if he even notices. I imagine he's tucked in tight behind drawn blinds and curtains.

Let's get this fucking over with. I knock quietly. I have the urge to cover up my watch. But that would defeat the purpose. I hate how this unwelcome excursion is messing with my head. I should have never gone along with this. A white woman answers the door. Thank God. My father is one of those Brown people who has a problem with other Brown people. I'm sure his racist tirades would have run anyone else out of here.

"Hello. Can I help you?"

She's clean and professional. She's in scrubs so as not to be mistaken for someone who would willingly be here in the absence of a paycheck. I don't blame her.

"Hi. I'm here to see—"

She cuts me off. "Mr. Melendez?"

That's rude. "Yes, my father—"

"No." She interrupts again. "You're Mr. Melendez, Tristan Melendez?" She compares my current face to a family picture on the side table by the door. We took that shot at Kohl's Family Portrait Studio per my mother's request two years before she died. I'm not smiling.

"We're in town for the reunion." Do I wait for her to invite us in? It's my house.

"Come in. Come in." She beckons warmly.

The carpets are worn and flat and the linoleum is chipped. In spite of that, the place gives off the impression of being well cared for. There's an almost overbearing smell of baby powder.

"It's so nice to finally meet you. I'm Nell, one of the rotating shift nurses. Can I just say, we all appreciate your generosity so much. Mickey is so lucky to have—"

"Yeah. Sure." Did she refer to my father as Mickey? He would drown me in a bucket of my own tears if I ever addressed him with such a soft-sounding moniker.

Lacey is casually snooping around. She won't find any insights into my past here. We might as well be in a Motel 6. No, I'm selling the place short. It's more like a Best Western. As I poke around myself, I find that my room has been converted, updated really, to house the night nurse. The *Independence Day* and *Goodfellas* movie posters Frankie made me hang up are long gone. I wonder what happened to my PlayStation? The place is both generic and homey. Sterile and cozy.

"Your father is on the patio." Nell sneaks up behind us. Nurses and their damn quiet shoes.

There's a patio? When did we get a patio?

Frankie pats me on the back. "You did good."

I did? What am I trying to be good at now? He must be able to tell by my expression that I'm not following.

"I know your pops wasn't always an easy guy to be around. No one would blame you if he was thrown in a home somewhere."

"It's wonderful," Nell tells us. "Seniors who have the ability to spend their final years comfortable at home have a much higher quality of life. Your father—"

That's enough. I don't need to hear any more about my father living it up in the lap of luxury or be ordained Best Son on the Planet. "Thank you. It's what anyone would do." My tone is curt, just how I intended it.

The nurse raises an eyebrow and leads us back to the living room where she slides open the glass door. Huh. We do have a patio. I remember now. I always thought of it as a concrete slab that took up half the backyard. We never used it. No barbecues or cornhole games. Until now, I guess. My father is relaxing in one of four wicker chairs around a small round table.

"Mickey, you have a visitor."

The backyard is as impressive as the front. "Who does all this? The yard?"

Nell seems surprised I have to ask. "The neighbors."

"Neighbors? Am I paying them?" That's a ridiculous question. This nice lady in scrubs is not my accountant.

"They do it for free."

"Why?" I'm dumbfounded.

"They own a landscaping company and your father lets them store some of their equipment in the garage."

What? Now I'm really stumped. My father, Miguel Melendez, is helping somebody? I guess Mickey Melendez is better at sharing.

"I do it for Sheba." My dad doesn't look up from his chair.

The nurse nods and gives me a smile. "Sheba is the neighbors' dog. Mickey likes having her over to play fetch."

Shut up. Am I being Punk'd? Where are the hidden cameras? My father does not help neighbors or enjoy animals.

We're all bunched up in the doorway. Nell

motions for us to come out and sit. "Can I bring you something to drink? Lemonade?"

We politely decline and take our seats. I don't plan on staying long enough to get thirsty. Though something cold would be nice in this horrendous wind. Why is he sitting out here? Lacey is working hard at keeping her hair out of her face. Have I told her how nice she looks? She and Frankie look at me to start the conversation. I don't. I'm pouting like a spoiled child. Frankie gets the ball rolling.

"It's nice to see you again, Mr. Melendez."

"Call me Mickey. Mr. Melendez was my father." My dad's overused expression gets a courtesy chuckle from Frankie. "Don't bother telling me who you are. I won't remember and I'll just forget."

Nell is back with bottled water. "Just in case."

"Thank you, Nell." My father fumbles with the cap.

She leans down to help. "This is your son, Tristan."

"Who, him?" He pokes a finger at Frankie.

"No." She points to my scowling face. "Him."

"You look like my brother Juan. Do you know Juan?"

I shake my head no. Nell moves to depart. "I'll leave you all to catch up. Your father takes his medicine and has supper at five."

"We won't be long."

Her smile tightens at my response. So sorry, Nell. Not all of us have made such *wonderful* memories in this place. God, go get your own fucked-up family.

"So, you're my son?"

I nod.

"Are you my daughter?" He studies Lacey's face.

"I'm Mr. Melendez's assistant."

"She's my friend. Good friend."

"I'm Lacey." She smiles and extends her hand. Gross. I do not like touching old skin. Lacey would be good with old people. I bet she's good with babies, too.

Frankie's phone blasts an obnoxious ringtone, making us all jump. "Jesus. Sorry. It's work."

He excuses himself from the table and takes large strides around to the front of the house. A bird passes by holding a long, unfurled party streamer in its beak.

"Must be from the party. It's Dylan's birthday." Dad looks at us like we should know who the hell Dylan is. "I went over earlier for cake. A little dry, but not bad."

I don't say anything. This is awkward, even for me. Lacey tries being a good sport. "What kind of cake was it?"

"Huh?"

"From the party?"

He shrugs. "I don't know."

Swing and a miss, Lacey. She gets credit for trying. That's more than I'm doing. Fine. "How about this wind?" There. Happy now? Have I done enough? Why did Frankie leave? I want to wrap this up.

"The Santa Anas." My father squints toward the mountains. "It's not natural for the winds to blow east."

"It makes me nervous." Lacey wrestles her hair back from her face.

My father smiles in agreement. "'It was one of those hot dry Santa Anas that come down through the mountain passes and curl your hair and make your nerves jump and your skin itch. On nights like that, every booze party ends in a fight. Meek little wives feel the edge of the carving knife and study their husbands' necks. Anything can happen.'" He takes a beat. "Raymond Chandler wrote that."

Lacey is impressed. "I recognize that name. What did he do again?"

"He was president of the Mystery Writers of America. You know. He wrote private eye–type

stuff. Humphrey Bogart. *The Long Goodbye.*"
He trails off.

"Dad always had a book in his lap." I forget to scowl.

"I like to read, too." Lacey has to raise her voice over the raging wind.

She starts talking about books. She's not doing her whole "nervous chatter to fill the space"–type talking. She's relaxed. Charming. I'm oddly jealous of the time the two of them seem to be having. My father is laughing. My father doesn't laugh. Is this what it's like bringing a nice girl home to meet your parents? It feels pretty good.

We move on to critique movies and TV shows. Nell doesn't like Dad watching anything too loud. Lacey thrills us with one tidbit after another. My dad tells us about a baseball game he went to with his big brother Juan and how he got lost. He's never told me a story from his childhood before.

All of us are surprised when Nell comes to collect my father for dinner.

"It's time to eat, Mickey."

"What's for dessert?"

"First pills, then vegetables, then dessert."

"She's the mean one." He points an accusing finger at her. "When do you go on vacation? Martha lets me eat whatever I want!"

"Yeah, yeah. Martha's everyone's favorite. Would you like to stay for dinner?" Nell gestures to me and Lacey. "There's plenty."

Lacey looks to me for an answer.

"We have to get back to the reunion."

We don't. In fact, I don't know what we'll do for the next few hours but staying longer would definitely be pressing my luck. This has been strangely . . . nice? My father is no longer my father. I guess that's all that needed to happen for us to spend a nice afternoon together. I've been wrong dreading old age. It's downright delightful. Still, glad I won't be rolling the dice. I'm sure I'm not lucky enough to have my brain implode in such a pleasant manner.

He notices my watch as we stand for good-byes. "That's some watch."

"This?" I realize in making such a hasty purchase I know nothing about what is actually adorning my wrist. Please don't let there be follow-up questions.

"My son, huh?"

Nell yells from inside the house. "Tristan! He's your son, Tristan, Mickey."

"I suppose I should thank you. I'm still smart enough to know I don't have anything to do with this." He waves his arms, indicating the "this" is his life. "I remember my father. I don't remember yesterday but I remember that son of a bitch." He looks at me and then Lacey. "If I was anything like him . . . Thank you."

He extends his hand. We have yet to touch.

Lacey's eyes are pleading with me to take it. I'm not a monster! I'll shake his damn hand, age spots and all.

"Good luck to you."

I appreciate the finality of his goodbye.

I mumble a farewell and Lacey squeezes his shoulder. "It was great to meet you, Mr. Melendez."

My father smiles. "You're a good one. She's a good one." He winks at me.

Lacey blushes. This is the first time she's blushed all day, or maybe it's just the first time I'm noticing.

The SUVs have pulled up in a line out front, their engines running. That seems wasteful. How did they even know we were ready to go? I don't see Frankie anywhere. Damn it, Frankie. What do we do now? Wait? I'm not doing a second goodbye. The road is covered in party debris. There's a still-intact piñata in the middle of the cul-de-sac. A rainbow tablecloth is wrapped around a streetlamp. There are red party cups everywhere. The party sounds like it's still rocking. Aren't they missing all of their crap?

"Where's your friend?" Lacey looks around for Frankie. "Can you believe all this junk?"

Does she want an answer? She's distracted trying to keep her dress from unraveling. She looks . . . she should wear red more often.

"Let's wait in the car."

Without thinking, I put my hand on her back and guide her to the car door. Is this okay? It must be. She doesn't slap me. She slides in and adjusts her top.

"Thanks. This wind is freaking crazy!"

The driver is listening to the radio. He goes to turn it off but I stop him. "It's fine."

The news is on. All of Southern California is on an extreme fire alert. The air is already hazy and smells like a cookout. This is hardly news anymore. Did you know, and I shit you not, that through the 1990s there were only five fire-related emergency declarations a decade? Decade, with a D. Since the start of the 2000s it's risen—I wish I was making this up— to one hundred fire-related emergency declarations *a year*. That's one thousand declarations a decade. That's a 99.5 percent increase over the last twenty years of devastating forest fires. We don't deserve nice things.

Mr. Chandler was right. The Santa Ana winds suck. I will not miss this. It feels like I brushed my teeth with sandpaper. I don't think my father should spend so much time sitting outside. I'll have to call Nell.

"Are we waiting for the gentleman in cargo shorts, sir?"

"Yes. Please."

The driver talks to someone in his earpiece. "This is Alpha One. Has anyone had eyes on Limp Lizard?" He turns to us and mouths "code name."

Code name? We have code names? Well,

what's mine? I sure as shit hope it's better than "Limp Lizard."

Lacey doesn't hesitate. "What's my code name?"

"Bunches of Oats." He listens for a beat. "Roger that. The guest in question was spotted heading this direction on foot."

A plastic pole smacks into the windshield. The driver jumps out of the car with his weapon drawn. That's a bit of an overreaction. What is up with these guys? For their sake, I hope they get to shoot something before the night is over. The offending object is a pointy yellow stick covered in dirt with a nylon rope attached to the top. I don't know why I'm describing this random flying garbage to you. Sorry. It's just with the wind and seeing my father, I'm all—holy shit. What is that?

Lacey smacks my leg. "What the freak?"

A giant inflated rainbow square is bouncing across the cul-de-sac.

Lacey hits my leg again. "Oh! Oh! It's a bounce house! One of those jumpy kid thingies."

She throws open her car door and clambers out. Great. That means I have to get out, too. We join the driver out on the pavement. The kids inside the bounce house (wait, there are kids in there?) are shrieking and laughing as it skitters toward us. Do they not realize they're in a colorful death trap that's desperate to take flight?

"Don't worry, sir, I'll handle this." The driver raises his gun toward the tumbling fun house.

Are you kidding me?! I can't believe this guy. I wave my arms frantically to stop him. "Don't shoot!"

Out of nowhere, Frankie dives through the air and slams into the driver's body like he's Tom Cruise in *Mission: Impossible*. They tumble to the ground and roll, while a huge gust of hot wind gives the inflated house the juice it needs to take off. Lacey and I duck as it floats over us, and Frankie helps the shaken driver back to his feet.

"That's weird." Frankie squints at the rainbow as it glides out of the cul-de-sac. "Well, should we head out?"

The man with the very square jaw—and still holding the gun, I might add—looks Frankie up and down. Oh, my God. Is he going to kill him? Please don't kill—

"Solid maneuver." He nods in respect and opens the passenger door. Frankie slides in, shotgun.

Lacey and I hesitate. Shouldn't somebody do something? Where are the kids' parents? I specifically did not reproduce so I would never find myself in a situation like this. Fricking Santa Anas.

FIFTEEN

Let's Party

Should we dive in deeper to Tristan and his father's estranged relationship? Nah. Go binge *Succession*. Complicated people have complicated children. Lucky for therapists, they don't cancel each other out. Tristan's father wasn't a complete monster. Deep down Tristan knows that. There's no law requiring him to provide such exceptional care in his waning years. Mickey Melendez is like most people. Being cruel is much easier than being vulnerable, and there is nothing more vulnerable than raising a human. Becoming an adult doesn't mean we forgive all our parents' faults but it means we start to recognize them objectively. This visit has slightly lifted a weight from Tristan's shoulders that he assumed was permanent.

Oh, and in case the thought of children floating to their death is distracting, they're fine. They drifted halfway to Palm Springs and touched down in a Big Lots parking lot.

Back at the high school, the party is slowly getting started. Brea and Harry are standing on opposite sides of the crowded gym. Harry keeps checking her out and she keeps checking to make sure he's getting a good look. If his eyes aren't on her they're glued to his phone. Is it his family? Work? She's only slightly interested in what her small-screen competition might be.

Brea's holding court with her old crew like nothing's changed over the last two and a half decades. She's too self-obsessed to notice their collective disinterest. She does them a favor when she leaves to grace Harry with her company.

"Hey, babe." She glides into her place at his side.

"Hey, babe." He doesn't look up. He's too busy sending an angry text message. Can't anyone just do their job? He finishes typing TAKE CARE OF IT! with his thumbs. He contemplates adding an emoji.

Brea bristles at his side and makes to leave. "Okay. Nice talking to you."

He almost drops his phone trying to quickly jam it back into his pocket. "Sorry. Work."

"I left my phone in the car. Fuck everyone. Am I right?"

He wishes he'd thought of that. "You've always been smarter than me."

Harry rests his hand on the small of her back. Her muscles tense but quickly recognize his touch and settle in. They stand there like the old days, quietly surveying the crowd. Most people have freshened up between the afternoon welcome events and the big party. Some have cleaned up better than others. Brea and Harry tug at their costumes in unison. Seeing their peers in suits and little black dresses, work pants and capris, they can't help but feel a tad silly. No one else has chosen to show their school spirit as proudly as these two. It's a brief lapse of confidence, but both would murder you before ever admitting to feeling self-conscious.

"Fucking losers." Harry offers Brea his flask. She takes it and drinks more enthusiastically than he remembers. He smiles once she comes up for air. "All right. Someone's ready to party."

"Fucking sheep. All of them. Why am I even here?"

"Totally. How sad. Everyone is the fucking same." Says the guy in a twenty-five-year-old jacket.

They haven't quite remembered how to talk to each other. It's not like they'd had a relationship grounded in communication, but they're both disappointed with how rough this small talk is going. They take a few quick drinks from his flask to hopefully loosen up.

The whole mood is tense and lame. The Backstreet Boys are playing. No one is dancing. A few people sway, waiting for an invitation to sway with somebody else. These people know they are adults, right? They have kids in college and preschool. They've made and lost millions of dollars. They own homes. They've survived tragedies. Yet here they are, right back where they started: waiting for approval, waiting to be picked.

Thank God I didn't go to my reunion. Any of them. Those fuckers don't deserve to see me IRL. And I could never afford a helicopter.

"Kristin got fat."

Brea smiles. "I know. It's fantastic."

"What was your beef?"

Brea shrugs. "Screw her. Screw all of them."

Round tables with white tablecloths are organized in clusters around the school's mascot painted on the middle of the floor. It's a profile of an Aztec in a headdress. I'd be a lot more comfortable if their mascot was a tiger or a gator but it's an Aztec.

"The place looks like shit." Brea reaches out for another turn with the flask. "Who organized this, anyway? The bar is in a terrible spot. Total bottleneck. That balloon arch is ridiculous. Adults don't need flipping balloons. I'm not ten. Streamers are fucking garbage, not to mention a hazard. We might have people here with fake hips, okay? A selfie booth? How basic."

Apparently, Brea has some strong feelings about the décor. I think the balloon arch is kind of cool. Maybe if she knew how much it cost, she would like it more. She needs to take a chill pill. There's only so much you can do to make a school gym sexy. I will say, the lighting is problematic. Whoever was in charge of the "being able to see" committee deserves all of Brea's wrath. In her rant she didn't mention the fake tea-light candles plopped on the tables or the sparse strings of twinkle lights lining the walls. The biggest turd burger is an off-centered disco ball that doesn't have any light to reflect. The room is disorientingly dim. People are crossing the floor like mummies with their arms out, ready to brace themselves for a fall or a boob graze.

Harry's pocket vibrates throughout Brea's hot take on the decorations. He's trying real hard to ignore the unwanted thigh massage. He needs this. Needs this time with her. He's doing all he can to make this feel natural, like they never skipped a beat. But it's clear they've skipped entire albums.

"Do you need to get that?"

Brea is standing close enough to his leg to catch some residual vibrations. He wouldn't dare take his attention off her. "What? No. No. How are you?"

"Never better."

He stays quiet and drinks. A little more liquid courage should do the trick and loosen those lips. But Brea can't wait that long. She can't shake the feeling that everyone is laughing at her and she's about to be covered in pig's blood. "Want to get out of here?"

"Yes!"

Of course, no one is actually laughing at her. It's worse. Nobody cares all that much. Sure, it's cool she's a fancy-pants lawyer who's hung out with the Supreme Court, but she's always argued for the wrong side. Makes sense. Most alpha alpha *alpha* bitches do not grow up to join the Peace Corps or give a voice to the oppressed. Brea grabs Harry's hand and they head toward the exit.

They don't get far before Tristan's security team busts through the doors. The squad of identical-looking white guys in identical black suits rudely sweeps the room for threats. The fascist assholes break up large groups of people and stop the music. There are at least two dozen of them. Nobody knows who they are or what the hell they're doing. Their symmetrical features and broad shoulders are enough to convince the crowd of their authority. They stand on high alert around the perimeter, holding flashlights to light a path. Tristan's arrival is literally lighting up the room.

Once again, Lacey has to stop him from running away. She pushes him through the doors. The music resumes right as he enters. How cinematic. Brea immediately drops Harry's hand and follows the lighted path to meet him in the middle of the gym floor. Time has stopped.

Brea approaches in slow motion with her blond locks blowing in an invisible wind. Holy crap. This is really happening. Under a spotlight from heaven, surrounded by adoring fans, Tristan Melendez has found himself standing on the Aztec with the prettiest girl in school. He can't believe it. Is he dreaming? Did he get shot in an attempted mugging and the last ten years of his life have just been a hallucination as his synapses fired for the last time and he's not really here but finally fading into oblivion?

Lacey doesn't understand why he's shuffling his feet like he's standing on hot coals.

"Tristan!" Brea clings to his arm.

Maybe it's because they can finally see or because Chumbawamba is blasting; people start to loosen up and get freaky on the dance floor. Tristan is surrounded by fans.

"Nice work, dude!"

"Holy shit, man!"

"You're a BFD, bro!"

Harry high fives his way into the crew. Brea pays no attention to him. She is quick to push everyone out of the way so she can claim her rightful spot as Tristan's plus one. She is finally getting the attention and respect she deserves. She points out her new date's watch to the former captain of the soccer team. "Check out the Rolex." She scolds a nobody for almost stepping on his fine leather shoes. "Watch it! Those shoes cost more than your house."

She leans in close. His skin tingles from her hot, boozy breath. "Thank God you're back. Everyone here is so lame. Oh, my God. Let's get a drink and catch up!"

They leave without saying goodbye to their inner circle.

Frankie feels for Lacey. He knows how it feels to be ditched for the hot chick. "I have to check in with the office. Can I grab you a drink on my way back?"

Lacey nods yes. She's pretty sure he just asked

if she wants a drink. It's hard to hear above all the yelling of *I get knocked down, but I get up again, you are never going to keep me down . . .*" She was four years old when this song came out and doesn't get the mass excitement. Harry, an oddly familiar face, comes to her rescue.

"Hey." He yells over the music.

"Hi."

"You're Tristan's assistant, right?"

"Something like that." Lacey doesn't want to play along anymore.

"You want to sit down? You really shouldn't be standing here."

"Why?" What's wrong with this spot? She's slightly alarmed. Is she about to get covered in pig's blood? Why can't she stand here?

"It's the Aztec."

"Okay." She's not getting it.

Harry yells louder. "You haven't earned it." He leads her toward an empty table on the sidelines. "It's a social hierarchy thing. You know."

"Not really." She turns away, expecting him to leave.

He doesn't. He plops down next to her but stops short of pulling the chair in close. He needs to scope this scene out before he commits. Even though he's at an appropriate distance, he can't help but manspread in her direction. He finally tends to his phone and sees a series of missed calls.

"Fuck! I told them not to call this weekend."

He throws the phone on the table. Lacey waves away the cloud of hard liquor wafting from his pores.

He notices. "You want some?" He holds up his trusty flask.

"What's in it?"

"I forgot."

"You forgot?"

Harry isn't used to being questioned. He likes it. It feels good to have someone interested in him enough to say more than "Yes, boss. Sure thing, man." Fucking lackeys. He's built an empire of dickless dipshits. Why do they keep calling him? He should murder every last one of them. He's getting good and drunk now.

She's waiting for an answer. "You forgot what you just drank?"

"It all tastes the same. Here." He holds the silver container in front of her face. "It's expensive."

"Okay." She takes a small drink and hands it back. "Yum. Thanks."

She looks around, trying to spot Tristan. He's leaning on the bar while Brea talks, inches from his face. They're the same height, which is perfect for Brea, who loves looking people dead in the eyes. It always bothered her that she had to look up to Harrison. In between giggles and whispers, she tucks Tristan's hair behind his ears and smooths out his jacket. Lacey doesn't appreciate his unclenched posture. This whole day has been a mind fuck, or as she would call it, a mind fart.

She holds her hand out to Harry. "Actually, can I have some more?"

Harry is happy to oblige. "Let's party, girl!"

His phone vibrates on the table. He hands Lacey the flask and answers with clenched teeth.

SIXTEEN

Odd Couple

What the heck is going on? It's bad enough that I'm his assistant, but that butthole up and leaves me the first chance he gets? Off he goes with Super Tits and I'm stuck breathing in Malibu Ken's toxic fumes. Why is he still sitting here? Ooooohhh, I better not stand on the Aztec. Heaven forbid I'm a human person with human feet standing on a floor built for humans to stand on. God! This is some grade-A BS even for Tristan. All the things I do for that jerk and this is what I get? I get to spend my night babysitting Sir Drunkington? I waste so much time thinking about him. Permission to swear? Tristan can go fuck himself. He's being a real cunt.

That was too much. Sorry. I tend to go from zero to a thousand when I'm stressed.

What is this dude's deal? This guy, what *is* his name? It's something stupid. He's hot but bad news. Totally bad news. Bloated, too. I mean, it works. It all works, he definitely works, but it's sad. He's like if Ryan Reynolds wasn't Ryan Reynolds but a depressed mattress salesman. That jacket . . . that's a man holding on tight to something. He must be lonely. I haven't seen him talk to anybody but those two freaking lovebirds over there. What is his name? Herbie? No. That's a car.

Harry! Yes! Harry is his name. Gross. What the hell kind of name is Harry? It's as bad as Herbie. It's a name that sounds like his breath smells. Shit. I'm having a hot flash. Swearing's not half bad. He's looking at me. Why is he looking at me? He just cussed someone out on the phone. I might be drinking a smidge-a-roo too fast. This dude is stressed to the max. I better give him back his medicine. He's leaning back in his chair, checking me out. I wish I had a sweater to hide under. No, that's a terrible idea. It is so fucking hot in here. I'm going to cuss for the time being. Seems reasonable given my current situation.

It's time to start drinking on the clock. Past time. Screw you, Tristan. Enjoy your new phony life and phony girlfriend. That bitch is crazy. Who wears an actual cheerleading uniform in public besides an actual cheerleader? Sorry, lady. You ain't no cheer—

Harry grabs the flask back. I forgot I was still drinking. Oof. That was a big gulp.

"Save some for the rest of us." He winks.

This guy can pull off a good wink. He scoots his chair a little closer. Does he need something?

"Can I help you with something?"

He sobers up for a millisecond. "Oh. Is this not okay?"

Interesting. Could he be a modern man actually concerned about invading my space? A few more sips and this night could get interesting. No. Something unbearable is about to happen.

"It's just . . . why are you still here?"

"We're hanging out. Do you want me to leave?"

That question isn't directed at me, but to the universe. Is it possible that a girl such as myself, so low in the social hierarchy, would actually not want his attention?

"Oh. No. I. Umm, didn't think you . . ." This is going really well.

"You don't hang out with a lot of people, do you?" He sounds interested but not judgmental. Huh.

"Not many. I guess I enjoy my own company."

"Fuck me."

What? Why?

"That's the most honest thing I've ever heard.

That's great. You're a real straight shooter. 'Enjoy my own company.' Fantastic."

He takes a drink and passes the flask. If I put my lips on this right after him, does it count as a kiss? I shut my eyes just in case. Man, this is good whiskey.

His phone shakes on the table. We both overreact to the sudden noise.

"Excuse me again." He answers without saying hello. "Take care of it." I can't make out what the person on the other end is saying. "Fuck. I don't care. Start with the fingers and keep breaking shit until you get an answer. Then use the blow torch. I gotta go."

I'm sorry, what?

He throws his phone down. "Do you like working for Tristan?"

Small talk. I can do this. But one quick sec. Was he referring to human fingers?

"Yes. Tristan is . . ." Don't look. Don't look. Don't look. I look. Tristan and Leggy La Rue are thirty seconds away from fucking. Harry follows my gaze toward the bar. He looks equally deflated. "He's a fine boss."

"An interesting guy, that's for sure. What do you all do again?"

"Um. Chocolate. What do you do?"

"Pharmaceutical sales."

"Yeah. Us, too. Ah. We do chocolate trading. Sales. You know. Milk. Dark. Hazelnut. I think I'm drunk."

Not shooting too straight now, am I? I've been on the verge of a total meltdown since five-thirty this morning. Another sip or two and there are only so many ways this night is going to turn out.

His elbows are on the table, propping his face up next to mine. Is this a drunk thing or does he always get this close to people? Is this something attractive people do? I don't like it. Is he waiting for me to say something? This is a lot of pressure.

I rack my brain for something to say. "How come you're alone here?" That's the best I can come up with?

Oh, God. He's not answering me. He might murder me. Or maybe he works for the CIA. Shit. Now that would explain the letterman's jacket and cheerleading uniform. Of course. Harry and Tits McGee are working some undercover operation. He certainly drinks on the job. Speaking of, I should have eaten more today. Did I eat anything today? I'm going to need some carbs to soak up this booze.

"Do you have a granola bar or anything?"

He shakes his head.

"That came out wrong. What I said before. I meant, why is no one talking to you? Oops. That sort of came out the same way. How about this: Why are you talking to me? Like, don't you have a ton of friends here?"

His mouth turns down into one of those smile-frowns. "Not really." He drinks as we both watch Brea suck a lime out of Tristan's mouth. "She was it. You know. I put all my eggs in one basket."

I do know. "That's not true. All those pictures. You were like the quarterback on every team. You must have had a lot of friends."

"No. Nobody likes the best. And I was the best. At everything. It was amazing. Now I suck. Everything sucks. It's the opposite of amazing. To top it all off, it looks like my best friend is going to go home with my girl."

I do a spit take but I don't have any liquid in my mouth. That kind of hurts. "Tristan was your best friend?"

"Sure. Probably. We never talked about it. I don't know if it's, like, official, but, yeah. We were total bros. It worked because he's not good at anything. Besides thinking. There was no competition. A real yin and yang situation. Fuck. I guess he won, though. Look at him." His voice trails off.

"It might not be what you think."

"You all do some shady shit. Obviously. Whatever he's doing, he's making bank. I would never sweat in those loafers. You have to be real fucking rich to go sockless in shoes like those."

"His T-shirt cost four hundred dollars."

"Total baller. And look at you, Miss Thing. Lady in Red up in here."

"This?" I look down to survey my dress but get distracted by the boob sweat in my cleavage.

He is also looking at my cleavage. "It's hot in here."

Oh, my God. Can he see my boob sweat? I should fake a seizure.

He moves his chair to get a better look across the room at Brea. "She hasn't changed."

"Nobody changes."

"Tristan did. You know, a lot of people thought he was retarded. Or would go postal."

Those are some choice words.

"Not me." He takes another drink. "I knew that kid would make it."

Should I tell this guy Tristan's secret before his liver explodes?

"What's your deal? How do you like being here with all us old fucks? What are you, twenty-two?"

Twenty-two! My, my. "Ha. I'm thirty. Almost." I like to round up.

"No shit. Good for you. I bet you're smart like your boss."

Smarter. "I guess."

He's talking to me but looking across the room. "I was looking forward to this. My big comeback. This could have been good for me, you know? Recharge the old batteries. Fuck. Just another point in the Epic Fail column. I have nothing left but to wait for my balls to be pureed and served with a side of fingerling potatoes."

Wow. He is a lot. My desire to fix him is

becoming overwhelming. "Buddha says life is pain when we spend our energy wanting things to be different than what they are."

"Deep. You're a good listener."

"Thanks." He should hang out with us normies more often.

He stands up abruptly. I must have finished serving my purpose.

"Come on." He holds out his hand. "Let's show off that dress."

He leaves his phone bouncing on alert on the table. Uh. Did I just become the most popular girl in school?

SEVENTEEN

But Wait, There's More

I thought it would be cute to stick with our unlikely couple—well, one of our unlikely couples, anyway—and get a look inside Harry's head. You know, a whole she said–he said meet-cute? But we're going to move on. You're too smart to waste your time with that convention (for now anyway . . . we'll see what happens in another forty pages). Besides, what else is there to discover? Once Brea ditched him, he needed to quickly find another receptacle to dump his shit into. Enter Lacey. "When Harry

Met Lacey . . ." That would have been a fantastic name for the last chapter. Damn it.

Meda Lucas. Remember him? He's waiting down the road at a delicious taco spot for word of Santa Ana. He sent his two most promising newbies to scope out the high school. And by "most promising," I mean the only two with enough facial hair to possibly pass for thirty, let alone forty-something. They were instructed to blend in, hang back, and send a pic of anyone who might fit Santa Ana's description. They were a bit jumpy and trigger happy. Meda Lucas had to tell them multiple times there was to be no shooting until he gave the orders.

He was not able to enlist the help of his A or B squad for this weekend getaway. Too risky. He doesn't want anyone to know he's in town. No one can know he's in California. That means no trips to the grocery store with a supermodel in West Hollywood and no tagalongs who could catch the eye of a beat cop. He's making a gamble that he can still get his hands dirty while making a *Forbes* Top 100 List.

He brought with him an expendable army. There are pros and cons to this sort of temp-for-hire workforce. Pro: They're hungry, both figuratively and literally. They'll do anything to impress their new famous boss and they are also in major need of calories. Con: They're malnourished street rats. (His words, not mine.) Pro: They're exceptionally good at killing people and improvising. Con: A would-be King Rat could go off script and try to take him down. Like what happened in Colombia.

A few years ago, Meda Lucas had to take care of some assholes in the jungle and needed a faceless crew to keep it under the radar of the dirty military. Nothing could be traced back to him, but by golly, he was going to go down there and slit some throats.

While he was knee-deep in jugulars, a kid

with permanently dilated pupils from huffing varnish came at him from behind. The boy wasn't after his empire, he just wanted whatever was in his pockets. Meda Lucas's spare change was enough to keep him high for years. A quick-thinking orphan with acne snapped his neck before he was able to swing his knife into the boss's back. Meda Lucas was grateful. So grateful that he let that orphan walk out of the jungle. The rest were told to drag the bodies into a shed and wait there until the coast was clear. The coast was always clear. He just needed a minute to grab the flamethrowers. Once the last dummy followed his orders, Meda Lucas barricaded the door and torched the place.

The whole attempted-stabbing thing had really soured him on the day. He wanted the entire trip in his rearview mirror. He was always planning on leaving a few of his temp guys' DNA behind to make it seem like a random attack gone bad but this was even better. The more bodies left to burn, the more it looked like a legit squabble between local dickheads. Any major player looking to fuck up the corrupt government's shit would have the means to get their guys out. He made it look like amateur hour on purpose.

Now he's prepared to blow his current company up with the rest of Azusa. Or things can go according to plan and everyone goes home after he sautés Santa Ana's testicles. Either way, the testicles will be sautéed. It's not that Meda Lucas wants to cut these possible up-and-comers' careers short; street rats have been proven to be highly trainable. And he certainly isn't interested in hurting innocent bystanders. He just doesn't care.

His two partygoers picked up on Harry right away. There was something about his jacket that caught their eyes. Isn't there a photo of Santa Ana wearing a jacket with letters like that? They took a pic and sent it over. Before Meda Lucas had time to get a good look, they texted: "Never mind. Too fat. Has limp."

Harry *was* limping. The winds always make his knee act up. And to be fair to the newbies, their boss did look at the text and agree Harry wasn't who they were looking for. That guy with the nice smile and dad bod definitely did not have it in him to wipe out a gang of skinheads. Santa Ana was a pain in the ass and a force to be reckoned with. A guy like Harry, you had to worry about him stealing your wife during a mutual midlife crisis, not making a dent in your violent drug monopoly.

They followed a nervous-looking jacked-up dude around until he went into the bathroom to snort some lines. Heads of this sort of enterprise don't stay in the game long if they get hooked on the product. A quick search through some stolen databases and he popped up as an inactive Marine with some minor misdemeanors being treated for PTSD.

They were about to give up when Tristan landed in their lap.

What an entrance! Of course, here was Santa Ana! They couldn't move their thumbs fast enough to get the news to their boss. He was intrigued, but the helicopter alone didn't convince Meda Lucas. There's plenty of rich assholes in SoCal. The security detail was a juicy touch but didn't seem to be on-brand for the type of person he thought he was looking for. This might be a man worth getting to know but he wasn't the man they were after. It wasn't until they sent him a close-up that happened to be a terrible shot of Tristan from the knees down that he was convinced he had found the thorn in his side.

"I have those shoes."

Meda Lucas needs to have a tense talk with his stylist. He was under the impression the shoes on Tristan's feet were from an extremely limited edition that was nearly impossible to find. Only those with incredible taste and exceptional bank accounts could possibly have the privilege of sliding their feet into that fine leather. Yet, here they are on Santa Ana's feet. Only a certain type of man can pull off a shoe like that.

Scrolling through snapshots of this strangely attractive, spritely built mastermind, he's not convinced that Santa Ana himself actually gets into the shit . . . oh, my God . . . that's it! He could have all sorts of jerks running around in that stupid mask. This hadn't occurred to Meda Lucas until right now. Could it be he's grossly underestimated his adversary? This newfound image of Tristan as Santa Ana feels like a much bigger threat. How has he missed this? Where has this boss bitch been hiding? This is worth the trip. Maybe he'll convince some of Santa Ana's guys to come back with him. They do pretty good work.

Tragically for the hungry street rats (again,

his words, not mine), just as nervous waitstaff bring out platters of delicious tacos, Meda Lucas gets a text, causing Lobos Gris to jump into action. No time for snacks.

"In the gym."

The crew clears out so fast their bewildered hosts feel a breeze. Meda Lucas is known for both his brutality and generous tipping. He leaves tightly rolled bundles of hundreds piled by the front door. At least someone is going to have a good night.

EIGHTEEN

That Was Unexpected

just killed a guy. Is there blood on my jacket? There better not be blood on this jacket. FUCK. This is not okay. One weekend. Forty-eight hours, that's all I asked for. Did I get it? Nope. Not even twenty-four hours.

"Boss. Boss. Boss." That's what it's been like all day, this fucking phone buzzing nonstop. Just take care of it. Get in your car and take fucking care of it. Is that so hard?

Shit. Hold on.

I just killed another guy. Great. Super. GODDAMNIT. Let me bring you up to speed.

Meda Lucas has guys in town. I'm rather disappointed that the guys I pay to follow the guys who follow me are nowhere to be found. If they were doing their goddamn jobs, they could have taken them out in the parking lot. Instead, I get eighty-six thousand voicemails that Dennis's cousin is some low-level out-of-town gangster who says he's in Azusa to take some dude out at some lame-ass high school reunion.

"Do you think they're talking about *your* lame-ass high school reunion, boss? Do you see them, boss? What should we do, boss?"

But there's a twist. I made Meda Lucas's guys the second they stepped up to the registration table. Somehow, someone figured out Santa Ana would be here at the reunion. I don't love that. There's a leak. I hate leaks. But, good news, the mask works! It really fucking works.

I thought I was dead. Right there across from fucking Jenny Kellogg, I saw these assholes and their fucking twitchy fingers and was like, yup. We'll both be dead by the time you fill out my fucking name tag. Sorry, Jenny. You were kind of a bitch and laughed when that kid fell out of his wheelchair, but you still don't deserve to die like this. But joke's on you, motherfuckers! That asshole still has no fucking idea who I am! And he thinks these two jerk-off street rats could handle me? Insulting. Good. Come and get 'em, Meda Fuckface.

What do you think of that Lacey? Is she too young for me? Are you shocked that I would care about such things? I'm not a total scumbag, you know. I feel like she gets me. Fuck. I shouldn't have bolted from the gym like that. I got to ditch these assholes.

But seriously. How did he know I'd be here? This may be naïve, but as retarded as they are,

I trust my guys. They would get eaten alive in a big shop operation. They know how good they have it.

This is hard, dragging this body. Is it always this hard? I think I did something to my shoulder. My knee has been fucked all day. I'm drunk. That's the problem. That's why these dickheads are so fucking hard to drag. I'm hard-liquor drunk. How on-brand. Poor, drunk Harry. Sad, drunk Harry. Has-been Harry hanging out with two fucking dead guys in the hallway. I'm glad Brea's with Tristan. That's the sort of man she deserves. I have a private island. I bet Tristan has multiple private islands. Fucking walking off a helicopter in those shoes? That's a man who knows how to take care of his shit.

Lacey and I should ditch this place. Forget this night ever happened.

This isn't even my problem. This is Tyler's problem. But who's the one dragging these dickheads to a janitor's closet? Not fucking

Tyler. Goddamn it. I'm getting their damn death sweat all over me.

Why didn't they try to kill me? I'm Santa Ana, like, literally Santa Ana. Sure, it's sweet no one knows who Santa Ana is, but who else would it be? Look around? Fucking Ryan Decker in his goddamn diabetes socks? I wasn't even fucking worth roughing up in the bathroom? You line up every fat bald fuck in this place and any reasonable person would put me in the top three suspects.

It's not like I have a death wish. Let's go, motherfuckers. I would have been fine. I would have chucked Jenny Kellogg at 'em and fucking run like hell to my car, which has two AR-15s in the trunk. These fucking twinks can't shoot for shit, I'm sure. Really, is it that much of a stretch that I could be someone important? A major fucking player, fucking up big man Meda Lucas's shit? I know I let my core get a little soft but my quads and triceps are fucking tight. Christ, this is a long hallway. Rookie mistake. Why did I lead the fuckers away from the janitor's closet?

I should've let Tyler wear the mask. Right off the bat I fucked up and didn't validate his leadership role. I have no one to blame for Tyler's lack of initiative but myself. Ah, shit. I've got the drunk rambles, soon to be followed by the drunk shits. God. I did not want to kill anybody this weekend.

These fuckers are heavier than they look. Great. Now I'm getting swamp ass. Should I bang that girl in the red dress? Damn it. What's wrong with me? Tracey is a good girl. Lacey. You didn't need to correct me. I said it first. I'm not the asshole everyone thinks I am.

Lacey is a good girl. She isn't a girl you bang because you're fucking sad and worthless. I should buy her a car. I'm going to tell her I drive a Tesla. Custom made. I'll take her to space. Yes! Finally, I'll call Elon and pull the trigger. Got to spend my money on something. I think she would like space. Who wouldn't? Elon lets you pay in cash. No questions asked. A lot of fuckers with that dirty Nazi money are headed to Mars. It's true. Look it up.

Fuck, this guy is heavy.

NINETEEN

This Is Also Unexpected

arry and Lacey were talking. Why were Harry and Lacey talking? I don't care. It's none of my business. I really don't care who either one of them chooses to converse with, but is this becoming a thing? I wasn't expecting this to be a thing. I don't even know what this thing is. You know what? It's not a thing. It's no thing. It's nothing.

The inside of my head feels sloshy. Like my brain is moving side to side in a Ziploc baggie. My tongue feels heavy, thicker. Oh, my God.

What if I'm having an allergic reaction to tequila? No. That's ridiculous. If anything, it's alcohol intolerance. In one study of sixty-eight people, 7.2 percent had allergy-like symptoms, but only two had an actual allergy. It's not a thing. I'm referring to Lacey and Harry again. Sorry. Tequila brain! To the 2.9 percent of people with an actual allergy to alcohol, it is indeed a real thing. I'm never one to minimize misfortune. Harry and Lacey are not a thing. They are just two consenting adults enjoying each other's company. Yup. That's it. No biggie. Why am I even thinking about them right now? No big thang. Did I say that right? "Thang." I'm one of the cool kids now.

Brea and I are in the bathroom. Can you believe it? It worked. The whole plan is going swimmingly. I'm watching her toss her hair back and forth in the mirror. I've never been inside a women's restroom before. It's terrible. I thought only men were this disgusting. It smells like urine and hairspray. There's wet toilet paper on the floor in the corner. The wastebasket is overflowing with brown wads of paper, and the mirror has a big crack running diagonally from the top left to the bottom right. All these years I thought girls relieved themselves someplace pink with throw pillows. It should smell like lilacs. Or, I don't know, have delicate peacock feathers in a vase. Brea is done primping. She pushes me up against the cinder-block wall.

Are we going to have sex in this bathroom? Should we look under the stalls first? Do we go into a stall? I don't know how bathroom sex works. I barely know how bedroom sex works. Tristan, you dog, you are really going out on top. That's confusing since I'm currently on the bottom. I'm on top, figuratively.

Lacey saw me leave the gym, right? I should text her. Should I assign her some sort of task? I am her boss, after all. No. That's silly. I'm about to bang the prom queen in the handicap stall. She can have a good time, too. Harry is an objectively attractive man. Way to go, Lacey. I didn't think hunk was really her type or that she liked dancing and having loud fun. You know what I mean. The loud "Look at me, I'm the first person in the world to have this much fun" fun. But, whatever. I'm glad she found something to do. Brea is kissing my neck. I have the sudden urge to balance my checkbook. Like I can't get intimate until I complete a chore.

Brea's actual boobs are in my actual face. She has clothes on, but, man, that is some thin fabric. Wow. The back of my neck is super sweaty. Are those hives? I hope her lips stop moving in that direction. Thank God. She's moved on to unbuttoning my shirt. What do we do when she's finished? I have on a very expensive undershirt. She notices. Yes!

"My, my, Mr. Melendez, even your under-shirts got an upgrade. You can't buy these just anywhere."

My T-shirt cost four hundred dollars. Should I tell her that? She sucked a lime from my mouth. Does that count as a kiss? It was weird and highly unsanitary, but I'd do it again in a second. I'd do it all night long even though citrus surface areas are notorious for being covered in microscopic fecal matter. I would shove a thousand dirty limes in my mouth to make Brea happy. That could explain the fat tongue. Citrus allergy or straight-up salmonella.

We haven't actually kissed yet. Should I be instigating the kissing?

Brea has me pinned against the wall. You take the lead, girl. Pin me, slap me, tickle my balls. That was uncalled for. Sorry. She could tickle my balls if she wanted to, but only if it was her idea. I would never *make* anyone tickle my balls— Her hands are moving all over my body. Rubbing, grabbing, pulling. I've never been with anyone this assertive before. Every woman I've been with (all three of them) had to be somewhat assertive because I'm, well, me, but this is next level. Is she enjoying herself? Am I meeting her needs? I try to be a sensitive lover on the rare occasions I have somebody to love. I reach out to touch the small of her back but chicken out and let my arms fall back against the wall. Don't blow this. I think she's happy. She's licking my ear. That's a pretty primitive and sensual way to communicate one's happiness.

Mother Fudgecracker. This is happening. She's reaching down my pants. Hello! Should we talk more? That's stupid. I don't need to know every detail of her life for the last two and a half decades. Remember, less is more. That's the only way this works. I'm pretty sure she's married and I'm more than sure she doesn't care about that right now. I wonder what her husband is like. A better version of Harrison? Can I just say it, that guy has aged. He looks like he's been rode hard and put out wet. Is that how the saying goes? Oh! She's really going for it down there. We are under the garments, people.

This is it. It's happening. This is what I came here for. After tonight, I can die a happy man. If she keeps moving her hand in those circles, in about forty-five seconds I can die a happy man. I'll have climbed my Everest. On average, eight hundred people make that epic trek a year. By the time you're reading this, more than six thousand different humans will have made it to the top of the world. That seems like a lot, like, what's the big deal, another extreme tourist trap, but if there are 7.9 billion people in the world, that means 0.000076 percent of us have reached the summit. Still pretty special.

Nice work, stats. The bulge in my boxers is a bit more sustainable now. Come on, brain, keep thinking. Let this last a respectable amount of time. Doesn't have to be a studly or impressive amount of time, I'm not looking for a miracle. Wait, hold on. She's reaching toward my butthole. I don't love that. Is that what people do these days? Please, universe, don't turn this into a joke.

There's a section on Mount Everest close to the top called Rainbow Valley. It's littered with dead bodies in brightly covered climbing gear, hence the name. Lacey and I spent a week of lunch chats doing a deep dive on Everest. The cheapest way to get up there safely is about forty-five grand. I should touch Brea. I move my arm again but this time she pins it behind me. Sexy? Fancy climbers with private tents and Sherpas spend at least a hundred thousand on the trip of a lifetime. Huh. Maybe I should have blown my wad on a mountain expedition.

What would that get me? A nice view? I'm moments away from blowing my wad all over Brea. That's a much better use of my finite resources.

How crass. I apologize. Gentlemen do not blow wads.

"What are you thinking about?" Brea's words come out in a breathy slur.

Should I tell her to steer clear of my butthole? "This."

Good one, idiot. "This." What does that even mean? She stops all her body parts from wiggling and looks serious. Sober. Goddamnit. I knew this was too good to be true. I knew I would ruin it—

"Tristan, am I pretty?"

"Yes. Oh, my God. Of course."

She smiles a tiny smile. "I know *you* think I'm pretty. But, like, am I *pretty*-pretty?" She sways a little. I reach out to steady her. "Am I prettier than everyone else?"

Is she seriously asking me this? "Brea. You're everything."

I'm not trying to make her feel better. I'm being honest. I don't know how else to respond.

Whatever I said worked. She slams her body back into mine and dives into my neck.

TWENTY

Crap Hits the Fan

Before we continue getting hot and heavy in the bathroom, I feel like for legal purposes I need to jump back a chapter and make very clear that Harry is incorrect. Nobody is paying Elon Musk to take them to Mars with Nazi cash. That there's proof of, anyway.

Okay. Back to Tristan and Brea.

She's biting now. Tristan finally gains control of his limbs and puts his arms up, gently nudging her off of him.

"What's wrong?" She contorts her face into an exaggerated pout.

"Nothing. Nothing—"

"I'm sorry. Was Mommy getting too rough?" She flicks him in the nuts. Oh, dear.

"No." He's wincing from both the assault on his nuts and the parental reference.

She morphs into a breathless kid. (Warning: This gets much worse before it gets better.) "Please, Mr. Melendez. Please, I have to pass this class. Is there anything I can do to bring up my grade?"

She gets down on her knees. Would it surprise you to learn that blow jobs make Tristan nervous? Because they don't. He loves blow jobs. Get real. Don't let that last chapter fool you. He's not some forty-year-old virgin.

"What's in there, huh?" She starts unzipping his pants. "What are you hiding from Mama?"

And we're back to Mama. Nope. This isn't going to work.

"Brea." He reaches down to help her up.

"What?"

He honestly doesn't know what to say.

"Don't you want me?" Her voice is equal parts threatening and terribly insecure.

"Of course. It's—"

She slams her body into his, causing the back of his head to smack the cinder-block wall. His hand instinctively flies up to his wounded melon. She grabs the other and places it firmly up her skirt on her ass. He gives the moist cheek a hesitant squeeze. She moans in ecstasy and grinds against him. Brea doesn't know how to do anything without faking it. That includes pleasure. God doesn't give one person everything, after all.

In another dark corner of the school, Lacey is alone in the boys' locker room trying to relax enough to empty her bladder. She's pee shy, which, if you ask me, is worse than being poop shy. Anyone can hold their poop and still function for a decent amount of time. One's bladder can only be so full before the whites of our eyes turn yellow.

She breathes deep and counts backward from ten. If you're thinking I must really be Lacey, you'd be wrong. I can pee and poop anywhere, anytime. I recently took a major dump in a crowded bathroom at the Mall of America. No. I'm not Lacey. And I'm not Brea either (what I wouldn't give for those legs, though). Don't try to connect all the dots. Most of life is random. Why should fiction be any different?

As her undies rest above her knees, she retraces the evening's events. Sometimes all she needs to do is get her brain busy. She needs to stop thinking about needing to pee in order to actually pee. Get herself in a urinary state of Zen. Is there a universe where she and Harry run away together? No, she doesn't want to do that. He's a flipping disaster. She knows this. So why is she dreaming up all the ways she can fix him? Evolution still says symmetrical faces make the best providers. Guess we can't blame everything on capitalism.

After she pees—please, Lord, let that happen soon—she's going to find Harry and possibly make out with him. But only if Tristan is watching. She's worried about him, Tristan. It's a deep worry, the type that really sticks to your gut. She can't put her finger on what it is exactly. Obviously, spending all his money and acting like an unhinged impostor raises some alarm bells, but she trusts Tristan. He's a reasonable, debilitatingly practical person. This must be one small part of a bigger, well-thought-out plan.

Uh-oh. Lacey is transitioning to weepy-girl drunk. How does *she* fit into this big plan of his? Why did he ask her to be a part of this crap show if he's just going to ignore her all night? And the billion-dollar question: why doesn't he like her? Every day he should be equally as in love with her as she is with him, but especially on this day, this night, how is he not madly in love with her? She's wearing her red dress! This dress is destined for greatness. This dress is supposed to change her life, and the only way she needs her life to change is to have Tristan in it as more than a friend. She should have tried harder to lose weight. Why didn't she get a spray tan? Why can't she be more like Brea? Brea doesn't deserve a guy like Tristan. A weird, messy, quiet, imperfectly perfect guy.

Oh, dear. She is really going all in on this downward spiral. Her heart is fully in Tristan's undeserving and nonobservant hands. Harry's catalog good looks can't compete with this crush. Ancient laws of attraction be damned.

Where is that handsome psycho, you ask? He's in the janitor's closet with two fresh corpses. He is also alone, feeling badly about himself. Brea wants nothing to do with him. Why would she? He's a fucking loser. Why can't he be more like Tristan? Confident. Mysterious. Living his best life. Harry could have shown up in a helicopter, too, you know. He could have shown up in three damn helicopters but nope. He's not allowed to spend his money. Fucking pencil-pushing Feds love to follow a trail of cash. Being a bad guy really sucks sometimes. And his shoulder hurts. He's an old, lonely bad guy who probably isn't going to get laid to-night. Stupid high school reunion. He should have never come. This whole thing is for fuck-ing losers.

Wait, he's not done. You know what else is really busting his ass? That Meda Lucas prick. Who does that fuck think he is? He's going to send two fucking street rats to take him down? Are these bozos old enough to drink? Can they vote? The nerve of that guy. Sending children to do a man's job. A motherfucking army's job.

Am I doing a good Harry? Poor Harry. He really has had a rough couple of years, and

nothing in his youth prepared him for this level of strife. Karma has pulled a nasty bait and
switch on him now that he's hitting mid-forties.
His violent and morally bankrupt choices haven't helped. He just wants to be noticed, you
know? Seen. And with that, his despair morphs
into the much more comfortable emotion of
being pissed the fuck off.

Fuck these two tweenagers, and fuck Meda
Lucas. Harry has been underestimated for
the last time. Yes. He feels good. His blood is
pumping. Testosterone rising. This is *his* fucking school! His house. Nobody is going to
come and make a fool out of him. He's going
to make a scene. Dangle Santa Ana right under
that fucker's nose. Santa Ana would never hide
out in a fucking janitor's closet.

What should he do? He has a small knife
in his pocket. He could make a pyramid of
body parts. No, it would take forever to saw
off even one limb and there's no guarantee

the blade would make it through bone. Dull knives make such a mess. No. He just got his butt-crack moisture back to base line, he's not looking to overly exert himself again. He could pull their eyes out, or maybe a tongue? Still too messy. He doesn't want to get goo on his jacket. Now isn't the time to be splashy. He's got too much other shit going on. He needs to leave a simple, restrained message: better luck next time, asshole.

Ask and ye shall receive. On a metal shelf right above one of the street rat's heads of dark curls, he spies a can of black spray paint. Yes.

As Harry works on his impromptu art installation, Brea is working on getting out of her top. She's stuck in the narrow polyester arm- and head-holes designed for children. She bends toward Tristan, yelling instructions.

"Pull!" It's endearing watching her forearms wave helplessly like a horny T. rex. "Yank it. Yank it off!"

Hundreds of tiny stitches pop as Tristan finally tugs it over her head. She laughs. "Tristan. I'm so happy you're rich. Now it makes sense for us to be together." She's having a rare moment of honesty, cruel as it may be.

The more time Tristan spends underneath Brea's gyrating body, the less amazing this moment becomes. He's confused. Shouldn't he be filled with pulsing endorphins? Cherubs should be strumming harps above his head. He should feel like two halves of a whole. Instead, his bones feel dry and the skin on his forehead feels stretched. He wouldn't mind lying down somewhere. Preferably alone. Is this what true love feels like? It's not that great.

Tristan has never been interested in Hallmark fairy tales, but if dreaming about the same woman for over thirty years isn't true love, what is? After meeting Breanna Davies at the age of thirteen, Tristan's brain formed around the idea of her being the absolute. He should be feeling the tangible rush of love right now, but it feels more like he's dehydrated. Life continues to be crushingly disappointing.

Lacey is finally peeing. Thank the Lord. She should really figure that out. There's got to be a meditation or podcast. Woo. She feels good, she's got an empty bladder and a new lease on life. Now that she's found a successful toilet, it will be easier to go the next time. She's not as drunk leaving the locker room as when she walked in. She no longer has the same tipsy sense of direction in the school corridors and gets herself all turned around in the maze of dark linoleum.

Outside, a line of cars races into the parking lot. For a minute the halls are bright from dozens of bouncing headlights. She covers her eyes. Being transported into a rave makes her dizzy. She never knows what to do when she gets this kind of drunk. Does she drink more and push through it? Will she feel better with a little more funny fuel in her, or will another sip plant her firmly in the head-spinning-and-counting-backward-trying-not-to-puke phase? Whatever she does next, she doesn't want to do it alone. Not here. Not in this creepy hallway. She steadies herself and continues walking.

A few steps and she sees a familiar shape walking toward her. Is that Harry? She feels warm and relieved. She's going to sit on his lap. Yup. She's making her move. She's going to give him a big sloppy smooch-a-roo and plop down on those meaty thighs. She mostly just hopes to find a place to sit down. Her feet are reaching their breaking point. She might need to amputate her left pinky toe after a night in these shoes.

Harry is happy to see her, too. To the victor go the spoils. Things are back on track. He majorly kicked some ass, and now he's going to have some good old-fashioned drunk loving. He feels like a caveman. Primal. Alive. He waves with his free hand. He has a tube or can or something in the other.

As he and Lacey come together, a blood-curdling scream interrupts their greeting. Lacey reflexively ducks for cover. When she looks up, Harry is hustling down the hall in the opposite direction of the screaming. Drunk loving will need to wait until he ditches the evidence.

Lacey pouts. That strange interaction did not help her mood. Gosh darn it and we're back to sad drunk. She just wants to go home and lie down. She's burning this stupid dress. Screw Tristan and screw Harry and screw all of these old pathetic assholes and their stupid Aztec. There must be a Change.org petition out there to change their stupid mascot. She's going to find it and sign it.

A few classrooms down, she spots the woman responsible for all the noise. The hairs on her arms start to tingle. Something is wrong. Why was Harry running away from the screaming woman? Lacey is young enough to have a grasp on gender fluidity, but what kind of man ditches two women in danger? Women in heels, no less? Harrison. And she was going to make out with him? Yuck. No, thank you.

She sees the outline of two large mounds on the floor at the screaming woman's feet. What is that? Oh, my God. She hopes it's not a dead bear or something. Is that some sort of mangled porcupine or wounded wolverine? Animals do weird shit when the winds start blowing.

That screaming is getting annoying. A switch flips, another alcohol-induced mood swing. Fine. She'll take care of this her damn self. She doesn't need a man. She doesn't need anybody. She's going to clean up this mess and then she's moving. Yup. She's out of there. She's going straight home to pack her bags and start a new life in the mountains. Tristan will be sorry. She'll meet a burly fisherman, and they'll live on a lake with a canoe in the mountains. Okay, so she does need a man, but only to make her happy in high altitude and make Tristan jealous. She doesn't need a man right at this moment. In this moment, she is large and in charge. She walks briskly toward the scene. I know, I never pegged Lacey as the type to run toward a burning building either, but, you know, whiskey.

"Are you all right?"

She grabs the screaming woman's arm. Holy crap! This is not a bear or badger. These dead things are definitely people. Dead. People. Dead people? Dead people! DEAD PEOPLE! If she screams that over and over again in her head will it somehow make sense? There's crude graffiti on the wall above the bodies. FUCK YOU M.L. Look at that, dumb Harry couldn't help himself. There's an outline of a devil drawn in blood. He used his little knife after all, slitting their throats to paint the floor and walls in red.

What are they sitting in? It's dark and thick.

Lacey gags as she tiptoes into blood. The woman starts screaming again. Lacey would be joining her but she's too busy trying not to heave. More headlights shine through the halls like strobe lights. The building foundation creaks and moans from the unrelenting winds. This whole thing is giving off real horror-movie vibes. God bless fermented grains. Lacey taps into some liquid courage.

"Shut up!" Opening her mouth to speak lets a gag slip out. It takes her a minute to compose herself. "We need to get out of here." Lacey pulls the screaming woman down the hall. Her diaphragm stops contracting once she's safe from the smell of blood. "Calm down. Where's the gym?"

The woman is barely coherent. I don't blame her. Really, what would you do if you came across two dead guys at a party? Hyperventilating is a very reasonable if not helpful response.

"If you pass out, I can't carry you."

The woman screams using words this time. "Were they dead? Oh, my God. They were! They were! They were fucking dead! What do we do?"

"Which way to the gym?"

"What do we do? What do—"

"Get your crap together!" Lacey does not appreciate this being a "we" situation. Or maybe she does. If she was all alone, maybe she would be the one hyperventilating in a corner somewhere. She has assigned herself the role of leader, and every leader needs a follower. She yanks her dead weight's arm impatiently and pulls the woman around a corner. Jeez Louise. Sorry, Lacey. We can't all turn into Chuck Norris when presented with a crisis. May I remind you that you're the one who can't go pee-pee in public?

Let's backtrack for a second. We're in the women's bathroom again and Brea and Tristan are having a moment. They're nose to nose and Brea is finally chill enough for them to actually have a second or two of intimacy. He leans in and kisses her, finally. She kisses him back like a normal human person and not some psycho alien sex addict. Still no goose bumps. Lightning doesn't strike. Maybe he's not trying hard enough. This has to be his fault. He needs to get in there and give it his all. They come up for air and blush like freshmen at church camp.

Okay, Melendez. It's go time. Go get what you came for. He smashes his face into hers. Yes. This is how they do it in R-rated movies. Eat her face. Eat her whole face. Time to turn up the heat. He awkwardly cups Brea's left boob. Seriously, dude? There something wrong with your hand? Squeeze that tit. As his hand starts to smush, a woman starts screaming bloody murder down the hallway. Tristan jumps back, thinking his aggressive hand had something to do with the stranger wailing.

"What the fuck? Shut up!" Brea turns toward

the door briefly, then goes back in for round two, or is it three now? How many times have they failed at making out?

Tristan tentatively reciprocates. With each pause in the screaming, he melts into Brea a little bit more. Finally, the screaming has made its way far enough from the ladies' room that he can give in to this long-awaited moment. Relax. Let it happen. What did Lacey say, just try being happy? If he can't be happy now, then he can't be happy anywhere. Wait, that wasn't Lacey screaming, was it? Of course not. Why would Lacey be screaming? Brea rubs his balls in a pleasing circular motion. Good job being normal, Brea. There we go. This is worth a Rolex. Yes. Yup. Right there—

Gunshots.

Hold the fudging phone. There are gunshots now? They both freeze.

"Were those gunshots?" Brea tightens her grip.

"I don't know. Were they?"

"I don't know! Jesus Christ! Should we hide?"
Tristan untangles himself from Brea and quickly organizes himself in his boxer briefs. Her nails have left tiny red indents on his forearms.

"I have to find Lacey."

TWENTY-ONE

What the Fudge?

I have news. Oh, my God. I'm out of breath. I found two dead bodies. And get this: It was those guys! The ones in the gray suits from check-in. Jesus Christ. I'd never seen a dead body before. A corpse. Two corpses. Corpsi? Do you have to be dead for a certain amount of time to be considered a corpse?

We're in the cafeteria hiding under a table. Unfortunately I'm in the plural tense right now. I didn't intend to find a buddy but I suppose it's better than being alone. Or not. This bitch will not stop screaming. Sorry. I never use that word. I'm still learning how to swear. Would asshole be a better choice? At least it's not gendered. Oh, my God! I don't have time to think about this now! What the shit is going on?

First we stopped by the gym to find help. Fun update: There are men with guns in the gym. Big guns. Real ones. Thank God I managed to pee. You know what's worse than hiding out during a mass shooting? Hiding out during a mass shooting while having to pee. I'm exaggerating. There's no mass shooting. There I go again, jumping to the worst-case scenario. If I went to a therapist, that's what she would tell me.

I should be in therapy. My mental health should have paid for someone's lake house by now. Is that a repeat zinger? Have I said that line before? It's something I say in my head all the time.

Focus, Lacey. We can't stay here. We need to find an exit. "Let's go."

"What?" My companion's reply is a cross between a whisper and a scream.

The entire back wall of the cafeteria is made of windows. Can we smash our way out? Only one way to find out. We both crawl out from under the table. I run to the windows and rub my hands over the glass. Why didn't that bitch follow me? There must be a way to open these stupid things. Come on. Come on. Nothing. Okay, fine. We'll do it the hard way. I grab a blue recycling bin on wheels and hurl it toward the glass. It bounces back toward me and spills empty Monster Energy drink cans on my feet. Great. Now my toes are sticky.

"The parking lot is this way!" The woman is over by the doorway waving her hands, encouraging me to hurry up.

Boy. I've seen that before. You encourage all you want, honey. This is as fast as I go. That's right, Lacey, great work. Keep it light. Sassy. No big deal. I'm so damn proud of my brain and my bowels. I have not lost my shit, literally or figuratively. I don't know which word means what right now, but I haven't done either. I should be a firefighter. Or a cop. Something dangerous. I'm good at this shit! I think we gave up on the window idea too quickly, but whatever.

I don't think I've ever been this aware of my surroundings before. I can see every green one-inch-square tile on the floor. I swear I smell mandarin oranges and honey. Makes me think of chicken nuggets. I'm going to McDonalds after this.

Something explodes, shaking the floor. My ears are ringing. I'm now close enough to the hall to see the bullets ping-ponging off the lockers. Perhaps we should pause and reassess. There must be a way to bust through that glass.

The woman at the door points. "That way!"

I stop. "Should we be running toward the bullets and explosions?"

She doesn't argue but takes off. I'm right be-hind her when a bullet bounces off the floor and hits her in the face. Huh. That's strange. How am I seeing the trajectory of a flipping bullet? It's like everything is happening inside of Jell-O. Oh. She's sitting down now. That must have hurt. She's lucky. It could have been a lot—

She's dead. Dead person number three. Oh, fuck. Thank goodness I've started swearing. Oh, fuck fuck fuck fuck. I don't have the language to process this. Fuck. She just got her face shot off. The opened side of her head looks like meat. Raw meat. That can't be real. Our insides do not look like Hamburger Helper. Something buzzes past my ear. I get swept into a crowd of running partygoers that escaped from the gym. We're like frantic wildebeests. If I fall in this hallway, there's no getting up. I move to the side and press my body into the lockers like Spider-Man. This hallway is endless! I feel like

I'm in a mirror maze with no mirrors. So a regular maze. But it's only going straight. So, not a maze at all. Oh, my God! The wall shakes next to me from a body ramming into it on its way to the ground. I'm sure he's fine. This is fine. We're all fine.

My legs are beginning to buckle like I'm on an invisible escalator. No. Stay upright. My muscles are folding in on each other. I have every intention of getting out of here, but I don't think I can stop my body from curling into a ball on the floor. The guy in front of me falls down and his intestines spread out over his sweater. I think those are intestines. I have no idea what intestines look like. Is *intestines* a weird word or does it sound weird because I keep saying it? There's a whooshing sound deep in my ears and my vision is getting all black around the edges. I raise my leg to step over him. It feels like there are cinder blocks around my ankles. Keep—I make it over and imagine I'm being operated by a remote control—going.

I almost slip in a purple puddle on the floor. I catch myself and wrench my back in the process. Tears spring to my eyes. I can feel the dams beginning to break. I'm moments away from bawling and barfing and crapping my pants. I put my back up against a locker. There are worse ways to die. This isn't so bad. I could be in Buffalo Bill's basement hole right now. That would be scary. This? No biggie. I'm sure group homicides are statistically more pleasant than individualized ones.

Hmm, the air seems quieter. Are we done with the guns? This hallway ends at another hallway, where a man rests against the wall with a pristine bullet hole in his forehead. Now that looks fake. Why didn't his head explode into meat like my friend back there? (May she rest in peace.) Because it's fake! Yes! Oh, my God!

Of course. He's not real! This isn't real! That's a gussied-up crash test dummy. Of course! Yes! Yes! None of this is real. Thank God!

This is one fucked-up party. Don't get me wrong, I love an interactive murder-mystery game as much as the next gal, but this has gone too far. What is wrong with these people? And millennials get such a bad rap?

Oh, thank God. Thank you, too, baby Jesus and grown-up Jesus. All the Jesuses. Thank you.

Holy crap! The sound effects are amazing. I swear it sounds like a car just drove through a freaking wall. These dicks spared no expense. Is Tristan in on it? Oh, my gosh, yes. I'm so stupid. Of course! He's playing the part of some rich mob dude, and I'm his sexy assistant. He should have told me. I minored in theater.

A few more people have found their way down this hallway. They have got to come look at this fake dead dude. A woman falls at my feet. Wow. She's good. She is very good. Do I have any cash? Should I tip her? Where did they find these people? So dedicated to their craft. I can't imagine improv murder pays very well. Phew. I can feel my legs again. This is wild. Now how did they get that bullet hole so perfect in the middle of this obviously fake person's fake head? Let me get a good look at it. Excuse me, nice lady sprawled out on the floor in front of me. Keep up the excellent work. Huh. The bullet hole . . . something red is pumping out of it. Must be, what, corn syrup and food coloring? It looks so real. I'll just stick my finger—oh. It's hot.

That's blood. Real human blood.

Night. Night.

I'm being dragged backward down the hallway. There are arms looped under my armpits. Whoever this is can barely hold me. "Hello?"

"Good. You're awake."

He stops and helps me stand. It's Frankie.

"Where the hell have you been?"

"Shhhh. When's the last time you saw Tristan?"

His words are on a two-second delay. I see his lips moving but have to wait to hear him. I'm not sure I understand him. I feel like I'm on a boat at high altitude. Did I make it? Am I here at my mountain paradise? No. Definitely not.

"We're not in a play, are we?"

"Tristan—where is he?" Frankie is all business. "Can you walk?"

I think I can. I nod and move my feet. They work. After a step I dry heave, hard. Then, whoopsie. There's a little vomit. "Sorry. It's the blood. The smell gets to me."

"Help is on the way. I need to find Tristan." He's pulling me by the arm. I'm glad someone else is in charge.

I heave again. I can't escape that smell. My dress is wet. Soaked.

"Is this . . .?"

"Blood? Yes."

Holy shit. I've been shot! "Am I hurt? Oh, my God—"

"It's not your blood."

That makes it much worse. My jaws open wide but I don't have a chance to puke before everything goes dark again.

TWENTY-TWO

Who's the Man?

Lacey isn't the only one questioning what's real. The hostages left cowering in the gym had at first cheered at the sight of their captors. Meda Lucas's shabby army barged through the doors, guns blazing, and Tristan's squad jumped at the chance to shoot at real people. The crowd caught in the crossfire played along, thinking this was the evening's entertainment. Finally, some excitement! The planning committee has outdone itself. Is this the setup for an escape room? Murder mystery? Is this some new immersive experience?

As the bullets grazed and burrowed themselves into some of Azusa High's most celebrated alumni, the hoots and hollers morphed into terrified shrieks and cries for help. I'd hate to have been the last asshole clapping and cheering.

Tristan doesn't know what he's walking into. The chaos is spilling out toward the cafeteria where Lacey was hiding. That's on the opposite side of the building from his makeshift love shack. Lobos Gris has arrived and is definitely crashing this party. They aren't bothering to make any sort of distinction between the armed security team and the soccer moms. They're shooting everyone. His brain isn't convinced that the rhythmic rat-a-tat-tat he keeps hearing is actually the sound of semiautomatic weapons.

Brea yells after him. "Tristan! Hey! Wait!"

He's relieved she's following him. He didn't mean to ditch her. Mixed in with his fear and

panic is a smidge of shame for unceremoniously deserting her.

"I shouldn't have left—" He stops once she's
caught up. She's holding her top.

"What?"

"Do you want to get dressed?"

She covers herself, surprised and embarrassed at his sudden propriety. "I'm wearing a
bra. What the fuck is going on?"

"How would I know! You were Prom Queen."

They continue speed walking toward
the action.

"What the fuck does that have to do with
anything?"

"Don't you know everything that happens here?"

"That was twenty-five years ago! You're the
one who brought security."

They're having their first spat. Cute.

Tristan scoffs. "What?" It hadn't occurred to

him that his fake security team might be using their very real guns. "This has nothing to do with me!"

They make it to the gym right as Meda Lucas silences the chaos with an ear-piercing whistle. He's got one heck of a whistle. That's sexy. Everyone freezes as he commands the room.

"Ladies and gentlemen! Calm down. We are not here to cause any harm."

Hmmm. The scattered bodies bleeding out might say otherwise, but please, go on.

"Any further harm. I apologize for the aggressive actions taken by a handful of my associates. We were not expecting an armed response and had no choice but to respond in self-defense. I regret I did not get here sooner." He glares over at one of his captains, whose ticket was just changed from round trip to one way.

Meda Lucas is not one to apologize but who knows, some of these terrified guests could be his constituents one day, or donors, or a city councilman he needs to buy in order to open up a weed warehouse. He's always planning two steps ahead.

"We will now put down our weapons." He motions to his crew, who hesitantly comply. "And ask for your help."

One of Tristan's bloodied security guards takes this opportunity to be a hero. He's badly hurt in a heap on the floor, using another body as a shield. He holds up his shaking arm and points a gun vaguely in the direction of Meda Lucas, who snaps his fingers and points. The employee standing guard to his left fires once, shooting the would-be tough guy in the head.

Meda Lucas continues over the gasps and screams. "I'm looking for one man and one man only. I have no interest in the rest of you. We do not want your money and will depart as soon as I receive the information I require."

Brea and Tristan are taking cover behind a garbage can just outside the open double doors.

"Holy shit." Brea surveys the scene in horror.

"Oh, my God." Tristan can't believe his eyes. "Do you know who that is?"

"Of course not! Do you?"

"That's Meda Lucas."

"The cartel guy?"

Tristan nods.

"We need to get the fuck out of here. These guys aren't known for leaving much evidence behind." She pulls on his arm.

Tristan shakes her off. "What is he doing in Azusa?"

"Charity auction? What the fuck does it look like! Come on!" Tristan doesn't budge. "Screw this." She sprints to the nearest exit.

Finally, someone is making good choices. Tristan doesn't notice. He doesn't know if he should run or try to get Meda Lucas's autograph. How could this be happening? Why on earth would Meda Lucas be at Tristan's twenty-fifth high school reunion? It's a miracle he's at his *own* twenty-fifth high school reunion.

"This is why I am here." Meda Lucas holds up his phone. "I'm here for this man and this man only. Turn him in—"

His big speech is interrupted when a voice from the crowd yells out, "That's Tristan Melendez!" The others quickly join in ratting him out.

Tristan doesn't understand why his battered classmates in the gym are now all screaming his name. As if he were in a trance being summoned by their siren call, he walks through the gym doors. His mind hasn't computed that his body has changed locations.

Meda Lucas raises his hand to hush the crowd. "Where is this Tristan Melendez?"

Those still standing murmur and look around, and it only takes a few seconds for someone to point in Tristan's direction. "There!"

Grant Barrett is the one who spots him. That guy has always been a tool. Okay, okay, I'm not being fair. If I were in Grant Barrett's leisure Skechers, I would be doing the exact same thing. He still sucks, though. He used to keep a journal of his favorite freshman VPLs. That's visible panty lines. You see what I mean.

Meda Lucas strains to locate his nemesis in the flesh. Could that hunched, shaking shape cowering in the dark be the cause of his recent restless nights?

Tristan is having a hard time wrapping his wobbly brain around what he's walked into. Why is Meda Lucas looking for him? It would make sense that his organization is in need of a few good actuaries but how did he find out about Tristan? Yes, he's the best but up until now he thought he kept a low profile. Word must be out on the street that if you're looking for a stats guy Tristan is your—oh. They're all pointing their guns at him.

This isn't a job interview, dummy! Run!

He does, right into the bleachers. And not in a slapstick sort of way but a good-for-you-that's-not-a-terrible-way-to-try-and-survive kind of way. He slides his svelte sample-size frame between the stacked-up rows of seats and the wall. Bullets dent and pummel the metal slats, while Tristan crawls on his belly toward the door like a lizard on hot pavement.

With their attention on Tristan, none of Meda Lucas's crew notice the remaining security guards flashing hand signs to each other from across the room. A few wasted and overly confident partygoers pick up on their cues and join them in taking up arms. They have an ample supply of dead-bad-guy weapons to choose from. Once again, the room erupts into gunfire. Amid the chaos, Tristan makes it to the exit and rushes into the hall with the screaming masses.

People are getting picked off left and right.

Tristan covers his head and keeps moving forward. He needs to remind himself to keep his eyes open and to breathe. Keep breathing. The shooting slows down as both sides pause to reload. Tristan turns a corner by the cafeteria and trips on a body. He catches himself before falling. What the . . .? The horror of the situation is starting to settle in. These are people. Real dead people. Which sounds confusing, but we get it. Why is this happening? Somehow in the middle of his shock and adrenaline he feels responsible.

This has something to do with him. Yes. He's on to something there and, well, Meda Lucas was pretty clear. Brea? Is this because he was hooking up with Brea? That makes no sense but brings his mind back to the bathroom where Brea was recently massaging his balls. Why did he leave the bathroom? Christ. All the screams and bangs and smoke and human splatter are making it impossible for him to think straight. Lacey! Yes! He left to find her. Shit! Was she in the gym?

He freezes mid stride. What if she's here in the hallway? What if she's one of these lumps on the floor? He doesn't want to look too hard and get an answer he doesn't like. He envisions her alone and scared somewhere. That's terrible but at least she's still alive. She's alive. She has to be. Lacey Hahn is not going to be murdered at his dumb high school reunion. What are the odds of anyone getting murdered at their dumb high school reunion? Right now, pretty high, obviously. Should he have factored this into his calculations when deciding to come? No. That's ridiculous. Is it, though? Eleven percent of mass shootings take place in a school, and there's on average over twenty mass shootings a year. (Way to go! U.S.A.! U.S.A.!) He can't recall a prior reunion massacre. He's desperate to think his way out of this.

The shooting starts up again. Tristan dives into a locker. Why didn't any of the dead people on the floor think of that? Tristan is two for two having ideas that don't suck. Maybe he'll make it out of this mess.

TWENTY-THREE

There's Something About Harry

This night is freaking awesome! Things have really turned around. I can't believe I was such a pussy earlier. Can we keep that between us? He's here! He came. That fucking dickhead Meda Lucas is in there with a whole gang of lunatics trying to find *me*! Santa Ana. I have to admit that was another baller entrance. His goons in terrible suits (my organization has a casual dress code, another perk if you ask me) busted in the doors, blasting lead. And I mean blasting! They wiped out half of Tristan's security detail and the lacrosse team before anyone knew what was happening. Woo! This asshole came to play!

Meda Lucas, now there's a good-looking man. God! I'm all tingly. I can't believe he's really here! All this fuss for me! It feels good to be noticed, you know? Only, funny story, he and his guys think Tristan is Santa Ana. Tristan fucking Melendez. That checks out, though. I can see how they could make that mistake. They're watching the wrong movies. This side of the border, you can't flash your shit around like Scarface. Nope, Uncle Sam doesn't put up with that shit. Haven't they seen *Breaking Bad*? Like I wouldn't want to cruise around in a private helicopter? Yeah. That looks fucking amazing. But to make it in the biz stateside, you've got to be sneaky with your money.

I have a storage facility filled with Viking artifacts that no one has ever seen. One year I spent New Year's Eve by myself drunk in Erik the Red's helmet. I give a lot of cash to super PACs. Pick the right candidate and they don't ask questions. I write off the donation and voila, the IRS successfully launders my money. I paid for a bill in Georgia that banned state-funded women's hygiene products. Why should the good people of the Peach State pay for some deadbeat's menses?

Tristan, you poor son of a bitch. This ain't going to end well for you. I have no responsibility in this, right? I didn't ask Tristan to dress up as my decoy. I love it, but I didn't ask for it. If he lives, maybe I'll take him to space.

I bummed a smoke off a dead guy and came outside. Needed to ditch out for a minute and take a breather. Don't judge me. I managed to shoot like seven scumbags and former yearbook editor Jared Connors, who I hear diddles kids. You're welcome. Oh! Don't forget about the two dudes I iced with my bare freaking hands. I'm carrying my weight in the killing department, thank you very much. I'll get back to work once I'm done with this cigarette.

Almost forgot. When I first came out here, and this is a true story, two fucking FBI jerks pull up in their shitty four-door sedan and I'm like, "Dudes, you're going to need a lot more firepower than your nuts and a service weapon. Do you have any idea who's in there?" And they're like, "Secure yourself in a safe location, yadda yadda yadda." These two idiots, and I'm not lying, then get back in their car and drive away. Can you believe that? This is why China is winning. Americans have no fucking balls. At least they left me to smoke in peace.

I hope Lacey is still alive. I dig her vibe. She's pretty, too. Like a little mouse from a cartoon or something. One of those chubby mice that made Cinderella's dress. You know, the round one in the green hat? Yeah. Lacey looks like that. Like a hot mouse. There's something hiding under those glasses so you just know that mouse likes to party. All right. I suppose I should get back in there.

It's dark and dusty inside. Kind of freaky. Amazing how fast an ordinary place can turn into a post-apocalyptic nightmare. I hope the end times is this cool. Tristan is getting his ass kicked. I found him in the hall by the cafeteria. I take that back. He's actually kind of holding his own. But not on purpose. He's getting in some lucky bounces. He just inadvertently headbutted one of his assailants.

"Fuck! Will you shoot him already?" Meda Lucas's guys are pussies.

Tristan backs away, holding his head.

"Meda Lucas wants him alive!" The other guy knees Tristan in the groin.

Ouch. Time for me to join the fray. This will be fun. "Hey, assholes! Why don't you pick on someone your own size?"

The big one punches Tristan in the gut and turns toward me.

"Why don't you mind your own business and take your ugly wife to Applebee's." He spits. "Stupid gringo."

That's not a bad burn. "Fuck you. I'm not married."

Shitbag number two, or the smaller one, joins the conversation. "Sad gringo with the small dick is all alone. Go get a Bloomin' Onion by yourself. You fucking loser."

Yikes. Why are they getting so personal? And joke's on that turd. You can't get a Bloomin' Onion from Applebee's. That's a tasty treat exclusive to Outback Steakhouse. I'm going to fuck this dude up. I reach for my gun—hold up, where the fuck is my gun? Shit! I left it outside. Harry, Harry, Harry. Oh, well, there's more than one way to skin an asshole.

I charge him, slamming his body into the trophy case. No! My trophies! What was I thinking?! Tristan takes a big swing at the taller one. He misses and spins off-balance. The dude pushes him to the ground and kicks him hard in the ribs. I elbow the shitbag in the face and duck as the other one, the little guy I just rammed into the trophy case, shakes glass from his hair and aims for my jaw.

"Fuck!" He hops, almost losing his balance from his major swing and a miss.

What a loser. I pop him in the side of the head and he goes down.

"Fuck!" The taller shitbag bends over, holding his nose. Ooh, I broke his schnoz. Nice!

Tristan crawls over to me and I help him up. "You good?"

His eyes bulge from their sockets. "No!"

He'll be all right. "You'll be all right."

He's not comforted. "What the fuck is going on?"

The wounded shitbags—I should have just asked for their names, that would have made this much easier—anyhoo, the wounded shit-bags have collected themselves and stand across from us like we're all waiting for the gym teach-er to blow the whistle so we can start chucking dodgeballs at each other.

Tall shitbag points at me. "Who is this fuck?"

"I dunno." Little shitbag is worried about the blood gushing from his hand. Sweet, that tro-phy case might have severed a major artery.

"Can we kill him?" Tall shitbag reaches for his gun.

"Probably." Little shitbag also reaches for his gun.

If this is confusing, all you have to know is both shitbags are now pointing their guns at me. Fuck.

"Tristan, you got a gun?" I know it's a long shot but maybe he's really playing the part. It's not crazy to think a guy with his type of mon-ey is packing heat, even if that guy is Tristan Melendez.

"What? Why would I have a gun?"

Figures.

The shitbags are enjoying having the upper hand in this standoff. Fuck. Fuck. Fuck. Weapon. I need a weapon.

A huge crash distracts them. We all cover our heads instinctively.

No fucking way! One of Tristan's rent-a-cops just drove through the fucking wall! Holy shit. Blasted right through the glass wall in the cafeteria! Shitbags! You dummies! You took too long. Ha ha.

A voice calls out from the SUV. "I got you bro!"

Oh, shit—this guy isn't stopping!

I grab Tristan and we dive out of the way right before getting crushed by the vehicle.

Fuck me! Ah. Christ. My ears. It's like a bomb went off. Tristan and I both struggle to stand back up. The SUV is still running, lodged into the wall. Tall shitbag and small shitbag are smeared across the floor. Shit. Did I rip my jacket?

"Hey, Tristan. Is there anything wrong with my jacket?"

"What?"

"My jacket?" I turn my back to him so he can fully survey the damage. "Is it ripped?"

He doesn't answer me. He's more interested in checking out the car in the wall.

"Holy buckets." He walks around to the driver's side.

"What?" I join him.

He's right. Holy buckets, this fucker is fucked up. Mr. Monster Truck Rally, his body flew halfway through the windshield and his head is smashed into the trophy case. He's all gargly and shit. Ugh. That is neither a quick nor painless way to go. Huh. This dude has an exceptionally square jaw. Wait, I probably need to put that in the past tense. *Had* an exceptionally square jaw. Fuuuuck.

"Should we help him?"

Bummer. The '96 Eastern Conference Championship Baseball cup is stuck in his face. That was one hell of a game. I pitched a no-hitter. Do you know how hard it is to pitch a no-hitter? I wonder, did I make a mistake lettering in multiple sports? If I had focused on one, really hit it hard, could I have played division one? Gone pro? Thank goodness my baby, the '97 Division IV Football State Championship trophy, is still beautifully intact. I had three touchdown passes that game.

"Harry!"

Is Tristan talking to me? "What?"

"Should we help him?"

I grab the football trophy. I wish I could communicate in emojis right now. "Let's check the car for weapons."

As we open the back doors all hell starts breaking lose. Again. I yell at Tristan to take cover. Jesus Christ, a lot of guns are going off.

What the fuck is going on out there? You can't tell me these dumb suburban pricks are fighting back. Who is doing all the shooting? How is there anyone left to shoot? I peek over the back seat and out the rear window.

No way! It's Tyler! And Rob! Or Bob! They're all here! Look at that! Excuse me while I have a proud papa moment. They did it. They're all grown up, taking care of shit without me. Dennis! Dennis is actually hustling. That fat fuck can move! Good for him.

People are running everywhere. Meda Lucas must have cleared out the gym. Where's that prick hiding? Big man can't get his hands dirty? Okay. We might be killing a few too many civilians. There's nothing wrong with aiming for specific targets, fellas. Seriously, try focusing on the bad guys. I'm not just saying this because I grew up with these people. Bullets aren't free. Especially the kind that have their registration numbers filed off. Seriously.

Trigger-happy much? We will definitely be having a staff meeting.

Shit. I better get out of here. It'd be pretty embarrassing to have my dick shot off by one of my own guys.

TWENTY-FOUR

Catch Me If You Can

I thought it would be helpful to let everyone catch their breath and step back to get a bird's-eye view of this gory shit show. The whole thing is getting way cinematic. Think *High School Musical* meets *Pulp Fiction*. Or what would happen if Quentin Tarantino directed *Back to the Future* without all the time travel but with loads of guns. So how do our friends get out of this? Obviously at least some of them walk out of here. We have seven chapters left. (Good for you! You almost finished a book!) Let's start with Harry. Oh, Harry. If this

story is ever made into a movie, Ryan Reynolds
has got to play Harry. I know he's busy with his
cell phone company, but he'd be perfect. Think
about it, Ryan. That's all I ask.

Harry is getting shot at by his own employees. It's not their fault. They have no idea what
their boss looks like.

He really should have a stern word with them.
They're killing everybody. Jim Thorp's pregnant
third wife just ate a bullet sandwich. Come on,
guys, clearly she wasn't a threat. I hope Tyler
and Dennis aren't doing that obnoxious thing
where the bad guys are trying to outkill each
other. That level of testosterone is played out.

Before leaving to find Lacey, whom he's apparently decided he would like to have inter-
course with, Harry sort of saved Tristan and
picked up a sweet souvenir, his precious 1997
Division IV Football State Championship trophy. In the amount of time it took Dennis to
kill Jim Thorp's third wife, Harry has resolved

to get back in shape and back on the grid-iron. Yes. This forty-three-year-old alcoholic who hasn't touched a football or taken a lap in twenty-five years is going to get back in the game. He may have hit his head when that car crashed through the wall.

What about those jerks who pulled up earlier, interrupting his smoke break? Crosby and Dillmann, of course! Should we blame them for running off with their tails between their legs? I can't blame anyone for anything. I have never been shot at; I can't imagine I would handle it well.

Meda Lucas made a mistake leaving his varsity team at home. Tristan's surviving security team is living out its video game fantasies and has joined up with Harry's crew. As the fighting spreads through the halls, Santa Ana may be gaining the upper hand.

I don't know where Brea is. Once Tristan left, she ran out of the building shirtless. A little gratuitous, I know, but she did not have time to stuff that sausage back into its casing. And can we acknowledge for a moment that Brea was the only one smart enough to actually leave the building?

Lacey, as you recall, passed out after sticking her finger in a stranger's head wound. Frankie (where the fuck has he been?) found her and dragged her down the hall. He's hoping she can lead him to Tristan. They are currently hiding outside of the band room. Frankie tried to kick the door in but it wouldn't budge. He blames it on the Crocs. Sure, dude. Sure.

And now we're all caught up. I apologize if that was repetitive, I've never written anything that's taken place in Nakatomi Plaza before. (For those of you Lacey's age and younger, that's a *Die Hard* reference. While I'm at it, I apologize for the steady stream of F words, but really, what other words would you use in this situation?)

Tristan and Harry are scurrying through the dark halls like rats. I should clarify. Tristan is scurrying. Harry is strutting. Tristan's feet might be moving but his mind is blank. He wants to take each bullet that ends up in the wall next to him and every dead classmate he jumps over and use it as a factor in some calculation that will save him. He can't. His hefty brain is in sleep mode. Nothing cool is about to happen. His head can't Jason Bourne his way out of this. Would that be better? Would it be satisfying to see him magically transform into a high-tech killing machine? Eh. Maybe in the sequel.

Tristan opens his mouth to yell out for Lacey but he can't remember the first sound of her name. Or maybe he's lost the ability to form any sounds at all. He stops moving. That was a mistake, but maybe it wasn't by choice? He tries again to call for her, but his tongue stays flat. What is going on? Why is this so hard? His eyes overflow with tears. He's not sad. He needs to blink, but he doesn't remember how. In this moment of life or death, the best he can do, the only command his brain seems capable of giving, is to breathe.

Harry notices he's stopped. "Tristan, buddy, we've got to keep moving." He jogs back to collect him.

Bodies are bleeding out next to them. Tristan summons all his courage and pushes out a weak animal call.

"Aaaaaaaaa. Eeeeeeeeee?"

Harry is strangely kind and understanding. Carnage isn't for everyone. "What's that, bud?"

Tristan tries again, and this time he manages to add an L sound. Harry nods. "Come on, we'll find her." He pushes Tristan's body forward. "So, what's the deal with you two? Do you mind if I—"

Tristan turns to him more terrified than before. Harry gets it. "Got it. Not the right time."

Lacey can't hear Tristan's half-human cries.

She smelled blood and passed out again. But Frankie's ears perk up. He knows that sound. He's heard that pathetic howl before. Once in tenth grade when the driver's ed car rolled over Tristan's foot and before that in eighth grade when Frankie's mother walked in on Tristan masturbating. Why was Tristan masturbating at Frankie's house, you might wonder? He was staying there while his parents were in Mexico for a funeral. That was when Tristan and Frankie still did kid things together and Tristan wasn't constantly mortified by Frankie's theatrics.

Frankie hopes they make it out of here. He's going to do all he can to help his friend.

"Tristan! Over here!" Frankie's hiding spot isn't all that hidden, and Tristan follows the sound of his voice around a corner to the thick wooden doors that lead to nerd heaven.

"Frankie? Where the fuck have you been?" Harry yells.

Tristan stumbles the rest of the way as fast as he can once he notices Lacey on the floor. "Lacey! Is she hurt?"

"No. Fainted."

I'm glad Lacey remained Lacey and did not have herself a Jason Bourne moment, aren't you? I thought that's where we were headed and was like "Yawn." She tried hard to be tough, though, she really did. And that was far more interesting than having her all of a sudden doing back flips over dead bodies. Plus, she made out better than most. And she hasn't sharted yet. That's saying a lot, given the circumstances.

"Tristan, can you stop this?"

Tristan doesn't answer Frankie; he's too busy trying to wake Lacey up. Now that he has someone else to worry about, his brain is firing a few more neurons.

"It doesn't have to be this way. Meda Lucas is who they want. Turn yourself in—"

Harry's ears perk up at the mention of his archrival. "Who wants Meda Lucas?" He tries to keep it casual.

"The FBI."

"The FBI?" Harry laughs. "Those pricks are long gone." He kicks open the doors to the band room. "Hide in here."

"What? What do you mean they're gone?" Frankie assumed at least some of the bullets were coming from good guys.

"Yeah, two pricks showed up and were like, no thanks. We're out."

"Two! They only sent two?!" Frankie kicks the air out of frustration and loses a Croc.

Tristan has assessed Lacey's vitals. Now that he's sure she's alive and sort of well, he joins in their conversation. "Frankie! What are you talking about? Why would I turn myself in? Turn myself in to who, Meda Lucas?" He's try- ing to pick Lacey up but can't get a good grip. She keeps sliding onto the floor.

Harry is standing guard at the door. "Frankie, you got a gun?"

"Why would I have a gun?" Frankie holds out his retrieved Croc for emphasis. "Do I look like the type of guy that walks around with a gun?"

"Chill. I'll try to find some firepower. Grab a clarinet or something."

Or, I don't know, you could all just LEAVE THE BUILDING. I swear . . .

Tristan drags Lacey inside by her wrists as Harry slips into the hall in search of a weapon. "Thank God she was with you."

"What does she know?" Frankie bends down to assist with the dragging.

"About what?"

"Is she your assistant or something more?"

Should Tristan come clean? What does Frankie mean by something more? Is there something more? No. Of course not. It's Lacey. His Lacey. There's nothing more to it than that.

"Maybe we could use her to get you out of

this. Tristan, you can tell me what's going on. I'm your friend. I can help."

"Frankie, why do you think I have anything to do with this?"

Remember when I said things were getting cinematic? Right on cue, here comes Meda Lucas, flanked by two tired-looking men regretting that they didn't ask for more money before accepting this job. Even the main man himself is looking less than perfect. Harry is going to crap his pants when he sees this, Meda Lucas, disheveled.

"You." He waits for Tristan to look at him. "Santa Ana."

"Santa what?" Tristan stumbles backward. He's the only one who hasn't realized his role in this wacky tale of mistaken identity.

Meda Lucas steps forward. "It's nice to meet you face-to-face."

"Me? Why? Thank you?" Tristan can't help

but grin. His eye twitches uncontrollably. Way to keep it cool.

"Kill them." Meda Lucas is beyond over this. He doesn't want to torture anybody. He doesn't want to deliver a monologue seething with vengeance. He wants to go home. He wants to take a hot bath and wake up refreshed in a world that no longer includes Santa Ana.

"You've got me confused with somebody else. Please. I don't know what you're talking about. Please, you've got to believe me. I'm a big fan."

Santa Ana's begging now? That's interesting. Meda Lucas is being too hasty letting his long day and sore feet get the best of him. He'll regret not having more time to get to know this once-masked pain in the ass. "Kill his friends. Make him watch, then bring him to me." He leaves to catch a moment of peace in the car.

The two men nod and take a dramatic pause before holding up their guns. How many dramatic pauses before these guys realize it's better to kill strangers quickly? I tell you what, their big egos are really causing them some problems. In that brief respite, Frankie takes center stage. He inhales and crane-kicks the gun out of one of the goon's hands. He then pushes the dude's nose up through his brain with his palm. (What sort of desk does he sit at, you ask? Not the same sort you do.) This catches Meda Lucas's attention. He's impressed as he watches his guy crumble to the floor.

"Very nice." Meda Lucas motions for the other goon to take them down.

"Please. Wait. We can . . ."

But Frankie knows Tristan's begging won't do any good. He comes up with a Plan B on the fly. "You don't want to kill me. Trust me, you don't want me in your body count."

After his showstopping takedown, Meda Lucas is inclined to believe him. Frankie keeps stalling. He's not sure what he'll do next or how they're going to get out of this alive, but he knows they need more time.

"I don't even know this guy. Go ahead." Frankie pushes Tristan forward. "Just take him and go." Maybe once their backs are turned he can get his hands on the recently deceased's weapon.

Tristan is not a fan of this plan. "What? Stop. No."

"What about the girl?" The goon asks Frankie.

"Her? Who's that? I don't know her."

"Does *he* know her?" The goon tips his head toward Tristan.

Why is this guy asking questions? Speed it up!

"Sure. Yeah. He loves her."

"No!" Tristan, don't say it . . . "No! No! I don't love her."

He said it.

"Should I kill her, boss?"

Meda Lucas is not happy with the pace of these executions. "For fuck's sake! Kill him." He aims a finger at Frankie. "And her." He points it next at Lacey.

Frankie is desperate. "He does! He loves her! He doesn't even know me!"

"No, I don't!" Tristan isn't doing this right. Any of it. But it's not fair that we keep expecting him to be a badass and save the day. I thought we got over that. Still. This all seems a bit lame, even for Tristan.

"He totally does—" Frankie is also getting lamer by the minute.

"Shut the fuck up!"

Thank you, Meda Lucas. Those two were starting to embarrass themselves.

"Why aren't you shooting?" He scowls at his goon.

Now pay attention, Ryan Reynolds. This is for you. Here comes your Oscar moment. Harry is going to do this right. Tristan closes his eyes and tries to shield Lacey's body with his own. Frankie is screaming like a small child.

And then . . . nothing. Where is the bang-bang? Where are the bullets? The gun clatters on the linoleum while the goon sputters out blood and lurches toward them. He falls to his knees. Harry is behind him, still holding the base of the trophy that's now skewered all the way through this gentleman's abdomen. It's a big trophy. Harry pulls it out slowly. The body in front of him sways for a second and then face-plants. The poor goon, he was just doing his job.

Harry, Tristan, and Frankie turn toward Meda Lucas. They are all big fans in one way or another. So they know Meda Lucas never carries a gun. Or a knife. Nothing. No weapons. If he's going to kill you, he's not using anything that can fit in his pocket.

My, my, the tables have turned. But Meda Lucas doesn't see it that way. Even though it's three against one, this tough SOB doesn't flinch. "I have more men. How fast can you run?"

Harry's not going anywhere. He spins the trophy in his hand and walks silently toward his nemesis.

Meda Lucas stands his ground, but the slightest tremor in his voice betrays him. "I have no problem with you." He gestures toward the bodies on the floor. "This? This is nothing. Go on your way and let me finish my business. Take the girl and the man in Crocs. I don't care."

Harry gets right in his face. Nose to nose. Look. Look at these eyes, motherfucker. This is who you came for. He presses the tip of the trophy into Meda Lucas's neck. Something left over from inside the other guy squishes onto Meda Lucas's skin. Harry's not an idiot. He's not interested in any sort of noble chase. He got lucky, and he plans to take advantage of the situation and take care of Meda Lucas once and for all. Holy shit. That's right. He wins. Harry—um—Santa Ana wins. David is about to send Goliath on a one-way trip to hell. Yes,

yes, we get it. You're the man, Harry. You've always been the man. Jesus, these men and their egos.

An SUV comes crashing through the wall. What? Another one? Well, why not. There's a massive firefight still happening on the other side of the newly formed hole.

"Get in!"

It's Brea!

TWENTY-FIVE

Born to Run

Let's all slow clap for Brea. She deserves it. That's some serious girl power busting in to save the day! Shame on you. You assumed she ditched her friends and saved herself the minute she could. Now that I think about it, that would deserve a slow clap, too. Sorry, but if we are ever in a situation with very final consequences, I'm doing whatever I can to get home. Does that make me a bad person or an honest one? I don't care. But way to go, Brea. You go, girl. She's still in nothing but a red push-up bra and cheerleading skirt. With all the murdering going on, I hope no one is offended by her partially covered boobs.

All the men have scattered while trying to dodge the armored SUV and flying rubble. Lacey remains cozy on the floor. Dusty debris now separates Harry and Meda Lucas. They stare each other down like two wolves fighting over a downed deer.

Brea is not interested in their pissing contest. "Jesus Christ. Get in!" She is the alpha in any situation.

Meda Lucas smirks and backs away. "Until we meet again."

Frankie dives into the back seat, leaving Tristan alone, struggling to move Lacey. Harry strides over bodies and chunks of cement and tosses her over his shoulder in one smooth motion. He puts her in the back seat gently next to Frankie then slides in, shotgun. Tristan is staring at the whole scene, pouting. Yes, Tristan. We get it. You didn't kick anyone's face in, and you are absolutely far less of a man than Harry. And Frankie. And Brea. Can you get in the fucking car, please?

Brea revs the engine. "Tristan! Let's go!"

He begrudgingly slides in next to Lacey, a cooler uncomfortably lodged at his feet. This night went downhill in a hurry. At least he's not bleeding out on the floor. Brea backs up, rolling over bodies, making the tires thump and bump. Harry winces, hoping he doesn't have too many open positions to fill after this disaster. Onboarding can be a real bitch.

Brea commands the vehicle with precision and grace. She zigzags down the hall, nailing Meda Lucas's guys like bowling pins. Harry is loving it! Frankie resumes his screaming. Sure, he smashed a guy's nose into his brain, but this is all way out of his comfort zone. He's screaming for Brea to stop the car, convinced that the cavalry is on the way. Tristan is squeezing Lacey's hand. He's not sure if he should be trying to wake her or praying she remains un-conscious. With each turn, her body bounces from Tristan's shoulder to Frankie's like she's the ball in a game of Pong, a reference these Class of 1998ers would get, but Lacey would not. That's your generational divide, right there. The tires squeal to a stop at the top of a staircase.

Wait a second, you ask. There are stairs now? Yup. It's a multilevel building built into a hill. The back half is like a walkout basement. Brea crashed through the wall on the main floor but has weaved her way through to the other side of the building and now they teeter at a cross-roads. Does she waste time turning around and backtracking? Does she floor it in reverse? Or do they hold their breath and see what hap-pens when you attempt to drive a vehicle down four flights of stairs?

One of Lobos Gris's finest walks slowly to-ward them, unloading his machine gun into the side of the car. Decision made. Harry yells for Brea to drive as they duck for cover. They all scream in unison as the SUV hops down the stairs, like a carnival ride from hell. Brea cranks the wheel as she crashes onto each landing. Once. Twice. Three times, and then finally they've made it back to the ground level.

A group of tired men in crappy gray suits are taking a smoke break. They frantically reach for their guns as Brea turns a corner, heading straight for them. She guns it, plowing into them, and the bodies fly into the air like confetti. One poor son of a bitch lands back down on the hood with a thud. He's missing chunks of his face but still tries to hold on with one hand and grab his gun with the other.

"Fuck!" Brea turns on the wipers, which do nothing, of course. "Get him off! Get him off!"

Harry leans out the window and grabs the guy one-handed. He throws him into a wall and his head explodes like a watermelon dropped from the top of a building. No biggie.

They continue speeding toward an exit. They finally take flight out of a glass wall by the main office and land on pavement. The tires smoke as Brea races out of the parking lot.

She turns onto the four-lane surface street without paying any attention to traffic. They cut off a bro in a Jeep Wrangler, who honks rather aggressively. Seriously, dude? Harry holds his arm out the window and flips him the bird. I love the middle finger. What a perfect form of nonverbal communication. The Jeep's driver makes a show of revving his engine and drives up close along their passenger side. Bro's jaw drops to his knees when he sees the damaged and smoking car filled with our crimson-stained occupants. (*Crimson* is lame, but I'm running out of ways to say *bloody*. I'm down to *imbrued* and *sanguine*, but I don't want to send you running for the dictionary.)

Harry smiles as they speed ahead. With each roll of the tires, relief sets in. The high school is getting farther and farther in the rearview mirror. Is this it? Did they make it? Look, they just passed a Shake Shack and T.J. Maxx. Life is back to normal.

"Hey, babe, pull a U-turn. I'm starved. You guys want some burgers?" Harry turns to the trio in the back, sorry to find Lacey still unconscious. She was hungry earlier, she'd probably kill for a burger. "Frankie, nice moves, by the way. Babe, you missed it. Fred totally killed a dude with his bare hands." Brea remains silent with her eyes focused straight ahead. "Thanks for saving us, by the way."

But Brea is suddenly distracted by a flash of light in her mirrors. "Fuck." She's the first to notice four motorcycles coming up on their tail. "We've got company."

Harry and Frankie both swivel to look behind them, while Tristan slumps down in his seat and shuts his eyes. Harry springs into action. "There must be something in here we can use. Tristan, look in that cooler, they got any hard liquor? Tristan!"

The second time's the charm. Tristan slowly commands his body to open the cooler and pulls out a bottle of vodka. He holds it up. "Here."

"Sweet. Make a bomb with it."

"Make a what? I'm not a chemist."

The motorcycle ninjas have caught up. They're probably not real ninjas, but it sounds cool. Don't ever accuse Meda Lucas of being unprepared. Harry grabs the bottle from Tristan's hand, takes a big swig, and then holds it tight, waiting for the right moment. As the first biker comes up alongside his door, Harry smashes the bottle in his face, causing him to wipe out. A helmet would have been a good idea, you dumb ninja. But who am I to judge? A pair of two-wheeled pains in the ass race up on either side, attempting to box them in. Frankie valiantly throws open his door, knocking one of them off-balance. His body skids under the SUV as the bike flies behind them. Crunch.

"Tight!" Harry reaches back and slaps Frankie's hand with a high five.

Brea jerks the wheel, driving them across the median and into oncoming traffic. They tip on two wheels as she cranks a one-eighty and lands with the flow of traffic. As grateful as the men are to have such a skilled badass behind the wheel, they can't help but scream. The tires straddle the sidewalk.

"Babe, what are you doing?" Harry smiles and waves at a woman out walking her chihuahua who has to leap out of the way, dragging the dog behind her.

Brea can hear the remaining motorcycle gaining on them.

"Hold on."

She swerves onto the walkway, weaving in and out of garbage cans and newspaper stands. Is there always this much crap lining the sidewalk? The lone cyclist is two lanes over. He can't get a good shot. (Not for lack of trying. He grazed quite a few innocent people.) She turns and barely squeezes the oversized car through a covered pedestrian path between an Anthropologie and LOFT. They continue to race through the adorable town centre. You know it's adorable because they spelled "center" fancy.

They cruise over cobblestones and fly by Jamba Juice, barely missing the fountain in front of the Victoria's Secret. Brea circles the stone cherubs on two wheels and they hop down a steep stone staircase. They land in the entrance lane for the parking ramp. Everyone takes a breath. They lost him. Really? That's it? One off-road excursion into an upscale outdoor shopping mall was all it took? Wow. This car chase stuff is easy.

"Great job, babe!" Harry claps loudly. "Wasn't that great, guys?"

Tristan and Frankie answer him by weakly slapping their wet palms together. It's hard to clap with Harry's level of enthusiasm when your hands are sponges.

Frankie attentively scans the back windows. "I don't think they followed us into the mall."

Brea backs out of the parking ramp entrance and rolls down a residential street. They pass by lovely one-and-a-half-story homes surrounded by cute square yards. Inside, families watch TV or play Saturday night cards. Frankie starts to relax.

"I've got to make a call. Does anyone have any bars? I've got two. No. One. Two, but one is flashing. What does that mean? Shit. Don't we have 7G by now?"

Brea slams on the brakes. "What the fuck is that?!" She leans over the steering wheel, staring intently at the road ahead.

"What?" Harry doesn't see anything out of the ordinary.

"There!" Brea points at a sturdy half sphere blocking their path.

Frankie looks up from his phone and cracks the case. "It's a turtle!"

"That's one big fucking turtle." Harry watches it for a minute before losing interest and relaxing back against his headrest.

"Shit. Where'd it go?" Brea struggles to see over the hood of the car. "Harry, do you see it? Did it cross?"

He laughs. "Why did the turtle cross the road—"

"Harry!" Brea is not in a joking mood.

He half-ass sits up again and glances out the front windshield. "All good."

"All good?" She's right to question him. "Do you see it?"

"It's just a dumb turtle—"

"Harry!"

"It's in between the tires. Pull straight ahead."

"Straight ahead?" She inches the car forward.

He encourages her. "Yup. Go nice and"—the driver's side rises in the air as the front tires roll over the turtle's shell—"slow." Then the back rises as the rear tires roll up and over before the SUV slowly plops back down on the pavement. "Oops."

Brea hangs her head. She's not crying, is she? "You fucking idiot."

Frankie's eyes are wide and filled with tears. "Turtles that size don't live this far inland. That was somebody's pet."

"Thank you, Frankie." Harry turns around, glaring. "That's helpful information."

Brea puts the car in park. "Go get it."

"What's that?"

"You heard me. Get your ass out of the car and get the turtle."

"Why? It's dead."

"We don't know that."

"What are you going to do, give it mouth to mouth?"

Brea has no idea why she gives a crap about this smushed reptile. She's been responsible for her fair share of roadkill and has never felt the need to deliver a eulogy. But right now she'll do anything to stop this little ripple of emotion she's feeling. She has to make this right. "We'll . . . we'll bury it."

"What if it's leaking stuff? I don't want to get turtle goo on my jack—"

"Go get the fucking turtle!"

Harry's lost this one. He opens his door and peers into the back seat before getting out. "Come on, Tristan. Let's go."

"Huh?" Tristan has been sleeping with his eyes open. His system is so overloaded he put himself in standby mode in an attempt to prevent a total meltdown.

Harry has been waiting all night for some alone time with Tristan. This weekend is about getting Harry's groove back, and the minute his old classmate stepped out of that chopper, he knew that's where he would find the answers he's looking for. A walking, breathing, badass fairy tale would certainly give him the pep talk he needs. Trade secrets. Life hacks. Some man-to-man Wall Street Zen Buddha shit. Apparently he hasn't noticed new Tristan's semi-catatonic state.

"Go! Both of you!" Brea never takes no for an answer, unless that's the answer she wants.

Harry and Tristan exit the car, stepping onto the quiet street. The air is smoky and heavy.

"Christ." Harry coughs. "We did it a favor."

Tristan is tucked way up into his own shell. Did somebody say something? He wouldn't know. He shuffles his feet next to Harry.

"You all right?" Harry finally notices his friend's demeanor.

Tristan turns his head in slow motion. Is he all right? No! He's not all right. He'll never be all right ever again! What sort of idiot monster would ask him such an insane question?

None of this makes it out of his mouth. When his parched lips hesitantly open, he answers Harry with a stream of vomit. He's a fire hydrant of puke. A bursting, barfing fountain.

"Ah, shit." Harry hopscotches out of the bile's path. "Let it out, pal. You witnessed some gnarly shit tonight. There's no shame in the throw-up game." He stretches his arm, giving Tristan's shoulder a pat from a safe distance.

Tristan heaves. "What." Heave. "The hell." Heave. "Is going on?"

Harry is genuinely surprised to see Tristan losing his shit. Obviously he's never been the heavy—you know, a guy who roughs people up. But wow, to be this rattled? How does he manage to keep his hands so clean?

Harry thinks on this for a beat. Tristan is silent and horrified. They both look down at the turtle. Its limbs and head are shut in tight. There's a crack down the middle of the shell.

"You ever shoot someone before?" Harry

squats to get a closer look. "You think anything is going to leak out of that crack?"

"I've never seen a gun in real life."

"No shit?" He stands back up.

"I've never seen a dead body before."

"Looks like chopped-up pizza, doesn't it?"

"What?"

"The insides." Harry mimes his guts falling out.

"No. Not at all."

Harry is skeptical. "In your line of work, things have never gotten messy?"

What does he mean by "messy"? Tristan wonders. Is he implying that something about this night should be familiar to Tristan? Why the hell would a person who spends their day toiling deep in the actuarial sciences ever—oh. Tristan gets it. Right. He's not a person who spends their day toiling deep in the actuarial sciences. He's a person who shows up to parties with armed security wearing freaking ridiculously expensive shoes, which are not comfortable, by the way. There's a variable or two he's left out of this plan. He's made a mistake, but he can't put his finger on it. Not yet.

"I'm, no, I'm not a violent person."

"Good for you. I'm proud of you, man."

Is that what Harry's been doing wrong? Does he need to delegate the violence more? That's kind of his bread and butter. No. It's bigger than that. Sure, he could outsource some torture here and there like that dumb fuck Meda Lucas tried to pull, but he still couldn't be out there living loud and proud like Tristan. No, Tristan was smart enough to keep himself and his money clean from the get-go. Harry's problem stems from his initial investment. Drugs aren't white collar enough. Well, not the drugs Harry markets.

"What do we do now?" Tristan is feeling marginally better now that his stomach is empty.

"I guess I pick up this fucking turtle corpse."

Harry scoops up the heavy shell and walks back to the car, leaving Tristan under the streetlights.

Lacey is awake. Harry smiles at her as he climbs into the front seat with his cumbersome cargo.

"Nice to see you, sunshine."

She blinks, trying to get her eyes to focus. "What's that?"

"A dead turtle."

"Where's Tristan?"

"Puking."

Brea can't help herself. "Fuck. Now the car is going to stink."

Tristan opens the back door. He doesn't know if he should laugh or cry seeing Lacey's half smile. He remains stoic but inside a ripple of normalcy creeps into his limbs. Lacey is okay. Maybe they will make it out of this. Whatever this is.

"Hi." She greets him quietly.

"Hi." He scootches closer to her than he

needs to and grabs her hand. His is damp. Hers is ice cold.

Harry tries to put the shell by his feet but there isn't room. "So, what? I have to hold this fucking thing on my lap?"

"Yes." Brea puts the car in drive.

"Can I just say"—they would rather he not, but nobody voices an objection—"I mean. Guys. It's a fucking turtle. A dog? I don't know. Maybe I'd go back and bury a dog but this is a damn reptile. Nobody really loves a pet unless it has fur. That's a fact."

"Wait, did we run over somebody's pet?" Lacey's eyes widen in alarm.

Harry continues before anyone can answer. "Half the people we grew up with are dead, and we're going to cry over this thing? Matt Fitzgerald got his fucking face shot off in front of me and I got to third base with his sister." He turns to Brea. "That was before you, babe."

"I don't care." Her tone is perfect indifference, and she means it. She genuinely doesn't care.

"I'm just saying. Keep it in perspective."

Harry has a point. All of them are guilty of having much stronger feelings toward the untimely demise of that turtle than that of Matt Fitzgerald. I'm sure if I took more than one basic psych class in college I could more eloquently explore the layered feelings of grief they are currently experiencing. But right now I'm with Harry and would be much more worried about the grossness that is about to leak out of that dead turtle's crack.

TWENTY-SIX

On the Run

Here in the back seat, I'm crying big, big crocodile tears for that poor dumb turtle leaking death juice on Harry's khakis.

"Fuck. I told you."

He blames the mess on Brea, who is also strangely shaken up about the poor dumb turtle leaking death juice on Harry's khakis. She's not crying, of course. I'm sure her tear ducts were removed years ago. Listening in on their bickering, I can tell she's upset, though. Are we in one of Tristan's cars? Is it over? Am I in heaven? My God, that's a depressing thought. Why is my face wet? Oh, yeah. I'm crying. The turtle. Makes sense. Sure. I've been to a buffet of carnage tonight and this is the thing that breaks me. Us, apparently. Frankie is also crying.

Holy crap! The mountains are on fire! "Where are we going?" Because it looks like we are headed east, directly into hell. "I think the forest is actually on fire?" Nobody is answering me. Nobody is looking at me. Oh, my bad. I forgot to say any of that out loud. So, like, when is someone going to fill me in on the last hour or four?

"Tristan, what . . ." No. That's not right. "How . . .?" No. How what? Oh, my God. I've forgotten how to make a sentence.

He squeezes my hand. "We'll be okay."

His hand is very sweaty. That's not overly reassuring.

"I found you in the hall by the cafeteria." Frankie is wiping his eyes. He's recovering nicely. Is his hand sweaty? I need a less-moist hand to hold right now. Moist. So many people hate that word. I don't get it.

"Was that . . . was that all real?"

The car answers in unison. "Yes."

"Are all those people dead?"

Another affirmative in unison. "Yes."

"Why?"

Brea floors the gas. "Fuck. We've got company."

Company? Can we get back to my original question? Brea is speeding toward the mountains. Did I mention the mountains are on fire? It's like the wind is blowing us right into the center of a fire tornado. The headlights are getting closer.

Harry looks over my head and out the back windshield. "Babe?"

"Yeah, babe?"

That was rather snippy.

"Go faster!"

"I'm trying!"

Sheesh! What's with all the yelling? It's like

they're an ordinary couple having a bad Saturday on their way to Menards. Wait, they would never go to Menards. Lowe's. They're just having some issues on their way to browse shower doors at Lowe's. A dark sedan has pulled up next to us. Am I the only one seeing this?

"Shit! Get down!" Harry holds the turtle shell up to the window, blocking dozens and dozens of sparking bullets. Oh, great. More shooting.

Brea cranks the wheel, pushing the four-door off-road. A motorcycle follows us. It must have special tires.

"Not this fuck again."

Again? Did I miss the other motorcycles? How long was I passed out back here?

Harry stands on his seat, exposing half of his body out the sunroof. Moonroof? I don't know the difference. His pants are smeared with dark substances, but we can't blame that all on the turtle. There's no way to distinguish between human and animal guts in this lighting.

Harry's body twists and turns as he dodges bullets. How is that guy behind us driving a motorcycle with one hand? Can a person do that? I could never ride my bike without both hands firmly on the handlebars.

There's a break in the not-so-friendly fire. Harry seizes the opportunity and hurls the turtle shell at our two-wheeled nemesis. It spins through the air like a medieval weapon and nails the cyclist in the throat. The bike instantly tips to the side and skids on the pavement. If there wasn't already a huge fire burning, those sparks could cause some damage.

Harry sinks back into his seat, a smug smile plastered on his face. "May he rest in peace."

Without an immediate threat, we slow down to only double the speed limit. It's darker as we drive out of town. Shouldn't we be driving toward people? Specifically, people in police uniforms? I'm starting to feel my mind thaw, but I know I'm not comprehending my current situation. My body is tingling, stuck on pause. My head is hanging low and I can't stop yawning. This is how dogs act around fireworks.

Brea looks in the rearview mirror. "Shit."

The car's interior is suddenly lit up way brighter than usual. I don't remember my dress being this color. It looks purple.

"Harry." Brea sounds tense.

"I see it." His tone is equally tense. This can't be good. Should I be offended no one is consulting us in the back? Kids' table for life.

Harry watches the cars gaining on us over his shoulder. Tristan is so pale he's translucent. Harry's face is flushed in all the right places. Did he lose weight?

"I can't go any faster. We'll flip." Brea must be worried our luck is running out.

"I know, babe."

Harry winks in my direction. Wait, am I the babe?

"Do something!" Brea is yelling, again.

He turns back around to face her. "What do you want me to do? I'm all out of shells."

We're racing up a two-lane road to nowhere. Brea can't pull off any fancy twists or turns here. If she jerks the wheel the wrong way we could be rolling back down to the valley.

"Take the steering wheel." Her toned arms look powerful as she flips down the visors and throws open compartments. "There must be something in here . . ." She reaches under the driver's seat and pulls out a gun.

I know I just got here, but no one thought to look under the seats earlier?

She tosses the revolver onto Harry's lap. Startled, he jumps like it's hot coffee.

"Where the fuck did you get this?"

"It came with the car." Having taken back the steering wheel, her eyes are frantically flitting between the road and the rearview mirror. The elevation is slowing the chase down. "Shoot!"

"Oh, my God. Babe. You're so smart. Why didn't I think of—"

"Harry! Shoot the goddamn people chasing us!"

He leans out his window and fires. I don't know anything about shooting people but he's sure making it look easy. Is it like in the movies? If I had the gun, would I be able to pull that off? Is there a stress hormone that kicks in, making ordinary dorks sharpshooters? I kind of want to try it.

We're driving the superior vehicle and thus able to gain some distance as the climb intensifies. Again, I'm new to all this, but should Harry be using up all the bullets right now? The landscape seems to be holding them back as much as our firepower. Finally, one of Harry's shots finds a useful target and blows out a front tire. After taking out one of the three cars—or are there four? I can't tell, and figuring it out by the headlights seems like too much math right now—he retreats inside and rolls up the window. The smoke is too intense to hang out there for long.

He coughs. "Fuck me. Now what?"

Brea jerks the wheel—I thought we decided we weren't going to do that?—and we race down an embankment on two wheels. Someone is screaming so loud! Oh. That's me. Tristan and Frankie join in. We bounce in our seats as Brea barrels through smoky brush, toward God knows what. We could be heading off a cliff. Wait, is that the plan? That better not be the plan. If that is the plan, shouldn't we all have been consulted?

Thankfully, Harry screams at her to stop. Except she ignores him (obviously) and accelerates. A flaming tree branch falls directly in our path. I told you the world is on fire, right? I want to make that clear. She slams on the brakes before we burst into flames. Brea, who has yet to break a sweat, expertly spins the wheels, throws the car in reverse, and miraculously backs us onto a dirt road. She turns off the headlights before resuming our ascent. I suppose she's using her Spidey Sense to navigate this hostile terrain. That sounded smart: hostile terrain. I wonder how I could work that into the conversation if I ever fully regain my powers of speech.

We breathe in silence. I'm not the only one monitoring my heart rate. Something feels wet and sticky. I need to soak in a hot tub of rubbing alcohol. Thirty seconds go by and Tristan breaks our quiet contemplation.

"What the fudge? What in the actual fudge is going on?"

Harry looks behind him. "Did you say *fudge?*" He turns from Tristan to Brea. "Did he just say *fudge?*"

He did. He did! That's really sweet. I've never heard him do that before. I'll have to tell him I swear now.

"What the heck!" Tristan is using a very loud voice. "Are all those people trying to kill me?"

Brea and Harry answer in unison. "Yes."

"Why?"

"Because they think you're the devil." Harry is calm as a cucumber.

Want to guess how Tristan responds?

"What?!?!"

Ow, dude, my ears.

The change in scenery is working for Frankie. He's no longer screaming like a child. He turns to his old friend. "Santa Ana."

Tristan shakes his head at the unhelpful explanation. "Who?"

Frankie starts to repeat himself. "Santa—"

Something appears to click in Tristan's brain. "That local scumbag drug dealer?"

This should make him happy. Tristan *loves* drug dealers. Who's that one guy he's always gushing about . . .

Harry is now strangely offended in the front

seat. "Scumbag? Entrepreneur might be a better description—"

Frankie ignores him. "Meda Lucas thinks you're his masked rival."

Yes! That's the guy. Meda Lucas. Tristan is always talking about him. He has a bit of a man crush, if you ask me. Is he the one chasing us?

"What? How could anyone, especially THE MEDA LUCAS, think I'm a drug dealer? That's insane!"

Frankie looks him up and down. "Is it?"

"Oh, my God. Do you think I'm a criminal?" Tristan is still talking very loudly. Must be part of his fight-or-flight response.

Frankie hesitates. "No. No. Of course not."

"Why are you hesitating? Frankie, I am not Santa Ana."

"Sure. Sorry. Forget about it."

Frankie is a terrible liar. It's very clear that he will not be forgetting about any of this. This is so funny. Why does he think Tristan is a drug dealer? Is it because he's Mexican? That's a little racist, don't you think? Frankie's Mexican, too, and, like, his oldest friend. Am I the racist one for not thinking Tristan could be a successful drug dealer? Wait, is Tristan wearing a Rolex? Now that is insane. When did he buy a flipping Rolex? Fucking Rolex. I forgot; I swear now. Frankie's hesitation makes total sense. I'm the dumbass for not asking where exactly Tristan got his small fortune. I wonder what kind of drugs Tristan sells. Stop it! He's not Santana or whoever the heck they're talking about.

"So, Frank, if Tristan isn't Santa Ana . . ." Harry drums the armrest casually. "I mean, obviously he's no criminal mastermind. Who do you think Meda Lucas is really looking for? I don't know, if you, like, had to pick somebody in this car, who do you think it'd be?"

Silence. What is Harry fishing for? It's

coming off as desperate, and that's not a great look for him. But more importantly: "Should we call the police?"

Oh, good. I made a complete sentence. I said that out loud, right?

"Yes." Tristan agrees with me.

"The police can't help us." Harry is quick to contradict us.

Okay, big shot. "What do we do?"

"We run."

That is neither helpful nor comforting. Brea has slowed down to an acceptable speed now that no one is following us. She puts her hand on Harry's thigh. Boo-hoo for you, Tristan. I guess your girlfriend has come to her senses and moved on. The two of them are completely relaxed and have moved on to enjoying their night. A bunch of old pals on an adventure. I don't know if I should be impressed by their quick rebound or terrified by their ability to be at ease after all the shit that just happened. My threesome in the back seat is having a harder time regulating our nervous systems. But in good news, I can see again. Everything was fuzzy for a while. Only . . . what is wrong with my dress? It's stiff. There's something . . . oh, God. I start to heave.

"Sorry. Blood." I can't stop gagging. Please let me barf out the window. Thank you, universe, for sparing my life numerous times, but I have to ask for one more thing. Please, if I'm going to blow chunks, let me get this window down. I reach over Frankie and hit the window button repeatedly. If he hadn't been dragging my limp body around half the night this might be too much touching, but after all we've been through, we're good.

The tinted glass rolls down slowly. Hurry. Hurry. Hurry. Finally, I can stick my head out. A cloud of hot sparkly smoke blows in.

"Sorry! Shit." Oops. I pound on the button but it doesn't help. Smoke covers us as the window slowly goes back up. "Sorry."

Harry laughs. "Classic Lacey." Classic what? Did he just say my name? He looks over his shoulder. "You know what, guys?" Nobody responds unless you count coughing. "This is nice." He turns back around, assuming we are nodding in agreement behind him. We are not. "Can I tell you something? Can I get something off my chest?"

Again, nobody responds.

"I'm not very happy."

Not happy now or, like, in general? I don't know if any of us are particularly happy right now.

"I haven't been happy for a long time."

Thank you for the clarification.

"Which is nuts! Right? How could Harry Sullivan not be fucking happy? I've got a rocking bod. A full head of hair. I'm successful. So fucking successful. I own a castle. With a moat. Elon Musk made my Tesla himself. By hand. True story. Do you know how many country clubs I belong to? I don't, but it's a lot. I'm a fucking baller and, oh, by the way, still a complete badass. Did you see how many dudes I murdered with my bare hands back there? In self-defense, of course."

He loses his train of thought.

Brea prods him. "Babe?"

"Yeah? Right. I'm so awesome, yet so fucking miserable. For months. Hell, years, I can't figure it out. Being with you guys tonight, hanging with the old gang, it clicked. Maybe high school truly was the last time I was happy, and now I know why. Happiness is about who you're with and how they make you feel."

Brea is not impressed. "Sure, babe."

I think he's kind of making sense.

He keeps going. "But also, how you make yourself feel. You know?"

Sort of?

"Tristan! Just look at Tristan. Sitting on a chocolate empire and still knows how to party. You made it, dude. To see the confidence in each step. You've come so far and still managed to keep that sparkle in your eyes."

When have Tristan's eyes ever sparkled? Speaking of Tristan . . . if we survive this, maybe he and I shouldn't be friends anymore. Harry might be on to something. I'm not too happy being around him these days. Not since I fell in love with him. He's never thanked me for making him dinner. For sending him home with decorated Tupperware. He didn't notice when I got new glasses. He only has lunch with me when I make him. And, like, who else is he going to talk to at work? Kevin? He sucks. Oh, and let's not forget the most recent and—most would agree—brutal snub of all. He invited me to come with him to the most important event in his life—*as his assistant.* I'm going to

die following him off a cliff as his motherfucking assistant. Swearing really does help punctu-
ate things.

"This whole clusterfuck aside, you have got
it figured out, man. Never doubted you for a
minute. I love you, Tristan. Thanks for being
you. And, Frankie, you're . . . you're surprisingly helpful in fucked-up situations. Glad to be
here with you, buddy. Lacey. Now this chick
gets it. I've never known someone for so little
time who's understood me so completely. You,
Lacey, are a treasure."

He's looking at me. Is he waiting for a response? Do I say something? What do I say?

"Brea."

Oh, thank God. He's moved on.

"Babe. You are exactly the person you were
born to be. All of you have inspired me tonight.
I'm blessed. Guys. Seriously." He turns around
again, getting as close to us in the back as
he can. He puts his hand on my knee. It's a

strong, dry hand. "This night has been a gift, and I'd be honored if you would join me on the run from that violent piece of shit Meda Lucas. Together—and I really do believe this—together, I think we're going to be okay."

Did Harry just become Ted Lasso? I would very much like to see him in a mustache. His slightly nonsensical monologue has brought my adrenaline down. It's amazing how fast and hard our brains work to establish normalcy. Okay. So, I guess I'm on the run now. Sounds good.

He smiles, waiting for some sort of acknowledgment. Brea finally says something.

"Whatever, babe."

Harry appears to take that as a yes.

TWENTY-SEVEN

Falling Springs

t's Tristan. Remember me? Like, where have I been? Isn't this book called *Tristan Goes Back to School* or some shiz? I'm being overly aggressive. Forgive me. I'm not quite myself right now. Meda Lucas is trying to kill me and, by extension, everyone around me. Funny story, he thinks I'm Santa Ana. Am I the only one who watches the news? I'm not walking around in a movie-quality devil mask. Duh. Santa Ana never goes anywhere without his mask. That's his thing. Meda Lucas is handsome and charming and is slowly buying his way into polite society, that's his thing. I have no things. I'm nothing. Why is this happening?

My shirt is hard with sweat. It went from soaked to solid. I smell like the bottom of a hamster cage. Brea and I kissed. In the bathroom right before everyone died. It wasn't great. The kiss and the everybody dying part. Now she's going the wrong way. Frankie tried to stop her, then we almost died three times, then Harry had some *Chicken Soup for the Soul* moment, and now we're driving into the fire.

"You're going the wrong way."

She's not listening to me.

"Harry, she's not listening to me. We should be driving west. Against the wind. The fire—"

"Did you want to get away from those pricks or not?" When Brea poses a question, she is rarely interested in an answer. "I'm getting us above the fire line. You're not the only genius in this car, remember?"

She might be right. Otherwise we wouldn't

have survived a high-speed chase down the main drag. We'd have ended up through the window of a Bed Bath & Beyond and those terrifying men would have skinned us alive. Speaking of terrible and odd ways to die, was I dreaming, or did Harry kill a guy with a giant turtle shell earlier?

Wait. This could work. I know exactly where we are. We're 12.2 miles up from Azusa in a state park. We used to come here on field trips. In just a minute or two we'll be in Falling Springs, which is nothing but a ghost town filled with abandoned vacation cabins. A cult once moved in and tried to set up shop. We cancelled our field trip that year. A rumor rippled through middle school that Polly Klaas was spotted living here. If you're not from California, Polly was a twelve-year-old girl who was kidnapped from a slumber party in 1993. Every female from my school had a cousin who knew her. I sound like Wikipedia. Good. About time I get my shit together. Falling Springs. Yes. This might be a good place to hide. That's what Harry means, right? We can't outrun Meda Lucas. We need to hide. I should be more involved with the decision-making.

"Stop."

Brea looks in the rearview mirror. "I'm not turning around."

"The police can't—"

Jesus, Harry. I heard you the first time. "Yeah. I get it." Seriously, Harry can just shut up for a while. "No, I mean keep going but stop."

"What, here?" Brea is actually humoring me.

"Not here. Soon."

"Okay."

"Sorry. No. I'm not being very clear. Stop the car—"

"Stop?" Brea takes her foot off the accelerator.

"—in one thousand two hundred and sixty feet."

"What?" Harry joins Brea this time. They must think I'm having a stroke.

"Springs! Falling Springs. From the field trips? At the state park?"

I think I *am* having a stroke.

Lacey leans between them and points out the front windshield. "There."

Harry is looking down her dress. Not a fan of that. Brea stops the car abruptly and Lacey lurches face-first into Harry's lap. She is quick to get herself upright and organized. We need to talk. I have so much to apologize for. Where do I even start?

Harry flings open his door enthusiastically. "Honey, I'm home!"

Creepy. Is he enjoying himself? The rest of us climb out with less vigor.

"Holy shit." Brea gazes around at the landscape.

I don't remember the place being quite this apocalyptic. Most of the two-room buildings have had extensive fire damage over the years. Some don't have much left but a wall or two. Anything still standing is covered in graffiti. There are hot pink dicks and balls and the usual ALL COPS ARE BASTARDS mixed in with scripture and a lovely portrait of Jesus and the Virgin Mary with tiger heads. Charred trees and branches cover what's left of any mini infrastructure the vacation hideaway once had. The overgrowth from being so close to the river has overtaken the rest. There's a little bungalow whose entire walls and roof are covered in green moss and vines. If elves went to hell, this would be it.

Harry claps his hands in excitement. "Well, this will do just fine. Nice work, Tristan. Let's set up camp."

Camp? I never took Harry for a Boy Scout.

"Can we call the police now?"

Thanks for looping back around to that, Lacey. Maybe Harry will be less dismissive if the suggestion comes from somebody with breasts. When exactly do we start doing the things that normal people would do in this situation? But I suppose normal people wouldn't have gotten into this situation.

"I told you. That's not how this works. For now, we hide. Give it a day or two and Meda Lucas will go back to his lifestyles of the rich and famous in Mexico. He can only stay stateside so long before he draws too much heat." At least Harry added some exposition to his reasoning this time.

Lacey's frowning. "We hide? Here?"

She doesn't camp. Or spend too much time outdoors. She told me how a snake once slithered by her feet when she was using the latrine on a canoe trip and she's never been the same since. This is going to be difficult for her.

"It will be okay." I try my best to sound positive. It won't be. Nothing will be okay, but that's what people say, right?

"Tristan! Yes! That's the spirit! Come on. It will be like that trip we took to Baja after prom. Babe, come with me. Let's find some wood for a fire."

I wouldn't know. I've never been to Baja or prom but I'm pretty certain singing around a campfire is not a good plan for our immediate future. "A fire? That seems like a bad idea given half of the mountain is already in flames."

"So, what's a few more? Come on. We need it to boil water."

Seriously, Harry? After all we've been through and he's still dismissive as shit.

Wait, did he say boil water? Is someone going into labor?

He slaps me on the back. "This is going to be fun. The universe has presented us with a gift. Now all we have to do is open up and accept it." He bows to me like we're finishing up a yoga class. He must have a head injury.

Frankie is walking away holding up his phone. Must be trying to get reception. Good luck. Between the location and the wind, he'd need a military satellite phone to get ahold of anybody. What's he trying to do anyway? Order a pizza? I think about yelling after him but he's not the one I need to talk to. I need to have some alone time with Lacey.

Brea points to a clearing that must have been some sort of community spot. There are remnants of a fire pit and tree stumps purposefully placed in a circle. "Let's set up over there."

"Can I stay in the car?"

Good for Lacey. She's the only one making sense. She also needs to get more involved in the decision-making around here.

"What fun would that be? Come on." Harry holds out his hand and helps her get out of the back seat. "Why don't you and your boss grab the waters and shit from the rear. I think I saw some Fritos. You're a classy guy, Melendez. Riding around in a car stocked with snacks. Nice work."

Melendez? Harry and I are on a last name basis now? That's a big deal in Man Land. Should I pass out some Fritos and open up? Accept what's coming my way? Could this night turn out to be fun, after all? Fuck! What is wrong with me! I'm the one with a head injury. How many dozens of people did I see slaughtered tonight, and I'm getting goose bumps at the thought of roasting marshmallows with my boy Sullivan?

Brea and Harry walk off arm in arm. They're up to something. Are they a couple now? I'm not sure what the vibe is now that we're living life on the lam. I don't really give a shit. I need to focus my attention on Lacey. I've got to fix this. Finally we're alone. This is the first time it's been just us since we got off the helicopter. God. That feels like it was three years ago.

"Hey."

"Hey."

Uh-oh. A hollow echo is never a good start.

"Lacey, I'm so sorry I dragged you into this. I can't believe this is happening and I hope you'll forgive me. I promise I'll make it up to you. I've been a huge prick and I should have never brought you with me to the reunion." There. I put it all on the line.

She doesn't say anything right away. She's no doubt in shock. I still can't feel my feet.

When she finally speaks, her words sizzle. "You should have never brought me to the reunion as your assistant."

She's still mad about that? After everything that's happened? I mumble something lame about it not being a big deal, that I was just pretending.

"I don't care that you lied, Tristan, that you put on some big act for your friends. Do whatever you want. But why did you have to lie *about me*? Why can't I be friends with this version of you?"

"You *are* my friend. My only—"

She's shaking her head and looking at the ground. "No. You made it very clear we have a working relationship."

"Well, we do work together—"

"And you ditched me the first chance you got. You left me all alone—"

My turn to interrupt her. "I had no idea Meda Lucas was going to show up with an army and kill everyone!"

"I'm not talking about that! The second you saw Brea, I was promptly ditched in the gym to fend for myself. I didn't know anybody. The music was terrible. I was starving—"

"You and Harry seemed to get along just fine."

She pierces me with an icy glare. "Fuck off, Tristan."

Wow! Did Lacey Hahn tell me to fuck off? To my face? This is about Brea. This has to be about Brea. Is Lacey jealous?

She starts toward the vehicle. "Should we get this crap out of the car, or what?"

I help her open the back door. "I'm sorry." I say the words softly, and I mean them.

"Yup. You said that." She still won't make eye contact.

I don't often apologize. Is it supposed to work like this? How long until she forgives me, and do our current circumstances speed up the forgiving or slow it down? I'll try again.

"I'm sorry I upset you."

She spins around. "I'm not upset. I think I'm behaving quite calmly. Do I seem upset?"

"Ummm—" That was a rhetorical question. I think.

"What could possibly be upsetting me, Tristan? That you lied to all your asshole friends and told them I was your assistant? That you ditched me all night with a bunch of old, sad fucks? That you left me to die with a bunch of old, sad fucks? That I'm currently covered in the blood and brain matter of the aforemen- tioned old, sad fucks? Maybe it's that I got to watch you get your dick sucked all night by Psycho Barbie. Or how about the fact that you involved me in your fucked-up midlife cri- sis at all?"

She's really taken to using the F word. Good for her. She does it well. I should tell her that throughout the course of this bizarre evening no dicks have been sucked. Would that help? Worth a shot.

"Nothing happened with Br—"

"I don't care."

Obviously she does but she's done talking to me. She slams the back door, almost taking my head off, and walks away without any snacks.

"Don't worry . . . I'll grab the supplies."

She flips me the bird and stumbles toward the clearing.

TWENTY-EIGHT

You Can Still Trust Me, Promise

Frankie is not attempting to order a pizza. But he is deep in the woods, desperate to find a cell signal. He climbs a boulder and reaches up as high as he can without falling down the mountain, balancing on one leg as he stretches the other out far behind him. I'm not sure how that helps, but you do you, Frankie. Stretch. Streeeetch. Come on, come on, come on. Yes! Two bars. Way to go, T-Mobile.

You guys, I'm busting. Eeek! I'm so excited to tell you . . . I've been keeping a secret. I'm sorry. I never meant to betray you and I promise after this one teeny-tiny surprise there aren't any more. This doesn't turn out to be a Scooby-Doo ending where everyone takes off a mask, at least not literally, since Santa Ana left his at home. Plus, you already know who he is. But figuratively, well, we'll see. (Unlike Lacey, I do know what those words mean.) Anyway, back to the secret, and maybe you already figured this out: Frankie is the inside guy! He works for the FBI! Crosby! Dillmann! Uncle Jocko! Remember them!? Frankie is with those guys! Sort of. He works in archives. But still! Frankie is an FBI agent!

He was beside himself when he got the call. That's a bit ambiguous. Was he beside himself overwhelmed by fear? By joy? Let's go with both. It was a Wednesday. He usually watches *The Godfather Part II* on Wednesdays, but not this hump day. This hardest day of the week to spell, he didn't have time to pay homage to Francis Ford Coppola. Nope. He was going undercover.

Frankie DeLeon was going under-freaking-cover! Eat your heart out, *True Detective*.

There was so much he had to do to get ready. He needed to research nondescript casual wear for men in their early forties. He needed to clean and polish his service weapon. He needed to find his service weapon. So many things. All of the things.

Did your ears perk up when I mentioned service weapon? You're probably thinking, yeah, where is that "would have come in handy multiple times" service weapon? He left his gun in the trunk of his car. OOPS. He wasn't sure how to use the ankle strap and was terrified he'd shoot his foot off. He figured he'd just run out and grab it when the shit hit the fan. Easy peasy.

Great idea, Frank. How'd that work out for you? Not that it would have helped. He's a terrible shot. Top of his rookie class in hand-to-hand

452   ADDISON J. CHAPPLE

combat, though. All those nights watching *The Karate Kid* on repeat really paid off.

I'm coming off judgmental. My apologies, Frankie. He's actually been doing a pretty good job. Harry is right. He's been surprisingly helpful in this completely fucked-up situation. You didn't get to see this, but he strangled a dude with his shoelaces outside the band room. He bent another dude's arm all the way around in the wrong direction. It was gross. I don't know what movie he learned that move from. *Roadhouse*, maybe? I'm being too hard on Frankie-boy. He's definitely been pulling his weight.

Right now, while he has these few miraculous bars, he has got to get ahold of his boss. He needs backup. He needs ammunition and a tank to take out Meda Lucas. He needs an extraction point and handcuffs for his onetime best friend, Santa Ana. And he really needs to get out of these stupid Crocs.

I have some bad news for Frankie. It might be a while until anyone brings him a new pair of shoes. His boss, Special Agent in Charge Tom Spitz, is currently Special Agent in Costume Uncle Jocko. Sure, he's still a company man for a few more weeks and technically "working" an operation tonight. But there wasn't a snowball's chance in hell Tom Spitz was going to let his hungry understudy swoop in opening weekend. Which, sadly, is not trending to be a Certified Fresh debut.

Mamma Rose has food poisoning and Baby June peed her pants. Uncle Jocko has been killing it, however. He is currently living his best life, watching from the wings and counting down until his next entrance, doing face exercises in order to keep himself loose. Onstage, a real estate agent from Marina del Rey is belting out a tune as Mazeppa, a burlesque dancer past her prime, as she pretends to play the trumpet. Watch your back, Lady Gaga.

"Shit. Shit. Shit." Tom dashes into the hall when his phone goes off in the pockets of his colorful knickers. He's curt when he answers. "This better be important."

"Sir?" Frankie is yelling. "Sir, can you hear me?"

Tom rolls his eyes. Always with the theatrics, this one. No, wait. That's the other one. Crosby. Who's this yelling at him right now? Wasting his time and taking him out of character? DeLeon. Right. The skinny guy from digital archives. "Yes, agent?"

"Crosby and Dillmann. Have they checked in, sir?"

"No. I told them, like I told you, not to bother me unless it was an emergency. Either you are at a different high school reunion or they are the only ones capable of following my directions."

Frankie doesn't know how to respond. Bosses from his basement department are usually much more encouraging.

"Are you there? DeLeon?"

"Yes, sir. I'm here."

"And is this an emergency?"

"It's an emergency, sir."

"Then stop talking in riddles and tell me what the hell is going on!"

I know he's got opening night jitters, but Agent Jocko isn't exactly moving things along himself. He's interrupted before he gets a chance to completely rip Frankie a new one.

"Hi, Tommy." A perky chorus girl skips by. Have I mentioned he's a GILF? It probably goes without saying.

He flashes a hot grandpa smile and whispers. "Talking to my wife."

"Don't forget the steps at the top of the first act finale." She stops and demonstrates by pointing her leggy leg in each direction as she says it. "Front. Side. Back. Side. Back. Side. Front. Got it?"

"Back. Side. Front. Thanks, Jody."

Satisfied, she pats his arm and continues on her way to the dressing room.

"Sir? Sir? Who's Jody? Is this a secure line—"

"Agent! How bad is it?"

"Very bad, sir."

"Civilian casualties?"

"Yes, sir."

"How many?"

"The soccer team. Half of the yearbook staff. Amy Donna and her twin sister—"

"What?"

"The chess club. The girl that turned me down for homecoming. The girl that turned me down for prom. The girl—"

"I get it. Shit! Dillmann? Crosby? Where are those assholes? Why hasn't anyone called me? Goddamnit!"

"Sir, I quickly assessed the situation and called for backup. In fact, I sent multiple texts requesting—"

"I'm sorry, agent. There must be a problem

with our connection. It sounded like you were about to question my authority?" Tom Spitz can take feedback from Jody the teenage dance captain just fine. He will never be questioned by a subordinate agent.

"No, sir."

Spitz covers the phone and yells down the hall. "Fuck!"

Frankie doesn't have much field experience, but he knows this is not going well. Poor Frankie. Is he the unsung hero of this whole thing? "Sir?"

I hope that trumpet lady can vamp. Agent Jocko has some work to do. "Where are you?"

"Falling Springs up the San Gabriel Trail. I have Santa Ana."

This should make Spitz happy. Maybe Frankie should have led with that.

"Alive?"

"Yes. Meda Lucas is in pursuit."

"No shit. Welcome to the party, DeLeon.

Meda Lucas was supposed to take out Santa Ana quietly at the reunion before we hauled his ass in."

"It was not quiet, sir! Not quiet at all! Santa Ana was waiting for him, sir. He had security and heavy artillery. He . . ."

Wait a sec. That doesn't sound like the Santa Ana described in the thick file Frankie read last weekend instead of enjoying his typical Diane Lane marathon. Santa Ana has gone to too much trouble trying to be being inconspicuous to all of a sudden show up and dangle his balls in Meda Lucas's face now. (Was that too much? Frankie is new at being a badass.)

It hits Frankie like a lightning bolt or—more specific to his situation—like a burning ember flying up his nose. He jumps down from the boulder. Tristan isn't Santa Ana. Shit! He has no idea if Santa Ana was even there tonight.

"Is Santa Ana in custody? Has your cover been blown?"

Frankie's wheels are turning. What are the chances he still has time to save the day and perhaps his job? There's no way Meda Lucas is going to stop looking for them. What if Frankie nabbed him in the woods? He's the real prize anyway. Too bad Frankie will have to use his friends as bait.

"Sir—"

"Fuck! I do not want to waste a day going to your funeral."

"Sir. I have a—"

"Don't interrupt me. Ping me your coordinates and we'll get you out of there."

"Do I have authorization to call in SWAT?"

"Christ! No."

"I can get you Meda Lucas."

Spitz is listening.

"I'm listening."

"Give me clearance to call in a tactical team. If I can force him to the—"

"Hey! Jocko! Where have you been?" Another

teenager, this time in a headset, is shouting out the backstage door. "What the heck, man?"

Frankie can hear that he's lost his boss's attention again. "Sir?"

Spitz turns to the teen. "Sorry. It's my wife. Dog got ahold of a chicken bone."

"Do you bring your phone onstage?"

"No. Of course not."

"Sir?!" Frankie is yelling into his phone now. "Sir! Do I have clearance—"

"Dude! You go on in like thirty seconds!" This kid is one hard-core thespian.

"Sorry, sir. On my way."

"Sir?" Frankie is even more confused than we are. "Do I have—"

The attitude in a headset shuts the door, leaving behind a cloud of mild BO and Axe Body Spray.

"Damnit, DeLeon." Spitz spits into his early model iPhone. "Yes. Fine. Do it."

Frankie is honored to have his boss's trust. "Thank you, sir. You won't regret it."

"I already do." Agent Jocko aggressively jabs his phone to end the call and runs to make his cue.

TWENTY-NINE

White Rabbit

F rankie has been gone a long time. Brea and Harry are back and working on a fire. Let me go on record saying I think that is a terrible idea. I'm giving Lacey some space. I'm not being mature. I don't know what else to say to her. I wonder when she started swearing? Our self-appointed fearless leaders have fashioned some sort of tea kettle out of a stainless-steel water bottle that was left in the car. I don't understand what is going on with this beverage situation. The car was nicely appointed with all sorts of food and drinks. Chips. Fritos. Beef jerky. Crackers. Chocolate bars. Bottled water. A shit ton of beer. Harry is chugging beer so we can use the empty cans for this tea Brea insists on making. Sure. Why not? With everything that has happened tonight, this seems like a perfectly logical plan.

Brea is wearing Harry's letterman jacket. Guess some things never change. Amazing how a few dead bodies can put things back in perspective. I don't care about any of that anymore. Besides, being with her in that bathroom was not the end-all be-all moment of moments I was counting on. Oh. Shhhh. Here she comes.

She hands me a can of tea. "Careful. It's hot." She raises her can in a toast and we take a sip.

My God! That is fucking awful. Maybe stress has changed my taste buds. We take a seat on a dirty log around the fire. Am I sitting in ash or ants? I'm going with ash. Harry is drinking alone, taking breaks to stretch into warrior pose. Oooo-kay. Lacey's leaning against a tree, her can on the ground next to her. She won't look in my direction. Brea and I sit silently, sipping. Where is Frankie? I hope he didn't get attacked by a mountain lion.

"Are there mountain lions here?"

Brea shrugs. She tips my can toward my face. Jeez. Why so pushy? I don't know how much of this I'll be able to stomach.

"Babe." Harry yells from across the fire. "How's my form?"

Brea gives him a thumbs-up.

He grins. "It's all about the mind and body connection, you know? That's what I've been missing. I need to live in my bones. I need to release the power held captive in my muscles."

"Sure, babe." She turns her attention back to me. "When we were collecting firewood, oh, my God, he would not shut up. I was about to fuck him just to get some peace and quiet." She pauses. "I'm kidding."

"Oh. Ha. Ha."

"He thinks he's going to be a football player now."

"What?"

"Yeah. The trophy's in the car. The whole night was a sign pointing him back to his true calling. What a dumbass. How's your tea?"

"Terrible."

This makes her smile. "Chug it."

"I don't think so." I smile back. I've never been this relaxed around Brea before. It's almost more unbelievable than our foiled makeout session. I like this better.

"Were you at Fat Kristin's party when we convinced those freshmen to drink piss?"

I shake my head no.

"Or that time Jeff Lewis was so messed up he ate a piece of shit wrapped in a Snickers wrapper?"

Jeff Lewis. He was nice. He was in the A.V. club with me and Frankie. We signed up so we could get out of gym. Around Christmas we got to hit the nursing home circuit with the choir.

Frankie was very proud of his cutting-edge cinematography. I wish Frankie hadn't disappeared. I could have been nicer to him tonight. I could have been nicer to him for the last thirty-seven years. If he's not eaten by a mountain lion, I'm going to give him a hug. Did I see Jeff Lewis there tonight? I hope he wasn't murdered.

"Was he at the reunion? Do you think he's okay?"

"Who, Jeff? He died in Afghanistan."

I didn't know that. I feel like I should have known that. "That's awful. Did he have a family?"

She shrugs and then laughs. "He ate the whole turd even after Harry told him it was a piece of shit."

That's too bad about Jeff. Junior year, some lacrosse pricks tossed my locker and he helped me pick it up. We were both tardy to our next class. My teacher was an old hippie who refused to keep records for the "man," but Jeff got detention. Why would anyone risk detention for me?

We're quiet for a minute, then Brea smacks my leg. "I've missed you, Tristan." She drinks. "How many bathrooms do you have? In your main house. Nine? Ten? Clarence Thomas has thirteen."

She's waiting for my answer. I have one bathroom with a stained tub, tepid water, and a hole in the ceiling. My clothes. My watch. The fucking helicopter. It's all a joke. A horrendous long-winded joke without a punchline. I give her a number instead of coming clean.

"Five."

"Five?"

Five appears to be a disappointing number. Seriously? Okay. Screw it. "The main floor bath is thirteen hundred square feet with a plunge pool."

Her eyes light up.

I saw that in a spread *Architectural Digest* did a few years back on Meda Lucas's desert estate. He doesn't have hippos, but he sure has nice bathrooms. It's rumored all his houses have torture chambers built underneath connected by a maze of tunnels. That part wasn't featured in the glossy pictures. He's going to find us, right? That will spare me from having to kill myself. I'm prepared to meet my maker or whatever nonconscious void awaits, but I don't want anyone else to die. That was never part of my plan.

"Tristan." It takes Brea a while to get out her next thought. She starts to say something and then changes course. "Tell me more about that girl." She nods toward Lacey. "The one you left me for?"

"Huh?" Oh, yeah. That might not have been one of my finer moments. "I didn't mean to ditch you."

"That's okay. I caught up."

"That was my first time in the girls' bathroom."

"There have been a lot of firsts tonight." She

stops to think. "My first time being shot at. First time seeing a dead body."

She'd never seen a dead body before? I take a sip from my can, forgetting what's in it. Jesus Christ, this is terrible. I can hardly get it down. I count to three after I swallow to make sure it's not on its way back up. "You seem like the type of person who's seen a few dead bodies." I instantly regret saying that. I don't even know what that means.

"Thank you." She accepts it as a genuine compliment. "I think she likes you." She tilts her head in Lacey's direction.

"We work together."

"I know she's not your assistant. I get paid to spend my day with liars."

"No. She's not my assistant."

"The way you took off looking for her. I think you like her, too."

What? What is all this "like" bullshit? What's

next, we're all going to pass notes to each other in study hall?

"I'm sorry. I shouldn't have left you—"

"Don't worry about me. I can take care of myself."

"Obviously. Where'd you learn how to drive like that?"

She smiles again. It's a wide and real smile. She should let her face move more. She's aging much better than she thinks. "TV. Years of pent-up rage and aggression." She notices my sips have stalled. "Drink your tea."

I take a small, painful sip. "Well. Good job. I'm glad we didn't die."

"Me, too." We clink cans. She calls over to Harry working on his downward dog. "Looking good, babe."

"Yeah?" He swings one leg into the air, going for a three-legged dog, but since he wasn't quite in an upside-down V to start with, he looks more like a dog lifting its leg to pee.

Brea keeps talking. She's talking to me, still, I think. My body is churning out some serious endorphins or cortisol or something. All of a sudden I'm feeling rather unmoored. Unmoored? My, my. What am I, some sort of liberal arts professor? My father hated those sissy pricks. His words, not mine. I can't hear anything but I can hear everything. What the hell? Should I be freaking out? Nobody else is freaking out. Don't freak out, Tristan. This is the crash from almost dying seventy-two times tonight. I'll be okay. Keep it together. Just ride the wave. I've made it this far.

I'll try reading Brea's lips. They're so sparkly. Bright. Blinding. How can lips be blinding? No. It's not her lips. When she opens her mouth, it's like a spotlight. Open. Shut. Open. Shut. Open.

"You know what I mean?"

I nod in agreement and try my best to

mumble "umhum." It comes out more like "ffzzzzzzuuuuuuup."

She's talking about her husband. About the last twenty-five years. I bet it's interesting. I should try harder to listen. Wait. What is that? Over by Lacey. The sky is brighter, like there's more than one moon. The tree Lacey's leaning against is suddenly lush and green. If I shut my eyes I can see each leaf growing. When my eyes are closed I see the tree bloom in stop-motion animation. When I open my eyes I see Lacey relaxed against a vibrant, triumphant example of birth and renewal. I get it. I understand why people like plants.

Something is darting around, like a centipede running across the room. I hate centipedes. Nothing needs that many legs. I brush imaginary bugs off my limbs. *Am* I sitting on a pile of ants?

"Tristan?"

Act normal.

"Yup?"

She thinks for a minute, winding back around to her original thought. "I owe you an apology."

Apology? Focus. I want to hear this. Something leaps out from the green tree next to Lacey. Fuck. I hope it's not a raccoon. I can't have Harry save her again. It's not an animal. It's a tiny person. What the . . .? A tiny little man in a sparkly green suit. He's the size of my pinky. I don't know how I can see this much detail on something so small. In the dark. There are at least three moons out, but it's still dark, and the little man is far away. But he's clear as day. Whatcha doing, little buddy? I should get up and introduce myself.

"Tristan." Brea stops me. Her eyes look like hard-boiled eggs.

The apology. Right. I'm all ears. What if I was all ears? Can you grow a random earlobe? Some people are born with tiny tails. They cut them off when they're still babies. What about an ear? What if you had an ear sprouting out of your shoulder? The little green man is hopping around. Is that a harp? He strums a tiny stringed instrument. Glowing hot embers blow in a rainbow arc out the back to accompany the sweet, spritely notes. If this is PTSD, it's not so bad. I wave. "Hello. Hello, little dude."

"That day, in the dressing rooms—"

He's a good little dancer. That's right. Left foot. Right foot. There you go. He leaps and skips toward Lacey. I want to see her face when she notices her miniature visitor. If anyone is going to appreciate this delightful mini green man, it's Lacey. Shoot. Where did he go?

"I'm so glad somebody found you."

Is Brea still talking to me? I was going to apologize to her for something. No! She was apologizing to me. Focus, Tristan! Wait. Where did he go? Buddy? Buddy? Come on out. Oh! There he is! He's sitting on Lacey's shoulder. He wraps himself in her shiny hair. He is loving it! What does Lacey's hair smell like? I can't believe I don't know that. I'm going to get up and sniff her head.

"I didn't know what to do."

What is Brea talking about? Should I tell her about the little green man? Something tells me she wouldn't appreciate him.

"I didn't want to get in trouble. You understand, right? I act like I don't care, but I do. I couldn't get in trouble. You know that, right? People expect things from me—"

"What are you talking about?" My voice sounds like it's in an empty auditorium.

"When I left you passed out in the dressing room."

Dressing room? What's that? Something happened to her face. I lean in, trying to get a closer look. She looks so . . . so . . . old!

"Oh, my God. Brea!"

The muscles on her face are shifting like melted wax. I reach my hand out tentatively. "Are you okay?"

She grabs my fingers and plants my palm on her cheek. "Enjoy yourself. Let it happen."

Let what happen? Her skin is gray and flakey. Her entire body is deflating in front of me.

"Are you okay?" Does she have cancer? She looks like someone with stage four cancer. We need to get her help. "Harry!"

"'Sup, bud!" He's moved on to a surprisingly agile cobra pose.

It's getting worse. Under Brea's jacket her tight midriff has turned spongy. Like Play-Doh. I poke it with my finger and it sinks in with a slurp. She takes my can.

"You've probably had enough."

Don't worry about me, Brea. You are literally dying in front of my eyes. Why is she smiling? This can't feel good. Her teeth are jagged triangles. Jesus Christ. What's next? Where's Lacey?

Is she okay? What's happening? Phew. The little green man is twirling her hair, keeping her company. Thanks, dude.

"Brea—"

My voice must still be booming. It catches Harry's attention. "Give in to the moment, Tristan."

Brea kisses me on the forehead and joins Harry on the other side of the fire. They both stare at me. My forehead buzzes from where her lips touched my skin. It's not a pleasant buzz. It's itchy and jumpy. Does that make any sense? This is what restless legs syndrome must feel like. No. This is much worse. This is the legs of ten thousand centipedes trying to burrow into my brain.

"Fuck!"

I think I'm standing up now. I should be lying down. I need to lie down. Do I remember how to lie down? I'm going to go lie down in the car. The smoke is getting so thick. I push through it like water. How come no one else is coughing? Lacey reaches out when I walk by.

"Tristan?" Her voice is like a choir of angels. That is not a cliché. That is fact. When she opened her mouth a dozen tiny chubby angel babies in diapers playing harps flew out and are now harmonizing around her head.

She stands up and holds both my hands, facing me. The sky around us is orange. Bright orange. The fire must be getting closer. A wave of panic seizes my limbs. Fire! Fire!

"Bananas! Bananas!"

Lacey squeezes my hand. "Why are you yelling *bananas*?"

What? Bananas? Who has time to talk about bananas right now? The fire is here! Brea and Harry are laughing like fat Cheshire cats. They've found top hats somewhere. Wow. My security detail truly thought of everything. I hope they're not all dead.

Lacey is inspecting my pupils. "Tristan. Tristan. Look at me. Are you okay?"

Her eyelashes are a mile long with stars on the end. Brea and Harry are chuckling in the shadows. The two of us are standing in a warm circle of light. The air in our circle is humid and fresh. We're in a greenhouse, not a forest fire. Lacey has changed her clothes. She's in a gorgeous white dress. I don't know anything about dresses, but that is a beautiful dress. She's standing on a mound of white petals. The same petals form an intricate crown around her head. Her lips are bright pink and there's perfect gold circles highlighting the apples of her cheeks. She's the most beautiful thing I've ever seen.

"It's all right. You can taste them."

Taste them? Taste what? She shuts her eyes and puckers her soft pink lips. I lean in close to lick her top lip.

She giggles. "Yummy. Huh?"

They taste like watermelon Jolly Ranchers. Lacey tastes like candy. Of course Lacey tastes like candy. A huge gust of wind lifts us both off the ground. Thank God. Somebody blow us out of here. I must have said that out loud. She laughs at me as we float back down to safety. We lay on our backs, sinking into the huge mound of white petals. I wonder what my lips taste like. Am I glowing? I roll up my sleeve. Nope. Not glowing. Wait. My forearm melted a little bit. I'll go ahead and cover that back up. If music was playing right now it would be a marching band. Something by John Philip Sousa. I love him. Did we cancel him? Did he write a march for the confederacy or something? I hope not. Up above, sparks pop and crackle like tiny fireworks. I'm losing my goddamn mind. It's wonderful. Everything around me is getting smaller. I'm a giant. A friendly giant. I will be a benevolent and generous ruler. I will take good care of the little green man and

his family. I want him to take me to his home-
land. I'd like to get to know the ins and outs of
diminutive forest culture.

Lacey rolls over and all I see above me is her
glowing face.

"I'm going to kiss you now, Tristan Melendez."

"I would like that very much."

She leans down and our lips merge, forming an electrifying seal. Little Dude hops out
of her hair and gives me a thumbs-up. I have
the sensation of flowers blooming under my
skin. There's a vibrant, growing garden where
bones should be. Lacey and I are more than
human. We're inertia. I have the sudden urge
to weep. To confess. I was willing to throw this
all away. My flesh. My spirit. Just up and pull
the plug. For shame, Tristan! For shame! I want
to live forever.

We stop kissing and Lacey floats up in the air
and rests on an invisible swing. She pumps her
legs and starts to flow back and forth. We start

laughing like it's the most wonderful and hilarious thing that has ever happened. I'm going to spend the rest of my life with this woman. I'll never forgive myself for wasting so much time. It's Lacey. It's always been Lacey.

Brea and Harry start to cackle and howl. They are on all fours, circling each other. Where we are the light is a rich, creamy orange. Harry and Brea are dark cut-out shapes against an apocalyptic backdrop. Their edges are sharp, that's all I can really see. Their sharp, jagged edges. Harry stands and rips off his shirt. He roars like a lion with fresh blood in his mane. Then instantly sobs. Roars. Sobs. Roars. Sobs. Brea's sharp shape is covered with random thick pointy hairs. She's standing upright but hunched to one side. Her curled fingernails are longer than her fingers. She swipes at Harry each time he sobs and rubs her crotch every time he roars. She moans and yips.

I wonder what Lacey thinks of all this. I think

it's pretty fucked up, but I've been wrong before. Thankfully she's not bothered. She's juggling hummingbirds. Nobody freak out. The hummingbirds like it. We're standing on a perfectly trim patch of grass. The sky is still a lush orange but feels like gingham. You know what I mean. It doesn't look like gingham; the air around me feels the way I think air feels on a ranch. A happy, happy ranch with happy horses and a happy sun shining down on a really happy day. Lacey and her bird balls are communicating with each other using lyrical whistles. I move closer. It's hard to hear their pretty tune over the snorting and grunting coming from the other side of the fire.

I'm going to tell Harry and Brea to keep it down. Oh. Huh. I can see them clearly now, and they're both back to being humans, but they're dressed in some sort of deer costume. Scratch that. It's not a costume. They're standing inside a hollowed-out deer carcass. Oh, God. They're trying to fuck. I'm going to throw up. If you are the type of person who throws up when other people throw up, now would be a good time to put the book down because I am going to fucking hurl chunks.

Behind me, Lacey hiccups. It's adorable. Fuck those two. That's it. For the rest of this night—this life—I'm only interested in Lacey. A huge, smoky, hot gust of wind smacks me in the face. Once it passes, I see Lacey standing in front of me. She's her again and I'm me. She smiles. I look over my shoulder and Brea and Harry are them again, too. They look embarrassed. They should be.

The ground starts to shake. Really? An earthquake? This freaking night . . .

It's men. Men on horses. They're headed right for us. Shit! Meda Lucas! He's found us. Lacey screams and pulls me into the air. Will I ever save anybody? God. We're running. We're so fast! I like running five feet off the ground.

You should try it sometime. Still, the horses are gaining on us. We're being herded deeper into the forest. Into the fire. I can smell my clothes singeing, but I can't feel anything. Lacey is leading the way, splitting the flames like she's fucking Moses and this is the Red Sea. The men behind us don't have faces. That's good news. Meda Lucas's guys definitely all had faces. Maybe these are friendly horsemen. Could they give us a ride home?

We've come back down to the forest floor. This is handy. The forest is bending and changing to grant us safe passage. The burning tree limbs bend to make an enclosed system of tubes. Our own magical transit system. Lacey is managing to guide us from one fire-free tube to the next. I can hear cheers from little green men on the other side of the fire. Their bright green bodies are doing just fine standing up to the flames. High five. High five. High five. Thanks, fire gods. We make it out to safety. I'm standing in a huge charred clearing. The bottoms of my shoes are hot from running above the flames. Wait. Where's Lacey? I can't see her; it's too smoky. Something tugs hard on my arm and then . . .

THIRTY

Rock Bottom

Tristan collapses. A trio of jeeps—you know, the kind you would drive through a jungle—surround him. The blast from the headlights jolts him awake. He's been face down in the burnt grass for a while.

"Lacey?" He scrambles to his feet. "Lacey?!" She's gone.

Car doors slam. Tristan circles in a panic. He needs to pick up his pace putting these pieces together. Those weren't friendly or faceless horsemen. In fact, there were no horses. Just jeeps filled with pissed-off murderers.

"Fuck!" He screams in primal defeat. Lacey is gone. They took her. They must have Harry and Brea, too. It's over. It's all over. He holds his arms out on an imaginary cross. Come and collect, motherfucker.

Meda Lucas steps in front of the floodlights. He yells, but Tristan can't hear him. Tristan falls to his knees, blocking his ears. All he can hear is a terrible ringing. A steady, high-pitched hum. Is this real? A man and a woman are dragged out of the cars and thrown next to Meda Lucas. Is that . . . is that Brea and Harry? It is! Wait, are they really kneeling next to Meda Lucas or is this some hallucination caused from the pain in his screeching eardrums? If Brea and Harry are a hallucination, then this whole thing could be nothing but a hallucination. This whole night. His whole life! He's not here. He's not him. He's a tadpole in a tide pool dreaming about a sad, lonely man and the unraveling of his sad, silly plans.

In slow motion, Meda Lucas swings a samurai sword and chops off his captives' heads. Tristan screams in a beautiful falsetto. That's embarrassing. Meda Lucas gloats next to Harry and Brea's headless bodies.

"It's time to take off your mask."

One of his guys grabs Tristan by the hair and drags him closer to the headlights, holds his face toward the light. The man takes out a long, dirty knife and presses it into the side of Tristan's face. Blood drips down his cheek in a steady stream. Before everything goes dark, he hears Lacey scream his name repeatedly.

Tristan is tripping balls. Is that phrase overused? Well, that's what's happening. He's fucked up on mushrooms. Obviously, that's why Brea insisted on having her stupid tea party. Harry often travels with a few shrooms in his back pocket. Can you think of a better time than tonight to open up to the universe and reconnect with some old friends? Those two are something else.

But don't worry. Tristan hasn't been sliced by a Meda Lucas goon. Not yet, anyway. The jeeps really are after him, though, and being in an altered state is keeping Tristan alive. He's back on his feet, running through the woods. His forest friends and fire bros cheer him on and guide him down the mountain, which is unfortunately on fire but fortunately farther away from the bullets. He needs to get out of here! He needs to find Lacey! Her screaming. That was real. He can't get the sound out of his head.

Is he running toward safety or running toward her? He has to come up with a plan. Okay. Think, Tristan. Large bands of color swirl around him. Yes. This is it. He needs to multiply purple by yellow and divide it by chartreuse. Hmm. That answer explained the ending of *The Sopranos* but it's not leading him to Lacey. He stops to talk to an owl. He'll know what to do. But this isn't some wise old owl in glasses, no, this owl is straight-up Antifa. Can you picture an antifascist owl? Me neither. We're not the ones on mushrooms.

Tristan follows the owl's detailed instructions and crisscrosses down the increasingly slopey slope. He gets himself trapped at the edge of a steep drop-off. Headlights are getting brighter behind him. Meda Lucas will be here any second. Maybe he surrenders and he and Lacey can at least die together. He looks over the edge. Jump and maybe they'll let Lacey go. He can't win. How did he even get this far? The ground gurgles to his left.

"Over here."

Who said that? Tristan dives behind a rock. Fine cover for now but he needs a better plan before the jeeps show up.

"Don't be shy."

What? Tristan whips his head around trying to find the source of this soothing voice.

"I'm nice and warm."

A muddy hole in the ground is trying to get Tristan's attention. Are mushrooms fun? This doesn't seem like a great time. Perhaps they work better when taken on a beach with friends and not in the middle of a forest fire with a cartel in pursuit.

"Come on in. Let's pull a fast one on these fuckers."

I like this muddy hole! The headlights are almost through the last line of vegetation, though.

"Jump in, you dumb motherfucker!"

Tristan plugs his nose and jumps into the mud pit just as the jeeps crash to a stop on the edge. Two guys get out quickly to survey the scene. "I don't know, boss. Maybe he jumped."

Meda Lucas doesn't think so. Santa Ana has proven a worthy adversary. He's not going to give up and neither is Meda Lucas.

"Back in the cars. He's still out there. I want him alive."

Everyone follows his orders and they speed off. Tristan slowly rises to the top of his muddy hiding spot like a hippo on the hunt at a crowded watering hole. He waits a minute and hoists himself out with a little help from a delightful salmon. That's one strong land fish. He takes a few steps into the night. Tristan has been replaced by the Creature from the Black Lagoon. He feels good. Confident. Strong.

And then he slips and falls down the mountain.

He tumbles for only a tumble or two before he hitches a ride on a slide. This is not a drug-induced shortcut. This is real. In this area of the San Gabriels there's a 250-foot concrete slide built into the mountainside that drains to the river. He flies down the terrible waterslide without water and is dumped into the river. He emerges from the reservoir clean.

It's been almost five hours since he drank Brea's tea. He's not rolling as hard. The sun has come out but the sky is a dark gray. He can't stray too far from the water or he'll be consumed by flames. This is his penance. For all the life he's wasted. For all the time he's spent thinking about the wrong things and the wrong people. The years he couldn't love his father. The thousands of times he rolled his eyes at Frankie. The millions of seconds he spent ignoring Lacey's affection. He deserves to die alone in this climate catastrophe.

A huge smoldering log falls in his path and bursts into flames. As the wood hisses and smokes, it sounds like it's saying "Lacey" over and over again. Then the smoke in front of his face, which is burning his eyes, curls into a cursive string spelling out "Lacey" over and over again. Okay. Those magic fruits might have a little magic left.

Lacey. Yes. He can keep going, for her. He may deserve to die alone at the bottom of this boiling river, but if there's even a chance she's still alive, he has to find her. She does not deserve any of this. He trudges on, heading east into the heart of the fire. Portions of the river are too close to the flames and cooked fish float by belly-up. Others jump out of the water onto land thinking they might have a better shot making a run for it. How long has he been walking? Three minutes? Five months?

Two maniacs come screaming out of the blackened woods toward him. He ducks, waiting for bullets to fly overhead.

"Tristan! Tristan!"

It's a woman and a man . . . It's Brea! And Harry! They still have their heads! This is fantastic news. They rush into the water next to their friend. They're covered in soot and sweat, and their hair is singed. Brea smells half cooked and extra savory. Harry's skin is pink and warm in the places not covered with dirt and ash. They're both sobbing and gasping for air. Brea falls into Tristan's arms. He holds her for a moment as they watch Harry's sudden drama unfold. He circles in the water like a puppy thrown off a pier. He slows down and starts awkwardly taking off his clothes. He proclaims something unintelligible as he slams each item of clothing into the water next to him. Tristan was relieved to have company; now he's not so sure.

"Done!"

"Done!"

"Done!"

Is that what he's saying? Tristan regrets walking closer now that Harry's stripped nude. Maybe you should try microdosing next time, pal.

"Tristan." Harry clings to his smaller friend's waist in the water. "Tristan. Help me. Help me, please. Kill me. I'm done. I can't go on like this. End my suffering, old friend."

Brea is close to sober and slightly alarmed. "Babe?"

Harry presses his naked body against Tristan.

"I've built myself a prison out of greed and deception. Help me break free! Help me—"

Tristan slaps him across the face. "Get ahold of yourself!"

Harry loosens his grip, stunned at Tristan's assertiveness.

"And please. Take a step back. I can feel your balls."

Harry obliges. "I'm begging you. Drown me in this river."

"You really want to die?"

"Yes!"

"You, Harrison Sullivan the Third, want to call it quits?"

"Yes!"

"So why did you run away from the fire?"

"Well, that seems like an exceptionally brutal and painful way to go—"

Tristan has lost his temper. "You. Harry fucking Sullivan, you don't think you have a good enough life? You have fucking everything! You always have!"

This resonates with Harry. Tristan has become a bit of a role model since showing up in a helicopter.

"That's it." Harry splashes the water out of joy. "That's it! Harry fucking Sullivan *does* have everything. Me. I. Harry. Harrison. I have a good enough life. That's it, Tristan. I don't need all that other shit. I don't need to be something I'm not. I'm good enough. Harry"—now he really breaks down—"Harry has always been good enough."

He doesn't care if he slaps Tristan with his dick. He's going in for a bear hug. Tristan reluctantly hugs him back.

Harry regains some of his composure. "That's right. Harry Sullivan is going to live, and that means Santa Ana has to die. From this moment on there is no Santa Ana. Santa Ana is dead."

Tristan and Brea both snap their heads toward Harry. "What?"

Harry picks up where his dramatics left off. "From this moment on, Santa Ana is—"

"What does this have to do with Santa Ana?" Tristan takes a step back, anticipating being super pissed at the answer.

"Really? Still? No one thinks it could be— you know what, it doesn't matter because he's dead. I will never put that mask on again."

Tristan smacks his forehead. He should have known. "You're Santa Ana?"

"Yes."

"*You're* Santa Ana!?"

"Not anymore. I thought I was pretty clear—"

"Oh, my God." Tristan puts his hands to his head and yells. If there were any birds around they would be flying away, startled by his outburst, which is saying something considering the outburst Harry just had. And the raging inferno. "This is all your fault!"

"I don't know if we're ready to assign blame—"

Tristan pushes him. "Meda Lucas went there looking for you."

"Allegedly."

Tristan pushes him again. "Lacey is gone because of you." He stops in his tracks. If Harry and Brea are standing here and he was sure he saw their heads get chopped off, Lacey could be safe somewhere. He's not going to spend another minute thinking about the wrong things. Harry can kill off his evil alter ego or have whatever sort of cathartic breakthrough he wants. Tristan does not give a shit. "We have to get Lacey back."

Tristan trudges out of the water. He slips in his first attempt at climbing up the embankment. In a fit of rage, he claws at the earth, chucking rocks and debris and forging a path. His sheer determination is keeping the flames at bay. Do magic mushrooms make you super strong or is that just meth?

The wind is finally on their side and has shifted course for the time being. Brea follows Tristan. Harry puts his wet clothes back on and catches up. They climb quickly and silently. Beating like a drum, Tristan hears "Lacey, Lacey, Lacey" with each step.

Finally, they've made it to a change in scenery. There's something up ahead that isn't burnt or burning. But it's not exactly functional either. It's California's famous Bridge to Nowhere, another popular field trip destination for Azusa kids. In case you didn't grow up at the bottom of the San Gabriel Mountains, let me clear my throat and try out my most official-sounding Wikipedia-esque voice to describe this scene for you.

The Bridge to Nowhere is an arch bridge built in 1936 in the San Gabriel Mountains north of Azusa. It spans the East Fork of the San Gabriel River and was originally intended to be part of a connecting roadway system from the San

Gabriel Valley to Wrightwood, California. Massive floods washed out most of the new construction in March of 1938. The rest of the project was scrapped and nothing remains today expect for the massive concrete bridge that goes, you guessed it, nowhere. (Phew! Glad that smart-person nonsense is over.)

It's a cool spot to hike to. Different tourist and adventure travel companies have tried to make it a thing. Some have been more successful than others. Harry, with his newfound lease on life, runs ahead to the latest start-up's equipment shed out on the bridge and kicks in the door. He jumps right in and begins to toss out random extreme-sporting goods: bungee cords, helmets, empty Gatorade bottles.

"Hel-*lo*!" He struggles to extract a huge wicker basket from the shed. No, they aren't high anymore. This isn't an *Alice in Wonderland* moment. It's actually a huge wicker basket:

the basket of a hot-air balloon, aka a floating death trap.

Tristan and Brea finally catch up right as Harry pulls out a giant wad of yellow nylon fabric. "What's this?"

"It goes with the basket, idiot." Brea has come down hard. Her head is throbbing and she would be throwing up if she had anything in her stomach. And, how can we forget, she spent the night on the run in the middle of a goddamn forest fire.

Harry starts to laugh as he shakes out the balloon. "Look. It's winking at you."

This isn't just a yellow hot-air balloon. This is a yellow, winking-smiley-face emoji hot-air balloon. How cool! And you'll never believe what Harry pulls out next: the propane tank that completes this whimsical mode of transportation. "No fucking way! Check it out, babe."

The three of them get to work putting the contraption together. They work fast and make it look easy. Don't shake your head. Don't be surprised. Harry excels at murdering people, Brea has been in one of Clarence Thomas's bathrooms, and Tristan is Tristan. They can figure out a junky hot-air balloon.

Tristan can't believe their luck. This will be perfect. They can get a bird's-eye view of the area and search for signs of Lacey.

Harry fires up the tank after they all climb into the basket, and the balloon begins to fill. They lift and Tristan lets out a triumphant *whoop!* But the balloon stops rising, its basket hovering a mere two feet in the air. That's as far as it will go. There's something wrong with the tank. It's not pushing out enough gas. Tristan clambers out to take another look inside the shed.

Suddenly, Meda Lucas and his remaining army come crashing down the mountainside, barely keeping their beat-up jeeps from flipping as they approach one end of the bridge. Harry and Brea don't have time to react before another line of less-beat-up off-road vehicles comes bouncing down and lands on the opposite end of the bridge.

It's the FBI! There's that SWAT team! They made it! Well, in reality they were part of all the shooting and chasing through the forest that went on last night, too, only Tristan was too preoccupied (read: tripping) to catch all the specifics of who was faceless, who was shooting, and who might be there to help. From inside the shed, he spies his old friend in a kick-ass windbreaker with FBI in big yellow letters on the back. Finally, Frankie gets to look cool.

"Frankie?"

"Don't move. We'll get you out of here."

Frankie is flanked by Crosby and Dillmann. Rows of men stand behind them in formation, ready to shoot. Meda Lucas and his boys are clumped together in a more casual format on the other side of the bridge. Brea and Harry are hovering in the middle.

"This doesn't concern you, Uncle Sam. Go home and I'll make a donation to the charity of your choice." Meda Lucas will attempt to smooth talk his way out of anything and, my God, is he tired.

"Drop your weapons!"

Meda Lucas whistles. Man, that guy is a top-notch whistler. A car door opens and Lacey is pushed out. He helps her up and holds on tightly to her arm. "I offer you a trade."

"Drop your weapons," Dillmann commands again. "We're not interested in negotiating."

"Me neither. I'm here for one man and one man only"—(everybody say it with me)—"Santa Ana."

There's slight murmuring from the FBI camp. That wouldn't be so terrible, would it? They could get home and out of these smokey clothes.

At least one drug-dealing maniac would be taken care of and do they really want to risk dying on this bridge for Tom Spitz's last hurrah?

Lacey's hands are tied behind her back and her hair is insane. Other than that, she looks intact and unharmed. Meda Lucas shakes her slightly. "A life for a life. Santa Ana for—"

Harry interrupts what was shaping up to be an epic bad guy TED Talk. "Tough shit, motherfucker. You're too late. Santa Ana is dead!"

Everyone on the bridge gasps. The fire is squeezing the two sides closer to each other.

"What did you say?" Meda Lucas yanks Lacey back.

"I said you're too late, motherfucker. That asshole is dead."

Meda Lucas thinks for a second. "Okay. Kill her." He drops Lacey's arm and turns around to leave. "Kill them." He points across the bridge to the SWAT team. "I'm going home."

This whole trip has been a nightmare and his

back is freaking killing him. He hopes he never hears that stupid name ever again.

Tristan won't let that happen. "No! Stop. I'm here. Stop! Wait, I'm not dead!" He runs out from the shed.

Meda Lucas freezes momentarily, then he turns back and locks eyes on Tristan. There's that little fucker. "Shit." He sighs. He is so ready to go home. Fine. He'll kill him, blow up this goddamn bridge, and then put this entire annoying weekend behind him.

Tristan strides toward his destiny. As he passes Brea and Harry in the basket, Brea tries to stop him. "Tristan, don't! What are you doing?"

He knows exactly what he's doing. "Trust me."

Frankie also tries to stop him. "Don't do this, Tristan. We know it's not you."

It had taken only a few clicks on a keyboard for Crosby to determine that there was no chance in hell Tristan Melendez had anything to do with this. He turns to Frankie. "I'm worried about his spending habits. Total red flag."

In the sequel, I want a lot more Crosby.

Tristan stops a few feet from Meda Lucas and levels him with a steely stare. "I am Santa Ana, mother*fucker*."

I know this story is not hurting for F bombs. But that there was *the* F bomb of all F bombs.

He grabs Lacey and gives her a huge movie-star smooch. All hell breaks out while they kiss. The land around them is shaking from the heat and flames. A burning tree trunk rolls down the mountainside and takes out half of Meda Lucas's fleet. A boulder follows and flattens one of his best shots just as they were taking aim. Our lovebirds run, holding hands, ducking and zigzagging as the shooting picks up again. They race back toward Brea and Harry in the hot-air balloon and Tristan barks an order. "Go! Go! Go!"

Harry and Brea look at each other in ex-asperation. Go where? They're already two feet off the ground, and that's as high as that thing will go.

When they make it to the basket, Tristan tosses Lacey in like a boss. The basket sinks a foot, but Tristan doesn't lose his cool. He leans against the hulking wicker and pushes with all his might.

Brea screams in Tristan's face. "What are you doing?!"

His voice is calm and steady. "Saving the fucking day."

Okay. I was a little premature before. That *there* is the F bomb of all F bombs.

Tristan leans toward the edge of the bridge and . . . wait for it . . . wait for it . . . pushes the hovering basket over. It instantly starts to plummet toward the flames at the canyon floor. He shuts his eyes and dives headfirst after it.

"What the ffffffffffffuuuuuuuuuuuuuuuu . . ."

His voice booms through the forest and fades as he falls.

The good guys and bad guys on the bridge cease fire. They watch in amazement as the fully inflated balloon rises over them. It's not a winky-eye emoji at all. It's a crying-face emoji flipping the bird. It's stupendous. Tristan, you son of a bitch. You, sneaky Pete, know a thing or two about aerodynamics, don't you? I don't know anything about aerodynamics, and I have a hunch you, dear reader, probably don't either. So let's trust Tristan on this one. He knew exactly the right moment to have the exact correct amount of weight in the basket to catch an upstream or jet stream or whatever nerds call it, and off they go, floating up, up, and away to clear skies and happier days. If they squint, they can just maybe make out Frankie putting Meda Lucas in handcuffs.

Finally, the wind is blowing west, and the four of them relax as the basket gently rocks over Los Angeles. Don't overthink this. I told you that on, like, page one.

As they fly closer to the rooftops, one of Lacey's light bulbs goes off. She taps Tristan's shoulder and points below. They're about to fly over his apartment and the bowling alley. He peeks over the basket and smiles at the new neon sign: Holy Rollers: Bowling Alley & Pentecostal Church. As they float past, they are treated to the rocking celebration below. Praise Jesus, indeed.

THIRTY-ONE

Bye for Now

Yeah, buddy! We did it! A whole freaking book. Congratulations. I'll miss you. I'll miss the time we spent together on the porch, in bed, on the toilet, waiting in the parent pick-up line, on the bus, maybe a boat, wherever lovely people such as yourself curl up to read. Are you angry about the ending? The whole balloon thing? Remember when Sandy and Danny flew off in the convertible at the carnival on the last day of school? "I've got chills, they're multiplying"? We don't have to make this hard. Sometimes the stories we tell are just fun.

And you know what's really fun? Jumping ahead five years to see what everyone is up to!

Let's start with Tristan and Lacey. I love those two. Tristan was a bit much at times, but he really did grow on me. After their wild weekend in Azusa, Tristan fessed up to everything. He needed some sleep and a shower, but after spending seventy-two hours safe and sound together in Lacey's apartment, he handed over his letter and final instructions. It was a beautiful and cathartic scene. We'll have to put it in the movie. When they finished crying, they took off in Lacey's Hyundai for Vegas, baby! Lacey wore a long, beautiful white dress with a crown of white flowers in her hair. (Sound familiar?) Tristan wore one of his $400 T-shirts (he had to buy two, of course), and Elvis took care of the rest. They stayed in the honeymoon suite at Caesars Palace. Guess who's really good at blackjack? Tristan. Guess who's even better than Tristan at blackjack? Lacey. Why didn't they think of trying that earlier? Would have made for a very different book. After three days in Sin City, they drove home with over four hundred thousand dollars.

Hobnobbing with high rollers, Tristan made some interesting contacts. Sports betting pays a lot more than Longus Life. If that boring movie *Moneyball* taught us anything, it's that math can ruin everything. Including sports. And gambling. In a matter of weeks, Tristan and Lacey said goodbye to that rectangle coffin forever and moved into a gorgeous house in the Hollywood Hills. Not a cute Craftsman bungalow, either. They set up shop in a lovely estate previously owned by a Laker. Tristan now works with clients from all over the world. He is a legend. Lacey is busy chasing after their two-year-olds (yes, that's plural). Tristan had a hunch it would be identical twins. Three to four out of every thousand pregnancies end up with a matching set, after all.

Because tidy endings are the best type of endings, Brea and Harry are also living happily ever after. Both are off following their passions with new careers. Brea is a boss bitch entrepreneur, and Harry plays on the practice squad for the Los Angeles Rams. He's terrible and gets his ass handed to him every day but Tristan helped the owner out with a side project and got his old pal back on the green. Does anyone call a football field that? Anyhoo, his practice jersey has the number 666 on the back and his life is perfect.

You know how much I love my Crosby and Dillmann. Let's go ahead and add Frankie and Special Agent Now Retired Tom Spitz to the mix. The whole Meda Lucas takedown gave Frankie some much-needed cred in the bureau. Dillmann acknowledges his existence now. Here they are sitting together in the middle row, anxiously awaiting the curtain to go up on opening night. This night is extra special. Not only is Tom Spitz's name in lights as the producer and director, but who is about to rock out onstage as that bad-boy kitty Rum Tum Tugger? You know it! My man, Crosby!

Now that we've come to the end, I should probably spend some time waxing poetic about the mighty Santa Ana winds, the chaotic force blowing us from chapter to chapter and the name of our book. I bet you're sick of me and my musings.

Joan Didion sums it up nicely: "To live with the Santa Ana is to accept, consciously or unconsciously, a deeply mechanistic view of human behavior."

Sure.

EPILOGUE

Goddamnit. The Melendezes showed up to-night in their helicopter again. One time. One time I told Tristan it was okay to land it in the side yard. Now the rose bushes are destroyed and the dog will never stop shitting on the rug. That stupid dog. I should have never let Harry talk me into that drooling shit machine. Dinner was fun, though I'm bummed I have to leave early. Harry is now in charge of entertaining our guests and he's out there parading around like a fucking jack-o'-lantern. When is that concussion syndrome going to kick in so I can leave him drooling with a nurse?

It was nice to see my babies Sugar Bear and

Honey Bee tonight. They need more time with their Auntie. How those two almost-average-looking people could create such gorgeous offspring, I'll never understand.

Have you figured it out yet? By process of elimination, do you know who this is? It's Brea, bitches! It's about fucking time!

"Babe!" I would like to yell "Where the fuck are you, you fucking loser," but we have company so I keep it civil. "Babe! I need you!" I'm waiting like an asshole in my own foyer. I'll be grateful and happy and normal again as soon as I get back from my errand. I've found the secret sauce, the key to happiness, the holy grail of work-life self-actualization.

"What's up, babe? You headed to work?"

"I'm trying. Where's my mask?"

He's giving me guilty puppy-dog eyes. Damnit, Harry. That fucker has been wearing it around the house when I'm not home again.

"Babe! Come on. I told you. I can't be

trapped in there with it smelling like sadness and whiskey."

"Sorry. Sorry, babe."

"Go get it. Hurry up. My phone is blowing up like crazy."

Freaking Tyler. We've recently hit some major managerial setbacks.

Thank the lord, here comes my Prince Charming.

"Gross! Harry! It's still sweaty."

"Sorry, babe. Knock 'em dead."

I can't stay mad at that dumb face. I go in for a peck and he grabs me, planting a full-on smooch. This fucking guy. "Don't wait up."

See you in the sequel, bitches.

Other books by
ADDISON J. CHAPPLE

The Man Who Would Be King
In this hilarious satire on American
exceptionalism, two Midwestern idiots travel
to Somalia, impersonate Navy SEALs, and
steal money from pirates . . . what could
possibly go wrong?

Rambling with Rebah
When a leading travel blogger returns to a
bed-and-breakfast she blasted years ago, the
owner must go to extreme—and hilarious—
measures to ensure her stay is perfect, or risk
going bankrupt. Even sworn enemies can fall
in love in wine country.

Pre-Order Addison's latest book:
Con Crazy
The con is on!

Prewitt Paltry used to be the best con artist in NYC. But fate has left him divorced, broke, his glory days behind him. . . . And then a golden opportunity falls into his lap.

Ranger du Courtemanche is the aging patriarch of the centuries-old French aristocratic Courtemanche family. Despite the filthy-rich façade, the family's fortune is quickly dwindling and their ancestral chateau is secretly in ruins. Enter Prewitt, who cozies up to the reclusive family—Ranger and his two sisters—and warns them that their chateau and wealth have been targeted by an ancient secret society. Panicked and desperate, Ranger enlists Prewitt in the fight to defend his family's honor and fortune. Et voila! The trap is set.

With the help of an eccentric team of wacky French con artists, and three Corgies, Prewitt gets to work. But, the closer he gets, the more the con unravels. Ancient betrayals, priceless jewels, and forbidden loves . . . the Courtemanches turn out to be a lot more than Prewitt bargained for.

https://mybook.to/concrazy

Stay up to date with Addison J. Chapple:

Follow Addison on Amazon & Goodreads

https://amazon.com/author/addisonjchapple